A MOST FAMOUS FEMYNYNE SEA CAPTEN

Grace O'Malley, Reluctant Rebel

Dermot Keane

CONTENTS

For Brenda, with love

PROLOGUE

The cell lay deep underground in the dungeons beneath Dublin Castle. It was damp, it was filthy and it stank. There was virtually no light other than that seeping under the door from the candles in the guard room along the passage. This gave the many rats free rein to wander where they would.

The cell had one occupant, a woman. The rats did not particularly bother her, nor, indeed, did the rest of the miserable conditions: she was a hardened sailor, a hardened galley sailor, and these conditions, other than the continuing darkness, were frequently the norm. Her name was Grace O'Malley.

She sat against the wall to which she was chained and pondered her future or, more likely, she supposed, the lack of one. The signs were not good. In normal circumstances a person of means, and she could certainly have counted herself such a person before her capture, would be offered a ground level cell with a window and even some sparse furniture. She would also be allowed to send out for decent food instead of having to survive on the disgusting food, pigswill to all intents and purposes, served up to her in her present accommodation. Her guards might even show a little obsequious respect. She smiled to herself at that thought: little chance of this lot of bastards showing any respect, they were probably hand picked for their thick, unimaginative, black hearted view of humanity. Of more concern was the fact that the Lord Deputy, for whom she had a liking which she believed was reciprocated, had failed to visit her in prison. This did not auger well.

She had first met the Lord Deputy, Sir Henry Sidney, about three years previously, when he was visiting Galway with his son, Philip, and the Earl of Essex. She had liked the

Sidneys on sight but had taken strongly against Essex, although she would concede to being ill disposed to him in advance because of his participation in the massacre at Rathlin Island. At the time, Sir Henry was pursuing his policy, on behalf of the Queen, of Surrender and Regrant, whereby any chieftain giving nominal control of his or her land to the Crown was given a title by the Crown in return, while still retaining the land.

That was where her troubles had begun. One of the aims of Regrant was to undermine the often fragile alliances of the Irish clans in hopes of finally achieving English rule over the whole of Ireland and not just The Pale around Dublin, and to this end those chieftains who had participated in the Regrant scheme were being encouraged to attack and subdue those who had not, their reward being the land of their victims. Her husband, Richard, who had an agenda of his own had, despite her misgivings, signed up to it. Her own approach would have been to vacillate as long as possible, sitting comfortably on a fence until she was absolutely forced to climb off it on to one side or the other. The immediate result was that he became Sir Richard and she Lady Grace, not, as she wryly admitted to herself, that her being a Lady seemed to be of any interest to the gombeens in whose unfeeling care she now found herself.

The aspect of the scheme to which she had immediately taken was the bit about attacking her "disloyal" fellow countrymen, which she interpreted as giving her carte blanche to continue doing within the law as she saw it, what she had always done previously outside the law. So, while Richard pursued his ambitions on land, she had pursued hers by sea. Local scores were settled and then she set her eyes on wider horizons, choosing as a particularly lucrative potential victim the Earl of Desmond. In choosing the Earl, she was not only hoping for rich pickings, she was also intending to increase her credit with her friend, Desmond's deadly enemy, the Earl of Ormond.

To begin with, all had gone exceedingly well. She had attacked his ports, seized his ships, and stolen his cattle. And then her luck had run out.

Venturing further and further inland, she finally made one foray too many and was captured by Desmond's men. The three companions with whom she was captured were summarily hung and she waited daily for the same fate herself, but some of her luck returned. The Earl, made aware that she was now Lady O'Malley and in some favour with the Lord Deputy, was unwilling to upset Sir Henry. And so, after keeping her in suspense a while, he had sent her to the Lord Deputy himself in Dublin to deal with her as he saw fit. But she had been here some months now and, other than a brief meeting on the road to Dublin, she had seen nothing of Sir Henry. No, the signs were not good.

She had the real sailor's instinct for time, and even though she was living in fairly continuous darkness and her meals were being delivered in the most haphazard fashion, presumably to disorientate her, this instinct now told her that it was night. She also had the real sailor's innate ability to rest in almost any place and at almost any time and so she now composed herself for sleep, which came almost instantly.

She was woken from a particularly unpleasant dream in which she was being viciously kicked to find that it was not a dream. She was being kicked, and also shouted at by her jailers.

"Dear Jesus," she thought," they've finally come for me."

In the brief moment between sleep and full wakefulness, she experienced a desperate terror in the pit of her stomach. It passed quickly and she rose, as steadily as she could, determined not to let her brutish captors know what she was feeling.

Her chains were removed and the head jailer addressed her,

"Get out, you bitch. I don't know who your friends are, or who they're paying, but you're free. Get out, I say".

CHAPTER 1

Thomas Butler, 10th Earl of Ormond, rested back in his chair feeling pleasantly benevolent.

The Earl, Black Tom to his friends, was seated with a number of those friends in the great hall of his newly built castle at Carrick-on–Suir, the first and, so far, only unfortified castle in Ireland. He had spent long years in England – he was a cousin of the Queen – and he had fallen under the spell of the new architecture and the building of great houses in which elaboration replaced austerity, the advances in artillery having all but made redundant the grim thick walls of older dwellings. The bawn and two of the towers built by his forebears still remained, ready for instant occupation should he wish to retreat from less sophisticated attackers, but it was generally unoccupied, the Earl and his household preferring the bright airy elegance of the new house to which it was attached, and in which he now entertained his friends.

They had spent the day hunting the stag, had feasted to the accompaniment of music provided by accomplished musicians, both Irish and English, and had finally sat down to cards, this last activity giving rise to the particular reason for his feeling of benevolence: the neat pile of assorted coinage on the table in front of him which, by virtue of his having held the dealership longer than anyone else in the game of One and Thirty at which they had been playing, he had taken from them.

The night was by now well advanced and the effects of the day's exercise, the heat of the great fires in the hall, and the wine which had not ceased to circulate throughout the evening, began to tell on the members of the company, not least on the Earl himself, who now announced that they might all consider retiring.

As the game broke up, the serious silence which had prevailed for the previous few hours was broken, and a general hum of conversation ensued as the various gamblers rehearsed their plays, and the luck, good or bad, by which these plays had been attended.

The company rose. Money was collected, discarded cloaks thrown loosely over shoulders, wine goblets emptied, and the guests slowly drifted from the hall towards their chambers. They were almost entirely a male gathering, there being only one woman amongst them, Grace O'Malley (one of the best gamblers in Ireland, a nation devoted to gambling), and it was to this woman that the Earl now addressed himself,

"Stay a moment please, Grace."

"Bigod, Tom. You must be more drunk than you look, if you're hoping to bed me on top of taking my money."

This raised a smile from the Earl and laughing comment, some of it verging on the coarse, from the departing gentlemen.

When they were alone he said, "I wished to speak privately with you, Grace."

She interrupted him. "Hang on there a minute now, Tom. Before you say anything, can I speak? First, can I apologise for being late (she had joined the hunt when they were already on their second stag), but I'm at the whim of the tides, as you know. Secondly, and much more importantly, ever since I did arrive, I've been dying for a private opportunity to thank you properly, in person, for getting me out of prison. I know that I wrote to you, but that's not the same. You know that Desmond wanted me killed. Well, of course you do. He had already hung my companions and if you hadn't intervened when you did, he'd surely have had me hung too". She shuddered involuntarily at the thought. "Anyway," she finished soberly," I'll be forever in your debt, Tom. Thanks again."

The Earl held up a hand:

"Don't be worrying yourself about it now, Grace. I'd always look out for a handsome woman like yourself," he said with a smile. "Besides, anyone who causes trouble for Desmond is sure of my assistance, handsome or not. That said, if you do insist on raiding his estates, plundering and pillaging like a common cattle thief, and you're caught at it, you can't really expect to be welcomed with the fatted calf."

She made to interrupt, but again he held up his hand:

"As a matter of fact, it's about the same Desmond that I particularly wished to speak to you.

Walsingham has been in communication with me. I don't like that man, I find him something of an upstart, but he's adept at keeping his finger on all possible threats to England, and particularly to the Queen herself, and nobody can doubt his utter loyalty to her. Anyway, the essence of his news was this: James Fitzmaurice has been active on the continent and has finally managed to drum up support from both the Pope and the King of Spain for a landing and uprising somewhere in Desmond's territory. He's currently hoping to get to sea with a fleet of ships and an army and, if successful, will be in Munster before we know it.

A year ago Phillip would have had nothing to do with such a venture, but he's becoming more and more annoyed by the activities of the English Navy, or English Pirates as he prefers to think of them, and is now thought by Walsingham's informants to have reached a point where he might well give serious thought to one. The Pope, of course, is entirely in favour of anything that might help restore Papism in England. Unfortunately, his excommunication of the Queen and her imprisonment of the Catholic Scottish Queen, makes a bad situation a whole lot worse by giving religious trappings to what should be a simple war for territory, with all the fervour and excesses that that implies. It's not at all certain, of course, even if Fitzmaurice does succeed in landing an army, that Desmond will join him in rebellion. He's already been to the Tower and, though he was fairly leniently treated there after the last rebellion, he'll be chary of ending up there again. However, if he does decide to throw in his lot with Fitzmaurice, he'll not lack for troops. Since Affane, there've been large bodies of armed men wandering Munster looking for employment. They'll never join with the Crown since the Crown massacred so many of their fellows but, if Desmond should rebel, they'll flock to him, hard seasoned soldiers all. In addition, there's no shortage of minor client chieftains of Desmond who were dispossessed of their lands after the last rebellion by people like Spenser. They would dearly love to repossess those lands and will happily join any endeavour which might hold promise of such a thing."

The Earl paused, swallowed a draught of wine and continued:

"I tell you all this as a kind of a warning Grace, because I'm aware that already, since your release from the Castle, you've had a major skirmish with English troops. This can only leave the authorities even more ill disposed to you than previously. I'm also aware that your husband Richard is fairly unhappy that the English have not been meeting his expectations since his declaration of loyalty, so, if there should be a rebellion, I would urgently impress upon you the need to dissuade Richard from joining with Desmond to redress any perceived slights."

He paused for a moment in thought before continuing:

"and that brings me to a subject which gives me some difficulty. The fact is, Grace, your release cost me a great deal of gold which, I suppose, I would like repaid."

Grace paused in turn before replying.

"I'm very thankful, Tom, for your good interest in my affairs, though you do seem to forget at times that I'm a grown woman and not some silly little chit of a girl. Furthermore, you should know that my skirmish was not with official Crown forces but with an independent Captain, a right peacock by the name of Martin, employed by the merchants of Galway."

Ever since she had married her first husband Donal, as much a man of the land as she was a woman of the sea, Grace had taken charge of the O'Flaherty boats with his blessing and commenced on a semi-piratical career which had included taxation of all sea borne traffic in and out of Galway. She had always supposed that they would finally get fed up with her depredations and try to put a stop to them. They had not succeeded on this occasion and the brash Captain Martin had been sent running with his tail between his legs and considerably less strut in his step. She smiled inwardly at the memory and resumed,

"So, though you needn't worry about the authorities on that particular score, I do agree that I should adopt a lower profile, and therefore I'm intending to get out of the country for a while. Hopefully, they'll forget about me in time. I may even do a bit of honest trading while I'm away."

He smiled at that.

"As for Richard," she continued, "when I see him again, I'll advise him as you say but he's his own man and won't necessarily be counselled by me.

Now. The gold you had to pay for my release. I might have expected that the thieving English, may they be eaten by crows, saving your presence Tom, wouldn't have let me go for free. You'd better let me know how much is involved and I'll see what I can do. I suppose my trading might have to be a bit more aggressive than I was planning."

"I was thinking," he replied slowly, "that you might be able to make some of the repayment in kind. Not in the way you may be thinking, I hasten to add, please don't think that of me, but by looking out for Fitzmaurice on your travels for instance, and getting word to me of his activities."

"You want me to play the spy?"

"No, no. Nothing like that. Just keep your eyes open. Don't interfere with him. But, if you could give me anything which might be of interest to Walsingham, it might be of great benefit to both of us."

She gave a noncommittal nod. She was a realist and would do anything necessary for her own needs and that of her O'Malley clan but she would not necessarily let the Earl know that, might even go against him if expedient, fond though she was of him.

She changed the subject.

"But what of yourself, Tom? If Fitzmaurice should start a rebellion, why not join with him and Desmond and take the whole of Munster for yourselves? The whole of Ireland? I'd support you in Connacht."

"It would never do, Grace. The ill feeling between us runs too deep and, besides, he's a Catholic and I'm Protestant. We could never work together. Anyway, the Queen herself is my cousin, and I wouldn't wish to embarrass her by rising up in rebellion against her now, would I? So you may also view it as a family obligation if you wish."

He said this last with a somewhat complacent smile, before commenting that without that Royal connection, and the undoubted moral advantage that it gave him over Desmond, and even Sidney, he might not have been able to intervene so successfully, if belatedly, on Grace's behalf, no matter how much gold was on offer.

"I must meet this Queen of yours someday, Tom."

"I shall certainly sponsor you, maybe even here in Carrick, if she ever makes the visit for which I hope."

He looked at her critically,

"If you live long enough, that is."

"If the English leave me alone, I'll leave them alone. Anyway, as I've said, I'm off a-voyaging for the next few months, so you won't have to worry about me until at least the Autumn."

"I'm very glad to hear it. But do bear in mind what I've said and, even if you're not prepared to welcome the English, at least do your best not to be too antagonistic to them. Keep your head down, in fact, and you may just hang on to it a bit

9

longer"

The fires in the grates were by now almost out and, with a quick sidewards glance at him, she said that it was about time for her to be getting to a warm bed before she got chilled.

He offered her his arm and they left the hall together to go upstairs.

CHAPTER 2

A few mornings later, shortly after dawn, in a light but persistent mist, the galley Dana of 40 oars moved slowly down the river Suir towards Waterford and the sea, her early departure being designed to catch the tide on the ebb where it met the downward stream.

At the tiller, Grace, her captain, scanned the heavily wooded banks. This was Munster and the Dana was a Connacht boat with no rights of passage should the owners of these banks and the surrounding countryside decide that they were trespassing. Therefore, Captain O'Malley scanned the woods, as did the men on watch.

Their vigilance was justified by the sight of two big boats coming out of the mist, each containing about twenty armed men. There came a shouted order from the leading boat for them to haul to. With an inward sigh, Grace called back that they were just a trading boat, but with empty holds. They had discharged a cargo upstream and were intending to take on a new one in Waterford. This was a relatively true statement. She was intent on trade and although, in fact, her holds already carried a valuable cargo of hides, tallow, frieze and various animal skins, she did intend to augment that cargo downstream with bales of Waterford rugs to be supplied by her friends, the deLacys. However, she also carried considerably more powder and shot than might have been deemed necessary for the defence of a mere trading vessel. Furthermore, her complement of nearly 260 men exceeded by ninety or so the amount of crew, sailors and oarsmen, that would normally be needed to work a galley, even one as big as the Dana. Most of these crewmen were conveniently out of sight at this moment, doing their best to catch up on their sleep on the galley's benches, and her main armament was hidden under its canvas covering, which gave added veracity to her reply. It did not satisfy the leader of the boats, who again ordered them to stop, emphasizing his order with a display of arquebuses with which he threatened them.

It was not at all in Grace's plans to get involved in an affair which could bring no possible reward but would, on the contrary, only complicate future excursions upriver towards Carrick. She was about to reply again with a warning that they were taking on more than they could handle when one of the arquebuses was discharged, accidentally or not she would never know, the ball missing her so closely that she could feel the wind of its passing.

"Alright, alright," she called, and to her oarsmen, "Avast rowing."

In a quieter voice she directed some of her hidden crewmen to doubleshot one of their patereros and mount it when ready.

The boats approached. The paterero was loaded and mounted. She gave the order to fire at their leader and watched impassively as its bows were shattered to pieces.

"That should have been grape, but I've no desire to kill you. Bloody pirates."

She ordered her crew to resume rowing and watched the struggles of the men in the water, some of whom she knew would not be able to swim. Stupid unnecessary deaths. She was thoroughly out of temper, furious with herself for not having had the patereroes mounted from the moment they slipped moorings, but she had to accept that these Waterford men were only doing what she herself did in Connacht. They were merely less professional.

The incident did confirm her opinion, unspoken to Black Tom, that a country in which even a simple river trip was a hazardous undertaking, such was the belligerence of its inhabitants to each other, was not a country which could ever present the united front that a proper rebellion would demand.

This line of thought brought her back to Tom's warning and her declaration that she was embarking on a peaceful trading voyage. She had omitted to add that should a suitable opportunity for a bit of piracy arise, she would not hesitate to follow that course also. She was not under any illusion that the Earl did not suspect as much, particularly now that she had to raise the gold to repay what it had cost him to buy her freedom. Tom was rich but this was business, entirely divorced from friendship, and Grace herself would not have had it any other way. Of course piracy, even the mild forms practiced by the O'Malleys, was a dangerous business, both in its commission and, particularly, in its consequences, and she was well aware that the English could be quite duplicitous in their understanding of what constituted piracy. If it benefited the Treasury, it was lauded as enterprising Naval activity and, as such, attracted the support of countless investors including, it was rumoured, the Queen herself, all determined on profit, no matter what the means employed. If carried out by anyone else, it was liable to be dealt with very summarily indeed, and Grace fully appreciated that were she ever to be caught at her piratical activities she might expect, not the praise of a nation, but a hangman's rope.

"God Bless you, Tom", she thought warmly, "for trying to keep me on the straight and narrow."

The rest of the trip downriver was uneventful and they were soon mooring on the Waterford quays below Reginald's Tower, from which it was but a short walk to the deLacy house, a large new stone building which had a warehouse at ground level surmounted by spacious living quarters on the first and second floors. It was a conceit of the deLacys that their house very much resembled a Venetian Palazzo, memories of which deLacy senior retained from a visit in his youth to that city and, even if the reality did not quite live up to the conceit, it was certainly one of the finer buildings in Waterford. Grace, who had visited the house before, enjoyed its spaciousness and proximity to the sea. All of her own dwellings existed from the age of castle warfare and were thus built entirely for defence with little allowance being made for gracious living, although her own room at the top of Rockfleet, her favourite castle, had fine views over land and sea. These views were obviously primarily designed to prevent the unseen approach of any visitor, friend or foe, but could still be enjoyed for the rugged beauty of the vista they commanded. Of course, neither of these dwellings, Grace's or the deLacy's, could stand any comparison with Tom's castle at Carrick.

There were warehouse men already at work and one of them escorted Grace upstairs to where Hugh deLacy, head of the house, was sitting down to breakfast. He jumped to his feet at her entrance.

"Good morning, Grace. Good morning. How good to see you. You're well, I hope?" he cried with unfeigned happiness, before inviting her to join him.

The O'Malleys and the deLacys had had a mercantile connection for some years and the mutual bond which had existed between the families had been strengthened by Grace's rescue of young Hugh deLacy junior when his ship had foundered in a gale on Achill Head. The lad had subsequently been murdered by the MacMahons of Doona while hunting deer on Achill, to avenge which Grace had tracked down and executed those responsible, subsequently seizing their castle for good measure. In other circumstances this might have put the deLacys in debt to Grace, but her fondness for young Hugh (they had, in fact, been lovers, but this was tacitly ignored) precluded this possibility and had merely strengthened the ties already existing between the two families.

"I'm very well indeed," replied Grace, "in spite of having been on the end of Tom Butler's hospitality for the last few nights and then attacked by some clowns on the way downstream, just when I could have done with a bit of peace and quiet."

He was instantly solicitous.

"The Powers. It must have been the Powers. The old man is sharp as a pin, but the sons would be just sufficiently stupid to try to take on the Dana. He married badly, you know. Anyway, you're safe and that's the main thing. Come, sit down here with me."

Over breakfast, family, the Powers and business matters were discussed until, putting his napkin down, Hugh paused, glanced at Grace, and inquired what her immediate plans might be.

"We're off to Corunna as soon as we complete our cargo. Why do you ask?"

"I'll get straight to the point. We've been having trouble with those villains from Baltimore again, most particularly with the O'Driscolls."

"Sure, I've never trusted those O'Driscolls, far too friendly with the English," interrupted Grace, before nodding at her host to continue.

"Well, during last week's storms, a Portuguese ship carrying 72 tuns of wine for Waterford was blown off course and ended up off Baltimore. She was tricked into harbour by the offer of a pilot and was then, of course, seized. She's now being offered back to us, through the agency of those same damned Powers, for a great sum of money. We, that is to say the deLacys and the other merchants involved, thought to swallow our pride and raise the money, even though it's quite likely that most of the cargo has by now been drunk or carried inland. Then I heard that the Dana had been seen going up river and, knowing that you would probably call on us on your way back down, I persuaded the others to wait on the possibility that, you being willing to lead it, we might raise an expedition to retake the ship and teach the O'Driscolls a real lesson that would finally put an end to their capers. There are two carracks in port at the moment for which I believe we could raise about 200 men to augment your crew. What do you think?"

Grace, with her debt to the Earl very much in the forefront of her mind, needed very little thought.

"I've no problem with handing out a beating to the O'Driscolls but, much as I honour you and your city, Hugh, my crew would need paying. They're an avaricious lot, you know. What might they expect?"

Hugh deLacy was as well aware as any Irishman with maritime inclinations that, in discussing payment for her crew, Grace mainly meant payment for herself. Grace O'Malley loved a profit. Hugh was sympathetic, however, being aware that when Donal had been killed, she had been cast adrift by his family without her dowry, having to undergo the disgrace of going back, penniless, to her own family, after which she had vowed that never again would she allow herself to be reliant on the charity of others. So Hugh was sympathetic. But he would not let his sympathy show. Smiling inwardly therefore, he made ready to bargain.

The matter of payment was quickly concluded, a guaranteed sum from Waterford, and any reasonable plunder that presented itself in the way of prizes to be kept by the Dana.

It was obvious that the success of the expedition depended entirely on surprise and so it was agreed that, to keep the O'Driscolls unsuspecting, Hugh would continue negotiations with the Powers, while the three ships would sail from Waterford independently. The carracks would embark their soldiers further down the coast, after which all three ships would rendezvous of Hook Head and thence, under Grace's command, proceed to Baltimore.

"On an entirely different matter, I've a favour to ask," said Hugh.

"Go on."

"We have a priest, a Cistercian monk, lately arrived with us. He's been in some way implicated in a plot to free the Scottish Queen, but escaped to Ireland just ahead of

Walsingham's spies who, even at this moment, seek him here in Waterford. Do you think that you might be able to take him to Spain with you?"

"Walsingham, eh? That man's name is turning up a bit too often for comfort. Well, I've no particular love for priests, but it was the Cistercians who taught me my Latin so, if he doesn't get in the way, and is prepared to pay passage, I'll find room for him. He may not like the accommodation but it won't be any worse than a monk's cell and, if he's not too pampered a priest, it should suit him well enough."

A servant was sent to fetch the priest.

The man who shortly entered the room was not the pale cleric expected by Grace, but a tall, tanned, strongly built man with a scar running across his right cheek. He wore the same white habit as the monks at Belclare and Murrisk but embellished with a cross on the front. On seeing Grace, he hesitated slightly before bowing to her with a cold smile. He addressed Hugh.

"Your servant told me that I was to meet a ship's captain."

"This is she" replied Hugh."

Any surprise felt by the priest was suppressed and after a moment he spoke again, this time to Grace.

"Forgive me, Madam. Unreasonably perhaps, I didn't expect to find a woman in command of a war galley."

"I hope you're not one of those priests who think women should be seen but not heard."

Grace turned to Hugh, with a coldly enquiring look of her own.

He hastened to correct the misapprehension,

"I do apologise. Father, may I name my particular friend to you, Captain Grace O'Malley. Grace, this is Father James Allen, who seeks passage with you."

The priest offered his hand to Grace, saying "Again, please forgive me. I'm delighted to make your acquaintance Madam, and would be honoured if you would consent to my sailing with you." She accepted his hand, giving her assent to his request.

He went on, "I don't wish to appear presumptuous, but I'd be happy to be away from Waterford as hastily as your commitments will allow."

Grace nodded in agreement.

"We'll be taking on cargo from downstairs shortly. I suggest that you clothe yourself less ostentatiously and you can then go on board as a workman."

The priest appeared to be about to protest, but Grace held up a hand to stop him.

"You're a hunted priest. I've agreed to carry you to Spain and so we'll do things as I dictate, not you. You may swallow your pride for the moment and consider that your marching onto my ship, dressed as you are, is as likely to put my head in a noose as your own, and I'm not yet ready for martyrdom. Mr. deLacy here will confirm that I've but lately escaped one hangman and I've no wish to risk the attentions of another so, if you want to travel on the Dana, you'll do it on my terms or not at all."

The priest bowed and said, "Madam, You're right, of course. I'm thoughtless. I will change immediately."

He left the room and, shortly afterwards, Grace saw him, in seaman's dress, shifting bales among the sailors and the warehousemen.

"There's more to that man than meets the eye," she observed to Hugh.

"I doubt not that there is, Grace, but I know little of him other than that he's a priest on the run and, though God knows that we wouldn't wish to draw attention to ourselves in these troubled times, he is still a priest and will burn if the Protestants lay hands on him. I wouldn't want that on my conscience."

"Amen," said Grace.

CHAPTER 3

The following morning, the little squadron could be seen moving westwards, just out of sight of land, the galley leading the two carracks.

The priest and his luggage had been safely brought aboard and, having replenished their water and completed their cargo, they had left Waterford, ostensibly for Spain, with no one, it was hoped, any the wiser as to their true destination. The carracks had also slipped quietly from port and had picked up their cargoes of men down the estuary, before waiting at the rendezvous. The two hundred odd were all hardened fighting men who had once formed part of the Earl of Ormond's private army. That army, and that of the Earl of Desmond, had been disbanded after the battle of Affane by order of the Queen. These unemployed soldiers, mainly Scottish gallowglasses, now lived in desperate circumstances, wandering in small bands, and keeping low to avoid the fate of the seven hundred of their colleagues who had been executed by Spenser and Drury in a harsh decision aimed at keeping the peace in Munster. As such, they had little to lose and lots to gain by joining the proposed enterprise.

The priest had been allotted quarters with the pilot in his very small cabin just off Grace's, and there he had stayed until they were safely at sea. He was now standing in the stern, taking in the ship, her crew and, particularly, her captain, who moved easily about the ship, obviously very much at home and, equally obviously, very much in command. She was taller than average and tanned in a way that a labourer's wife might be, a look which no lady of his acquaintance would countenance. Of course, he had to admit that no lady of his acquaintance would be capable of sailing a ship, and even less, for that matter, of commanding the rough body of sailors and soldiers that made up her crew. Her long red hair was tied back by a black ribbon but was otherwise unadorned. She had a strong face, firm mouth, and bright blue eyes which moved constantly and which, he suspected, could be unyielding in their gaze if surveying something of which she disapproved. She had exchanged the saffron coloured dress which she had worn in deLacys for the sailor's garb of her crew. As if aware of his scrutiny, she turned suddenly and, with a half smile, asked, "Well, do you like what you see?"

He was surprised to find himself discomfited by the question, but replied smoothly enough, appearing to misunderstand.

"It's a well ordered ship, Madam."

"And have your priestly duties given you much experience of ships?"

"I have not always been a priest," he replied, guardedly.

"I didn't think you had," said Grace. "What else have you been?"

Again, he was discomfited. Such directness from a woman was as far outside his experience as her command of this galley.

"My past is not relevant, Madam. I am now a monk and that is what matters."

"Have it your own way," replied Grace.

She was in high good humour. The departure from Waterford had been followed by a night at sea to avoid prying eyes. In normal circumstances, without the need for secrecy, the galley would have found somewhere to moor for the night, in which instance Grace and the crew off watch could rest. But these were not normal circumstances, so last night they had kept moving. However, the difficulties of keeping station with the carracks in the darkness had meant a restless night for all, particularly the captain, and the priest had been left to his own devices. Now, with the big lateen sails drawing on a mild southwesterly breeze and the squadron moving easily towards its destination, she was able to give attention to her passenger.

"You must be hungry. Come and breakfast with me."

They sat under the stern awning where they were joined, at Grace's invitation, by some of the galley's more senior men, as well as her youngest son, Theobald, known to all as Tibbott, who had been born twelve years previously on this very galley while they were under attack from an Algerine galley. She told the priest how her pilot, Thomas, one of the men to whom the priest had just been introduced, had been wounded and all but lost control of the ship and, in desperation, had begged Grace from her cabin whence, coming on deck, she had led the counter attack which had forced the Algerines back onto their own vessel. Afterwards, despite his wound, which had left him with a permanent limp, she had soundly berated Thomas for disturbing her as she lay with her new born baby, had even threatened to turn him ashore but, as she admitted with a smile, he was much too good a pilot to be left on the beach so she had put up with him since. The other guests were Rory and Conor O'Malley, kinsmen who might well have challenged Grace's preeminence in the clan, but who cheerfully acknowledged, tongue in cheek, that she was a better man than either of them. There was also Fergus O'Flaherty, the young half brother of Thomas. The majority of the crew were, in fact, either O'Malleys of her own clan or O'Flahertys who, upset at her treatment by his family, had followed Grace after Donal's death.

"I see from the sun that we are heading west," said the priest, after all had eaten and drunk companionably for a while. "When do we turn south?"

"Did Hugh not tell you that we had some business in Baltimore first?" Asked Grace.

"No. My arrival at his house was both hurried and secret and my departure was as you saw. I wasn't aware that you intended to sail anywhere but Spain."

"Well, you needn't worry, Father. Our business won't involve you and, in fact, it would probably be better for you to remain on board if we have any need to go ashore."

She stood up, stretched and said, "You'll have to excuse me now, please. This boat won't sail herself and, the way Thomas is settling in, it doesn't look as though he has any intention of tending to her," and then she was gone before the priest could respond. The men, other than Thomas, also made their excuses and left the table. Thomas smiled.

"You mustn't pay her too much heed, Father. She can be pretty haughty when the mood strikes her." The priest, who had seen a brief glimpse of this haughtiness in the deLacy house, nodded. "And her moods can be quite unpredictable. It keeps the men on their toes. She is, though, very fair so they accept the squalls. Also, this is an entirely free crew. There are no slaves here, unlike on the galleys of the Spaniards or the Algerines, or the French, for that matter, so they could leave if they didn't like her methods. They don't, of course."

The priest digested this for a moment before asking, "and was her son truly born on this galley?"

"Yes, it was as she said, although the situation wasn't quite as bad as she now maintains. I doubt I'd still be here if it had. It has, however, given Tibbott his nickname, Tibbott –na-Long, Theobald of the Ships."

"And has he spent all his life at sea since?"

"Oh no. He was fostered out with one of his father's subchieftains who taught him his weaponry and tactics, as well as English, Latin and the Law. His mother though, intends for him to succeed her in time as a sea going chieftain, so she occasionally takes him on what she anticipates will be routine voyages, to expand his horizons, as you might say", this with a swift glance at the priest but, seeing no response, he carried on, "the languages - she also speaks Latin and English herself, as well as Spanish – are a prudency against the day when you English may finally, God forbid, have your way in Ireland, and, were that ever to occur, she would have him familiar with the arts of diplomacy as well as those of the sword. She herself has made it her business to meet any Englishmen who she feels might have influence in London, as well as keeping well with the likes of Black Tom Butler."

He changed the subject.

"And what of yourself, Father? Why the urgency to get to Spain? There are rumours about you, you know."

The priest sighed and explained that he had merely arrived in England on family business at the wrong time and in the wrong company. He was a Cistercian, not a Jesuit, and much though he would like to see a Catholic on the throne, he did not see that that end justified the murder of a Queen, heretic though she might be. When his companions were taken, he had managed to escape, but was tarred with treason by association. Finding the channel ports closed, he had managed to get to Wales and thence to Ireland on a boat belonging, by happy chance, to the deLacys. He would be happy anywhere on the continent, although the Cistercian monastery to which he belonged was a Spanish one.

Feeling that he had disclosed enough for the time being, he sought a new subject.

"I didn't know that the Irish built galleys."

"They don't. The Scots built the Dana. They normally build much smaller than this and more for transport than battle, but they built this, and a couple more like it, to a specification of Grace's father who was also himself once attacked by Algerine galleys on a voyage to Spain in a carrack. He was lucky with the wind that day, they couldn't use their oars, and he was able to disable them sufficiently with his sakers to allow him to make his escape. He liked the idea, though, of the larger galley with the two masts, and the oars as well so that he wouldn't be totally dependent on the wind. He did change the design, giving it a wider beam and deeper draught to make it more stable in the Atlantic. He also, as you see, abandoned the ram for the same reason. A handy benefit of all this is that it makes us look more like the merchantman that we're supposed to be most of the time. It doesn't make it any more comfortable unfortunately. The men still sleep in the open except in calm weather or at anchor. Come and see."

They walked forward along the central gangway. The oars were inboard and, other than the crew members attending to the sail trim, the men lounged on the benches or occupied themselves with their weapons, the usual array of swords, axes, crossbows, with the odd arquebus. On the forward platform, the gunner was busy with his mates around the ship's main weapons, a huge twenty four pounder cannon and two eighteen pounder demis. There were also, noted the priest, a number of swivel mounted patereros along the outer platforms above the thole pins. This, decided the priest, who did have sea going experience, as Grace had surmised, would be a very formidable fighting machine.

Two nights later they lay at anchor in a small cove to the east of Baltimore and a council of war was held aboard the galley. The captains of the carracks, both Waterford men, were familiar with the area but were content to leave arrangements to Grace. Their soldiers had nothing to contribute either other than a fierce demand that they get on shore as quickly as possible and sack the town. Of the crew, only Thomas, as pilot, spoke and he was listened to intently, at least by the sailors in the company. He produced a chart of the area on which he had noted tides and currents, on the basis of which Grace decided, that there being no intelligence of what other ships were in port or what numbers of men, and there being no opportunity to find out without risking the loss of surprise, they would avail of the existing good conditions to make a dawn attack on Sherkin Island to be followed by a landing in the town. The Portuguese ship would be attacked and seized wherever they found her.

Signals were agreed and the others returned to their ships to await the dawn.

That night final preparations were made. The gunner and his team checked their shot and prepared cartridges. The crew readied their weapons and the skiff was hoisted out from its normal position amidships to be towed behind the galley. A substantial meal was served and the crew, replete, settled down on the benches and gangways to sleep as best they could for a few hours.

At dawn the next morning, Grace stood by the tiller as the ship got underway, Tibbott by her side. The wind continuing favourable, they were still under sail. The advantage of maneuverability which the oars would have conferred was not yet felt by Grace to be worth the consequent fatigue to the oarsmen.

The priest appeared on deck where he was curtly told he might remain if he did not get in the way.

Grace put a hand on Tibbott's shoulder and squeezed it.

"Watch and learn, Tibbott. One day you'll also sail ships and lead men and the only way you'll learn to do it well is by experience. And don't be afraid to be frightened. Tis the very bad captain who doesn't feel fearful from time to time. He'll often make rash decisions. Just keep your fears in check."

She called for Conor to join them on the stern.

"I don't expect too much trouble today Con, but keep an eye on him anyway."

Grace was rarely introspective. She had, early in her sea going career, decided that dwelling on matters overlong gave rise to doubts, and where doubts existed, failure was more likely. Decisiveness was everything. This morning however, her thoughts were crowding in despite herself. She loved Tibbott dearly and had high hopes for him, as the MacWilliam, chief of all IarConnacht if the Irish way of life continued, or as a Baronet, even an Earl, if the English prevailed. She wanted him, therefore, to learn leadership at an early age, but intended to be careful of the risks to which he might be exposed. He was not to be lost by carelessness. Her other children, Owen, Margaret and Murrough, were now fully grown and almost beyond her influence, Murrough indeed, being of a violent disposition, his father's son, and totally unheeding of any counsel she might offer. So Tibbott was her last chance of a real successor to the O'Malley chieftainship.

She shook herself free of these thoughts – weak and womanly - and applied herself to the work at hand, not that there was much for her to do at this time, the crew being an experienced and seamanlike one, other than wait.

They rounded Toe Head and there, directly in front of them, over a sea sparkling in the dawn light, lay Sherkin Island. The final approach, when they were likely to be spotted at any moment, seemed to take an age to the impatient crew but, at last, they were within long range cannon shot of Sherkin's castle, Dun na Long, before which, rising and falling gently on the morning swell, lay the anchored Portuguese ship, the Santa Maria do Soci.

The fretting inactivity of the last hour was over. The big cumbersome lateen sails were lowered and the oarsmen took over to bring the galley closer inshore, where anchors were dropped fore and aft to bring her guns into alignment with the castle.

At the signal from Grace, the expectantly waiting gunner applied his linstock to the touchhole of the big cannon and, with a deafening report, the first ball was fired at the castle walls. Some slight adjustments were made to the springs on the anchor cables to alter the galley's alignment and, when the gunner was satisfied, the two demi cannon were also fired.

A slow, rolling bombardment now began, the three big guns being fired independently of each other to lessen the possibility of damage to the timbers of the galley, which shuddered at each recoil.

The surprise was complete. The impact of the first shot

on the castle had created consternation within its walls and also on board the Santa Maria. People could soon be seen rushing around the battlements of the castle and there was some ineffectual arquebus return fire which fell well short of the galley. Grace murmured a silent prayer of thanks. Until this moment, she had not known whether there might not be cannon mounted on those battlements. Had there been, she would have had to withdraw and consider a land assault on an awakened garrison. The contest between stone walls and fragile timbers would have been too unequal. In the event, she could leave the castle to the gunner and turn her attention to the Santa Maria. It was apparent that the ship had no more than an anchor watch on board and even as they watched, these men could now be seen hauling desperately to get their skiff alongside and, having done so, were tumbling into it in a panic to get away before the galley should turn its guns on them.

"They must all be bloody drunk," said Thomas with professional disgust, "not to have kept a look out at least, not to mind cutting the cables and running her ashore."

"Ours not to question, Thomas," replied Grace, laughing, "merely to be thankful for our good fortune."

By now, the carracks had also come up and anchored, closer inshore than the Dana, whence their few small four pounder guns could add their weight to the bombardment and, although fairly useless against the thick stone walls were, by virtue of their quicker rate of fire, making a considerable contribution to the noise and the demoralization of the castle's defenders. It was not long before these defenders could also be seen abandoning their positions and making for the boats tied up at the little jetty, from which they too were soon rowing hard for the mainland.

Grace called for the guns to cease firing and Rory was sent with the skiff and a prize crew to take possession of the Santa Maria. He was quickly on board and shortly sent the skiff back with the information that, although her logs and charts were untouched, most of her cargo had disappeared, and her captain and crew were also missing, presumably being held prisoner in Baltimore.

Grace called the other two captains on board again and updated them with her revised plan. She would leave Baltimore for the moment and head instead for Clear Island where, it was hoped, they would arrive before its inhabitants became aware of what had happened on Sherkin. The carracks meanwhile, would land their men here, take possession of the castle, burn all the O'Driscoll small boats, send foraging parties across the island to subdue any resistance, and collect any weapons that the islanders might try to hide for future retaliation. Finally, she expressly forbade that there be any killing or indiscriminate destruction of any property other than the boats. The priest now intervened to request that he be allowed to go ashore with the soldiers to tend to any defenders who might have been wounded during the bombardment. Grace, who was illogically thinking that she did not particularly like having a priest as a passenger, even a paying one, impatiently acquiesced. He left the galley with the two captains.

"Good riddance," muttered Grace to Thomas, who regarded her fondly as she turned away to issue the string of orders that would set the galley on her way towards Clear Island.

She had expected much greater resistance from Sherkin than had actually been shown. The O'Driscolls must have expected some retaliation from Waterford, despite the apparent success of their ransom demands. It argued a great complacency which she intended to exploit to the full. Baltimore would be alive by now to the calamity befalling it, and although it too was going to be attacked, that attack would be better undertaken with the islands subdued and the Dana's lines of retreat clear. Accordingly, all haste was made in getting under way and it was not long after midday that they were approaching Clear's north harbour. This time however, there was no surprise. As they dropped anchor, a deputation set out in a boat under a white flag.

"Keep an eye on the castle," said Grace to Conor. "It seems unlikely that they'll have cannon here if they didn't on Sherkin, but there's no point taking chances. Tell them to stop there," she continued to Thomas when the boat was about a half cable away.

"State your business," called Thomas when the boat had stopped, its oars being gently plied in a professional fashion to maintain its position against the flow of the tide.

"Ye're from Waterford?" asked the leader of the deputation, standing up in the boat.

"Yes," called Thomas back, murmuring in an aside to Grace that a fishing boat must have seen the carracks with the Waterford crests – the galley showed no identification at this time - and escaped to raise the alarm here: they would not otherwise have rowed out to address a completely unknown ship and risked death or slavery by an Algerine or other pirate.

The man in the boat sat down and there was a hurried conference before he rose again to call:

"Ye should know that we had nothing to do with that Portuguese ship. We live our own lives here, and it's a hard one, fishing and raising a few crops. Your quarrel is with Baltimore, not us. We can help you with provisions if you wish but there's nothing else here worth landing for."

"Who are you?" asked Thomas.

"Jeremiah O'Connor. And this is my son Seamus," he said, indicating a strapping youth who sat at one of the oars. "We're all unarmed," he finished.

"Aha," said Grace with a small smile. "Tell them to come alongside."

They rowed the remaining distance to the galley and threw a rope aboard to be made fast. Grace looked over the side.

"Name of the devil," exclaimed the man who had called himself Jeremiah O'Connor, "Tis Grace O'Malley, God blast it. I should have recognized the galley."

"Indeed it is," replied Grace sweetly. "And why would Fineen O'Driscoll be trying to fool us that he's someone else if he's got nothing to hide other than a few fish and some poor ould crops? If you ask me, Fineen, I'd say there's more here than you're letting on. Wine perhaps?"

She became businesslike.

"Yourself and your son can come on board, and you," she pointed to the others, "can go ashore again. We'll bring Fineen and Seamus back to you when we're ready."

Leaving the boy with Thomas, she led O'Driscoll into her cabin where she opened a bottle of whiskey, offering him a glass. He drained it quickly and held the glass out for more.

"I thought the Galwaymen had finally sorted you out," he said bitterly.

"Sure now Fineen, anyone would think you sorry that they didn't." She was enjoying this. "They did try, mind you, but we saw them off, so we did, and would probably have captured the lot of them if we'd had a few more men. I doubt we'll hear from them again any time soon. Anyway, that's by the way. It's yourself and your thieving clan that we're concerned with now."

"What do you want?" asked O'Driscoll.

"For myself and my crew, only the wine. We've already agreed prize money for the safe return of the Santa Maria. We've retaken her, by the way."

"There's no wine here," said O'Driscoll.

"You're here, Fineen," replied Grace, "so you'll forgive my doubting your word that the wine isn't here as well. In any event, I intend to see for myself."

She fixed him with a hard stare.

"The boy will remain here," she said."

"I wouldn't expect any different from a bloody pirate. It was the sad day that your father ever let you out of the house.

You should have been kept in the kitchen like any other decent woman, with the odd beating to keep manners on you. You'll get your wine, but leave the boy alone."

"Another poor deluded male, God help us. The boy will remain with me," she repeated, "while you go back with some of my men. If there are no tricks, you can have him back after we've taken the wine on board."

She dismissed him and called for Fergus.

"Take a dozen men ashore with the skiff. Have a good look around. Make sure that there are no cannon on the castle and that nobody looks to be organizing resistance. If you're happy, I'll bring the galley in and we can load the wine, whatever's left of it."

She jerked a thumb at O'Driscoll. "Take him with you but watch him closely."

"You needn't worry about me," said O'Driscoll. "I was a fool to bring the boy with me, but then I didn't expect to be dealing with a bloody bitch like you."

Grace smiled as she watched him go over the side into the skiff. She wondered whether she would harm the boy if O'Driscoll played false but decided, somewhat ruefully, that her reputation for cold hearted bloodiness was such that the eventuality would not arise.

Fergus and his heavily armed party landed, and followed O'Driscoll through the silent, hostile islanders to the castle. Shortly, he stood on the battlements and signaled that the galley could come in. They came slowly in under oars, the lead being heaved to confirm that they had sufficient water under their keel not to run aground. The shallow draught of the galley made her ideal for this kind of inshore work and they were soon tied up at the small stone pier, the swivel guns manned and pointed at the sullen crowd.

Loading the wine tuns was not easy, even with the low freeboard of the galley, and storing it was even more awkward. It would have to remain lashed between the benches amidships so as not to upset the trim of the galley and, even so, was going to make her top heavy, this apart from the very serious deprivation of most of their oars in an emergency.

"Let's hope that we don't meet an English cruiser in this state," said Thomas.

Grace, who had been thinking that very thing, was in an agony of impatience to get away but concealed it, only commenting to O'Driscoll,

"I'm sorry we won't be able to avail of the hospitality that you're undoubtedly going to offer us, Fineen. Perhaps another time."

O'Driscoll did not reply, but stood silently watching, clenching and unclenching his fists in impotent fury.

At last they were done. They eased gently away from the jetty, O'Driscoll back on board, being followed by the boat which had originally brought him out to the galley.

At a suitable distance from the harbour, Grace anchored and O'Driscoll and his son went over the side again to the waiting boat.

When they were about half way to the shore, Grace ordered the patereros to open fire on all the fishing boats in the harbour.

O'Driscoll stood up in his boat, screaming,

"You filthy heartless bitch. May you rot in Hell."

"Have a care Fineen, lest we sink you as well. We've been paid for this. Waterford wants you properly punished and, as a business woman, I have every intention of doing what I've been paid to do. You should treat it as business yourself. It may make you feel better."

When all the boats, save O'Driscoll's own, were sunk, the anchor was hoisted, the sails raised and they headed back towards Sherkin, O'Driscoll's invective getting fainter and fainter until finally disappearing as they sailed out of earshot.

They had not long rounded Cape Clear when they saw the smoke over Sherkin.

CHAPTER 4

"I shouldn't have trusted those Scottish raparees without supervision," fumed Grace. "They've been too long undisciplined to have been left to their own devices. Well, there's not much we can do now until we get there, and then it'll probably be too late."

They sailed on in silence, Grace studying the island intently from the bows of the ship and the rest of the crew watching from the side platforms. It was soon apparent to all that Dun na Long was in flames, but there was also smoke elsewhere on the island.

It was imperative that the galley be made properly battleworthy again as a first priority. Accordingly, Grace brought it right in to the jetty to unload the wine as quickly as possible, after which the Santa Maria could be brought in to reload it at leisure.

Even as they had been tying up at the jetty, they had been met by an agitated crowd, amongst whom was the priest.

"I must protest, Madam, at the behaviour of your men."

Grace held up a hand to stop him.

"You should understand that they're not my men. They are in the employ of the City of Waterford."

He interrupted, "You are in command of this expedition, Madam, and are thus nominally, if not de facto, in control of them. They have burned the Abbey of the Friars Minor, desecrating the chapel and stealing what they may. They are also burning the houses of the people, as well as their boats. They have certainly killed a couple of men who resisted, and wounded others. I insist that you assert whatever authority you have and put an end to this brigandage."

She waited until he had finished and then asked for the whereabouts of the Waterford captains.

"They've returned to their ships," he replied. "They were unable to stop the soldiers, saying that you were in command. I believe them to be frightened of the soldiers."

Grace asked Thomas to signal for the two captains - Rory had already joined them from the Santa Maria - and then returned her attention to the priest.

"You don't appear to have done much yourself to stop them."

"Madam, I am a priest but, even so, had I been armed, I should certainly have intervened."

She looked at him thoughtfully.

"At the moment, this is all irrelevant, regrettable though that may seem. What is relevant is that the galley be emptied of this damned wine as soon as possible and become a proper fighting ship again. If you want a quick end to this," she called to the people on the jetty, "you can help with the unloading."

There was a resentful stir but no movement to help.

"I didn't think they would," she said to Thomas, "but there was no harm trying. Alright, let's get on with it."

Unloading the tuns was no easier than loading them had been. The block and tackle arrangements which could be rigged on the mast of the Santa Maria, for instance, had no place on a galley: its beam was too narrow and its draught too shallow to allow the amount of ballast that would stop it tipping wildly when the load was swung outwards.

Night was drawing on by the time the work of unloading the wine from the Dana and restowing it on to the Portuguese ship was finally accomplished and, the men being fairly exhausted by this time, Grace decided that the Scots were better left until morning. The final task of the day was to anchor the galley where it would be safe from a night attack, although a full strength watch would be kept throughout the hours of darkness. Grace would have preferred to provide the men with a more comfortable night's sleep ashore but, with the Scots on the rampage, even drunk as she thought they probably all were by now, the galley's benches, although uncomfortable, were safer. They did, however, eat and drink well again and were quite cheerful about their sleeping arrangements to which, in any case, they were well accustomed.

The two Waterford captains, who had been kept uneasily waiting by Grace all this time, were now asked to explain their lack of control. They protested vigorously that, once the Gallowglasses were ashore, they had become totally un-amenable to orders. The priest added his weight to their protestations and Grace, with a proper show of reluctance, accepted them. It did, as she intended, make it more certain that she could expect complete obedience from them for the remainder of the expedition and she was content with that.

The galley was astir before dawn. Keeping a strong contingent of men on board, she divided the remainder into two groups under Rory and Conor, and sent them ashore to find the Scots, wherever they lay. The Danas began to make their way cautiously inland, where they soon began to come across their would-be allies. All, as Grace had anticipated, were in various stages of drunkenness, lying in ditches or in the few cabins that had not been fired, with local island woman in attendance, some as drunk as the soldiers but most in a state of terror.

The Scots were disarmed, generally without resistance but some reaching belatedly for their swords and battleaxes to try to ward off their assailants. These were cut down mercilessly, even the full length chain mail that they habitually wore being of little protection against the determined assault of Rory's and Conor's men. Of those who resisted, their captain alone was not killed but allowed to live on surrender of his weapons. He was, naturally, in a fury, demanding to know why he and his men had been turned upon by his allies. His family, the clan Donnell, had come for years to campaign for the O'Malleys in their frequent wars with their Connacht neighbours. He would expect large recompense from their bitch of a captain for this treachery.

His fumings were ignored and he was herded, with the remnant of his men, back to the harbour. There, they were met by Grace who, keeping him aside, ordered the others to be ferried out to the carracks, where they were bundled unceremoniously into the holds under the watchful eyes of the swivel gunners that Grace had already stationed. She turned on their captain.

"Why, Hamish O'Donnell, do you so flagrantly disobey my orders? You were strictly ordered to burn boats only. Instead, you have looted a monastery, fired the whole island, murdered, raped and pillaged like a heathen. Why sir, why?"

The Scot, whose excesses of the previous day and night were beginning to tell heavily on him, blustered:

"We were employed to punish these people enough to stop them ever again interfering with Waterford trade. You've done the same often enough yourself."

She regarded him very coldly.

"Do not try to reduce me to your own animal level. You're a very lucky man that I don't hang you this minute. Get out of my sight."

He was pushed roughly into a boat and taken to one of the carracks, where he joined his men in captivity in the hold.

She turned to the priest, who had watched this exchange, and said, "I don't owe you any explanation, but I should have foreseen this. They've always been ferocious in battle, rarely giving or asking quarter and, when on the winning side, behaving as badly as ever their Viking ancestors did. Once they get over their present dissipation, they'll start plotting their escape and revenge."

She indicated the pile of weapons and loot that her men had taken from the Scots.

"Please get the monks to go through that. The rest will be scattered across the island, and the islanders, in their piety, will undoubtedly return whatever they find," this last with just a hint of irony.

She turned to her men.

"We still have to visit Baltimore. It's a pity that we don't have the Scots. The O'Driscolls won't know that, of course, since there are no boats for the islanders to warn them, or should be no boats," she added, before continuing, "when the monks have found whatever is theirs, get the rest of that pile on board. We'll leave the Santa Maria here with a guard while we attend to Baltimore. I'd like to get this done before nightfall. I don't doubt that someone will have concealed a boat somewhere and will try to cross in darkness. I wouldn't want them to know that half of our troops are being kept prisoner by ourselves. They might be more inclined to resistance."

In the event, there was little resistance from the men of Baltimore. Fineen O'Driscoll had managed to find his way home in a boat that had escaped destruction and, although the younger members of the clan were all for putting to death the party that Grace had put ashore under a flag of truce, to negotiate the release of the Portuguese sailors, he, Fineen, reminded them of the force, guns and gallowglasses, that would be turned on them if they resisted. He also pointed out that the safety of truce parties was sacrosanct: they would recall what Genghis Khan did to the Persians after his ambassadors were mistreated and, if they thought Grace O' Malley any less vicious than Ghengis Khan, they were sadly deluded.

The Portuguese sailors were freed and the gold which had been demanded as recompense for the wine which had been drunk was paid, albeit reluctantly.

The remaining O'Driscoll boats were now burned, the clan's thirty oared galley alone being spared, to be taken as a prize.

They still had to deal with the Scots. Grace ordered that they be landed up the coast from Baltimore, sufficiently close not to find some other clan's boats to attack one of the carracks when they were all ashore, and sufficiently far not to be immediately set upon by the O'Driscolls when they realized what was happening. After the last of them had been landed, their weapons were sent after them, without which they would surely have been massacred.

She advised their leader, as he left in the last boat, that he should seek out the Earl of Desmond, who was rumoured to be looking to start another rebellion, and who would need all the troops he could get. This advice, which was offered neutrally, was met with a storm of abuse in which no words were minced, and to which, with a wave to the departing chieftain, Grace merely smiled and said, "this is becoming a habit."

"Are you not taking a chance, letting them go so easily," asked Thomas.

"No," replied Grace, "they're professional soldiers. When he cools down, O'Donnell will accept that he's got no more than he deserved. Soldiering will always have its ups and downs. They've not been paid but they're still alive and will hope to fight another day. Anyway, despite our best endeavours, there's no way they won't have managed to hang on to some of their spoils from Sherkin. They're also much safer from Spenser and Drury here than they were in Waterford, and if we ever meet again in reversed circumstances, I'll remind him of that. Not that I anticipate that ever happening," she finished, touching the rail as she did so.

CHAPTER 5

"By God," said Grace, "tis good to be on the ocean again."

The good weather persisted, and the Dana was sailing easily under her big lateens. The previous day they had parted company with the Waterford ships and the Santa Maria off the Old Head of Kinsale, the Dana to begin her Spanish voyage and the latter to return to Waterford with the captured O'Driscoll galley (of which Hugh deLacy would dispose, retaining the proceeds on Grace's behalf, to be paid eventually to Black Tom). The Waterford men were, in truth, quite relieved to be escaping Grace's command. They had only known her previously by her hard, hard, reputation and they had found that reputation to be more than justified on their slight acquaintance. The Santa Marias, on the other hand, were effusive in their thanks and salutations and had, when Grace visited them on their ship, pressed upon her a quantity of the wine which had been returned to them. At that parting Grace was, for once, followed out of earshot by good wishes rather than imprecations.

Now she was poring over the charts with Thomas while she planned their course which would, necessarily, involve re-provisioning at various points. Not for the first time, she mildly regretted not having a proper ship for these voyages, a ship with a capacious hold that would relieve them of this burden. Such a ship, of course, would be quite unsuitable for her home waters in and around Clew Bay so, as ever, she put the thought aside and concentrated on the charts. The weather, obviously, was the key to their deliberations and would dictate whether they would have to hug the coast or could cross the Bay of Biscay directly to their destination on the North West extremity of Spain. Grace had sailed both routes in the past and for speed and the sheer joy of deep water sailing would much prefer the latter. However, that part of the journey could be put aside for the moment. The question under consideration now was which French port should be their immediate destination. English ports, though more convenient, were unlikely to be as welcoming to them as one of the ports of Brittany, whose Catholic inhabitants could be relied upon to be more friendly than the English to their Celtic neighbours. The priest was another consideration. She half regretted the charitable instinct which had led to her taking him as a passenger but, now that she had, his presence probably made it imperative that they avoid England with its certainty of arrest for him, and possibly for herself and her crew as well.

She decided on Roscoff. She was familiar with it. It had a good harbour, indeed had been deemed sufficiently good to be chosen as the port of disembarkation for Scottish Mary on her way to Paris to become the child bride of the Dauphin. It had the added advantage of being smaller than Brest, her alternative, and therefore offering less opportunities for the crew to be led astray by the delights that existed in all ports for simple sailors. It was also less likely than Brest to have English visitors - the English raid on Roscoff's neighbouring port, Morlaix, in Great Henry's time was still remembered with great bitterness – a very relevant factor in the circumstances. In the prevailing South Westerly breeze, the eighty odd leagues to Roscoff should be handily covered in three days or less by the swift sailing Dana, well within the range of her water and provisions, and so, in the end, the decision was quite easily made. Grace then settled back to enjoy the glory of the sun in a blue sky, the bluer sea, the fine bow wave, and the straight foaming wake stretching out behind to the disappearing Irish coastline.

The following day, at the noon bell, the log was heaved and their progress established as a very satisfying eight knots.

Thomas was waiting with his cross staff and, with it and its accompanying book of tables, he quickly ascertained their latitude. Longitude was less certainly calculated using the compass, their speed, and the noon position of the sun, together with some dead reckoning of Thomas's aided by his instinct and knowledge of the waters. In all of this he was assisted by Tibbott, whose education in the finer points of navigation was considered by his mother to be at least as important as his formal education. Tibbbott was proving quite a good pupil to Thomas as, quite apart from a natural aptitude for the science, he had a healthy desire not to fall foul of his mother who, in her capacity as ship's captain, would show no more partiality towards her son than to any other member of the crew in the event of his acting in what she considered a slack and un-seamanlike manner.

The midday meal was served, and the men, other than those immediately concerned with the sailing of the galley, relaxed on the benches and platforms, some attending to their weapons, and some trailing fishing lines over the side, but most just enjoying the fine day. All were fairly experienced sailors, even those members of the crew nominally entered as soldiers, and being constantly, if subconsciously, aware of the perilous nature of their trade from the vagaries of elements and enemies, would always seize gratefully the all too seldom periods of relaxation available to them.

Grace, with Thomas and her sailing master, Rory, together with another kinsman, Donal O'Malley, who was responsible for the galley's discipline and rigging, spent the afternoon making fine adjustments to the trim, seeking to ring every last ounce of speed from the boat. They also gave consideration to the rake of the masts, trying to imagine them allowing the big lateens to draw even more wind, thereby increasing their speed as well as permitting them to sail ever closer to the wind, a major concern if pursuing, or being pursued by, a square rigged ship, to which a galley would normally expect to show a clean pair of heels in all reasonable weather conditions because of that very ability to sail closer to the wind. She also gave much thought to the perennial problem of tacking the galley. The nature of the lateens and their rigging meant that, on a favourable tack, the sails drew free, whereas when the galley changed to the opposite tack, the sails where pressed against the masts, greatly reducing their effectiveness. There was really only one solution to the problem, which involved brailing up the sails and then hauling the yards bodily over the tops of the masts, before again unfurling the sails on the other side, leaving the galley with decreasing momentum while the sails were furled. Grace was fairly sure that there ought also to be a way of swinging the yard around within the rigging but the mechanics of this always seemed to elude her, as they did everyone else. Frustrated again in her thoughts, she fell back on her usual answer to the problem, which was to leave the main sail alone and accept its loss of power but manhandle the smaller foresail around its mast, so that at least one of the sails was drawing properly, a hotch potch solution, but better than nothing at all and a conclusion that in no way diminished her good humour.

After the evening meal, Grace called for music and the men gathered aft. Whiskey and wine were liberally dispensed and all made themselves comfortable while the musicians readied themselves. Grace, like most Irish chieftains, had around her, in her crew, men who were proficient at pipes and bodhran. She even had a professional bard. The proceedings were opened by Donal, an excellent piper (his namesake, her illegitimate elder brother, had also been an excellent piper, preferring music to all else, even chieftainship of the clan). He began with some of Grace's favourites, the wild airs being enthusiastically accompanied by the bodhran players. These were followed by a selection of slow airs on the harp by a gifted young crewman called Carolan, not a regular member of the crew but who had joined the voyage in hopes of learning some of the music of the continent, particularly that of Galicia, their destination.

It was finally time for the bard's contribution and he rose properly to the occasion with a long epic poem detailing the exploits of Grace's father, Owen O'Malley, followed by a paean to Grace herself delivered, and received, with suitable solemnity. In the applause that followed, Grace mischievously asked in Gaelic whether he might have a few words for the priest.

"Sure, I know nothing of him, and anyway, what priest was ever worthy of the attention of a bard?" He asked in reply, being himself of a somewhat pagan outlook and resenting, as did most of his fellows, the activities of the monks who committed everything to writing, a situation which they all foresaw as leading eventually to their unemployment. Grace laughed and translated for the priest who, with a bow and a smile, acknowledged his own unworthiness.

"I had never been to Ireland before this recent brief visit," he said. "I was unaware of the depth and importance of music and poetry.

"Ah, you English," Grace replied, shaking her head in mock disapproval, "always surprised that anyone else might show a bit of a cultural inclination. The Sidneys were surprised, pleasantly I believe, as was their friend Sheriff Spenser of Cork, another man who fancies himself a bit of a poet. That would be the same Spenser, by the way, who assisted Drury in the murder of those seven hundred Gallowglasses whose friends we left in Baltimore."

"I grieve," said the priest, "to hear such a thing of Spenser. I've read some of his work and I believe him to be headed for great things. I must confess," he continued, "that my little previous knowledge of Ireland was gleaned from Edward Campion's short history and most of that, apparently, was based on the writings of Bishop Gerald, the Welsh cleric who was cousin to Strongbow and who, it must be supposed, had a vested interest in portraying the natives as being very savage and in need of civilizing. Campion, of course, is now a Jesuit."

"Savages, is it? Sure didn't we keep learning alive in Europe when the rest of you were scrabbling around in the dirt after Rome fell? And didn't we send monks to Iona, and Lindisfarne, and loads of other places as well, to educate you and drag you back out of the dirt? Savages indeed."

"I do apologise for my ignorance. I had no idea. But tell me," he went on, feeling an urgent need to get away from Irish history, "does your bard have to fight as well as all the other men on the boat?"

"Of course not." She shook her head sadly at his ignorance. "Bards have a place so important in Irish society that they're above fighting. They may well record the fighting to be later converted to epic poetry, but they themselves never fight and, even if their patron should be unlucky enough to be defeated, or even killed, they themselves are always spared and, if necessary, merely rework the epic to the satisfaction of their new patron. Besides," she looked critically at her bard, "just look at the puniness of him. He wouldn't have the strength to push a soldier off his sister, even if she wanted him to."

The priest bowed to Grace, in acknowledgement of his shortcomings.

"No matter," replied Grace, "I forget you're only English. Anyway, it's getting late, and I must take a last turn around the boat. Gentlemen, I'll wish you all goodnight now."

She ordered the stern lantern lit and then went forward on a quick tour of the galley before retiring to her cabin. The assembly broke up and the priest retired to his own cabin shortly afterwards, where he contemplated the events of the past few days, and the inscrutable workings of a God who could make a woman so capable that she could run, and with such authority, a vessel as powerful as the Dana with her large crew.

CHAPTER 6

Late in the afternoon of the following day, they made a very satisfactory landfall off Ile de Batz and were soon at anchor in Roscoff harbour. The skiff was lowered and Grace made ready to go ashore with her lieutenants to pay her compliments to the port authorities and organise the supply of fresh food to replenish their stocks, particularly of meat and fruit. Refilling their water casks had also to be organised although this was not a problem, fresh water being available in abundance, sufficiently so that they were able to indulge in the wonderful luxury of using it for washing, a function normally accomplished at sea with salt water and a rough cloth. Grace, in prospect of meeting the Roscoff merchants, some of whom had recently grown very wealthy indeed and would, consequently, be well dressed, as would their wives, had discarded her sea going garb in exchange for a dress and slippers that would not have looked out of place in Galway, or even Dublin.

Having taken them ashore, the skiff returned to ferry ashore, in relays, the half of the crew granted shore leave, the other half to have their leave on the following day. The priest, for whom Brittany was a new experience, went ashore with the last party.

Roscoff, which had existed as a port for hundreds of years, had lately grown prosperous on greatly increased maritime trade with the rest of Europe and, it was darkly hinted, less respectable pursuits. It was now a fine town with numerous new granite houses and a recently completed church, Notre Dame de Croaz Batz, in the Renaissance style. It was to this church that the priest now made his way, leaving his cheery companions to search out the taverns and entertainment possibilities of the town. He sat for some hours in the dark silence before an awakening feeling of hunger stirred him from his contemplation.

He made his way back to the harbour, where he hoped that the crew of the skiff might still be in attendance, and had the good fortune to meet the galley's captain herself, who had been invited, along with her lieutenants, by one of the town's merchants to spend the night ashore, and who was making a brief visit to the galley to make preparations for the night, accompanied by Rory who, of the lieutenants, had drawn the short straw and would have to send the night on board as Officer of the watch. He returned with them and dined quietly with Rory before retiring early.

The following morning, after breakfast, he set off with a packed lunch to explore the riverbank up to Morlaix, where he wondered at the temerity of Surrey, who had sacked the town sixty odd years earlier, and even more at the extreme good fortune which had prevented his rash expedition being a total disaster.

As he had left Roscoff in the morning, he had seen various members of the Dana's shore party wandering the streets, most in a sad, disheveled state, looking somewhat lost and, indeed, not that unlike the Scottish mercenaries when thy had been rounded up back on Sherkin. As he now returned, he met members of the second shore party on his way, some already well advanced in liquor and others with local bawds hanging from their arms, and all offering friendly, if occasionally ribald, greetings to him in Gaelic and Breton. The taverns he passed all reverberated with cheerful noise and snatches of song until he came to one from which, instead of mirth, emanated sounds of voices raised in anger. He listened at the door for a moment and then entered.

Inside the tavern, he found Rory and Tibbott, with three or four others, backs to the wall and swords drawn, silently facing a circle of angry Bretons who, also armed, shouted and gesticulated at the Irishmen. Trusting to his habit to protect him, he elbowed his way through the Bretons to find out what was happening. Rory tersely explained that Tibbott had managed to drink a jug of unwatered wine before anyone could stop him. It had gone straight to his head and he had tried to fondle a girl who, contrary to his befuddled assumption, was not a serving wench, but the landlord's daughter. Accusations were made, voices were raised, each side unintelligible to the other, the situation escalating until, suddenly, swords were unsheathed and battlelines drawn, which was where the priest had come in.

He turned to the Bretons and attempted, in French, to diffuse the situation, but the Bretons were determined that the boy, at least, should have a beating. This, when he explained it to Rory, drew an angry and absolute no.

"We'll have to fight our way out then," said the priest.

Rory looked at him in some confusion.

"Be patient," he said. "Listen now, I'm going to take Tibbott's sword from him. Thank God it's a man's sword. Don't interfere."

In a sudden movement, he seized the sword from Tibbott's limp hand and, swiftly turning, thrust at the nearest Breton, who fell back in confusion at this wholly unexpected turn of events.

"There are lots of Danas in the street if we can get out to them," he said to Rory before again addressing the Bretons:

"You cannot have the boy. He'll apologise and we'll be happy to pay compensation for any insult you may feel the girl has suffered, but he will be punished by us."

The landlord's response was a loud cry and a sudden lunge at the priest who, with a murmured "Lord forgive me," parried the blow and, in turn, lunged back at the landlord, slashing at his sword arm. With a howl of pain, the man dropped his sword and, before anyone else could intervene, the priest had grabbed and twisted the wounded arm and put the point of his own sword to the landlord's throat, drawing a trickle of blood. There was a stunned silence, broken by the priest's urgent demand that the other Bretons drop their swords and allow free passage from the tavern for himself, his companions, and the landlord, whom he was taking as hostage. At the latter's anguished request – his wounded arm was still twisted behind his back – this was complied with and the priest and Rory's party, they as stunned as the Bretons at the speed of events, left the tavern, dragging Tibbott with them.

"Don't follow us or I'll surely kill him," the priest coldly commanded the Bretons as Rory closed the door of the tavern behind them.

They made their way as quickly as possible back to the quayside, gathering up what crewmen they encountered.

"You'll need to get the captain and the rest of the crew back to the galley as fast as you can before the whole town turns on us," the priest said to Rory.

By good fortune, the crew of the skiff were still sober.

"Thank God for a hard captain," he thought, and sent them back to the galley with Tibbott, and with orders to have the guns armed and trained on the town.

Grace was found with her officers, fortunately before news of the event had spread to the house in which they were now being entertained, and she got back to the harbour in a blaze of anger to demand of the priest what the hell he thought he was doing.

A quick explanation chastened and slightly, though not entirely, mollified her. The priest felt a fleeting sympathy for Tibbott and what was inevitably going to shortly befall him.

The Danas were found in various parts of the town and slowly drifted back to the quayside, the more sober leading the less with as much urgency as they could, through an increasingly ugly mob of Roscoffians. Happily, the landlord seemed held in good regard by his townsfolk and not even the hotheads were prepared to risk his death at the hands of this mad priest. The rumour had by now spread that he was English, almost definitely a heretic, despite his robes, and quite certainly deranged enough to have the head of the landlord if provoked.

When the last of the laggards had been rounded up, they all returned to the galley in the skiff and various commandeered small boats, the last of which, rowed by a local, contained the priest, his hostage, Grace and Rory. When they were safely back on board, the landlord, pale and faint from his bleeding arm, was returned to the town, together with a small purse in compensation for his injuries and insult.

Grace had, by now, taken command of the situation. Tibbott had been banished forward and was quietly vomiting over the side. The more drunken members of the crew had been deposited amongst the benches, and a strong watch set in case of any attempt by the townsfolk at retaliation. They were still within cannon shot of the town, if the town had any cannon and the townspeople were inclined to use them, but Grace was disinclined to shift moorings in the darkness which had now fallen, unless absolutely necessary.

"Right, I want a full explanation," she demanded of Rory when all her dispositions for the night were in place. Rory ran stumblingly through his version of events, which was unstinting in its praise of the priest and his quick actions.

"You're a very lucky man, Rory O'Malley, that things turned out as they did. We'll say no more on it".

She turned to the priest.

"It seems as though I'm in your debt for saving my son, not to mention my useless kinsman here, and the others."

"It was merely my Christian duty, Madam," he replied, somewhat drily.

"Nevertheless, I'm in your debt and you'll not find me neglectful of my debts."

"Yes Madam."

She looked at him curiously.

"Would you really have killed the landlord?"

"Hardly. I'm sworn to protect Christians. Fortunately, the landlord's supporters didn't suspect that or things mightn't have run as they did. Might I ask, in passing, that you're not too hard on the boy. I suspect that he's had sufficient fright to make him more circumspect in the future."

"He must be punished, as would any other crew member, but I will bear in mind your plea for leniency."

She called to Thomas for a bottle.

"There'll be little sleep tonight. You'll join me in a glass? Or are you sworn to abstinence also?"

"No. I may indulge in moderation. It's permitted by my order."

"I've been wondering about that. Which exactly is your order? I know the Cistercians on Clare Island and Belclare and none of them would have the slightest idea of how to even hold a sword, not to mind using it. And, do you mind my asking, how did you come by that scar? That's also been intriguing me since we first met."

He looked at his glass for a moment before replying.

"I am a Cistercian, but of a knightly branch, the Order of Calatreva, formerly dedicated to the expulsion of the Moors from Spain and, I thought mistakenly when I joined in the rashness of youth, still active in the war against the infidels. This isn't actually the case any more so I'm now, more or less, a wandering monk. When you rescued me from Waterford I had been, as I said, on family business in England but, other than that, I've spent most of my recent years in the Mediterranean, generally with the Knights of St John, the order I should have joined," he smiled ruefully, "but I considered their discipline too harsh. For one thing, they don't allow alcohol."

He raised his glass and drank before continuing, "the scar is the result of a wound I received while fighting with the Knights at a place called Lepanto in the Eastern Mediterranean."

"Is it now?" Asked Grace thoughtfully. "I've heard of Lepanto. They say there were hundreds of galleys involved. I've often wondered if it were true, and, if so, how they could all be got to the same place at the same time and how any order could be kept once the fighting started."

"Well, there were certainly more than 500 ships involved, and tens of thousands of men. I don't suppose the world will ever see a bigger battle."

"Would you tell us about it?" Asked Grace, almost deferentially.

"Of course, although you must understand that mine was a very small view of the battle."

He paused to collect his thoughts.

"We were led by Don John of Austria."

"I wonder," interrupted Grace, "might that have been the same man that Desmond's brother and the Archbishop of Cashel were trying to have appointed king of Ireland by King Philip."

"That I can't say but, other than leading the Holy League fleet at Lepanto, which he did very capably, he has subsequently been fully occupied elsewhere in the Mediterranean against the Turks, and latterly, in Flanders, against the heretics. He is, you know, a half brother to Phillip and I suppose that Phillip wouldn't have particularly wished to have set him up as a rival king in Ireland. Anyway, he was our leader with a fleet made up of Spanish, Venetian, Genoese and Papal galleys, along with the galleys of the Knights. The French were in alliance with the Turks and hoping for a Spanish disaster and, sadly, our own Queen," "your Queen," interjected Grace. He bowed, "I should have said Queen Elizabeth, was also in negotiation with the Grand Turk, so no help was forthcoming from either of those countries. Indeed, we might have had more Spanish ships had Phillip been able to trust the French not to take advantage of the situation.

We were to have relieved Cyprus but it fell to the Turks before we got there so we carried on eastwards, eventually catching up with the Turkish Fleet at Lepanto. They were more numerous than us and offered battle without hesitation. Don John divided the fleet into four, a line of three squadrons facing the Turks with a reserve squadron behind us, each of the line squadrons having two galleasses towed out to front it. I was in one of the Maltese galleys in the centre division. The Turks went for the galleasses straight away, thinking them transports, and took a terrible beating; they have cannon mounted along each side as well as fore and aft, you know. Those that survived, however, came right on. Admiral Doria, on our right, was outflanked by the Turks, and a gap was created between the squadrons so that we were attacked simultaneously from both front and side. Our flagship, with the Prior on board, was taken and we ourselves were boarded. We had very heavy losses but gave as good as we got and eventually drove the Turks back onto their own galley, which we then boarded in our own turn and eventually forced to strike. That was when I got the scar," he stroked his cheek, "but, in comparison with some of the wounds received by others, it was nothing. In the meantime, the reserve Squadron had arrived to relieve us and that turned the battle. The Turkish flagship was taken and their commander, Ali Pasha, was killed and his head displayed on a pike. This act, barbaric though it was, took the heart out of the remaining Turks and they fled the battle as quickly as they could. We sank many of their ships and took over 100 as prizes. We also freed thousands of Christian slaves, which was a great consolation for the losses we had suffered. But, in the aftermath, one could not help but feel depressed, so many dead and dying, the decks red with blood and the sea heaving with corpses. Our flagship was recaptured, but the Prior, with five arrows in him, was one of only three survivors, it being the policy of the Knights to fight to the death, knowing that capture by the Turks is, for them, a fate worse than death."

He paused. "The Turks quickly rebuilt their fleet but it will be generations, if ever, before they replace the experienced sailors and soldiers that they lost that day and hopefully, I pray, they will never replace them."

While he had been speaking, a small crowd from the watch had gathered around the afterdeck, his words been softly translated by Rory for the Gaelic speakers. There was now a sympathetic, not to say admiring, murmur from these men, and glasses were quickly raised to him.

"And what happened afterwards?" Asked Grace.

"Oh, we returned in triumph to Messina, whence we had set out, to great acclaim. Church bells were rung, celebratory masses said, Te Deums sung. Very strangely, the Pope had had a vision of victory during the battle, long before the actual news could have reached him, and declared the day a feast to our Lady of Victories.

We met their new fleet the following year but, although they were much superior in ship numbers, they declined battle. That was probably just as well because the Catholic Alliance was a fragile thing at best, with the Venetians not trusting the Genoese and vice versa, and the Spanish not trusting either, and the Knights being more intent on their own agenda, which is to seek out and kill Moslems where ever they find them, rather than cruising in a large fleet in hopes of another great battle. And, although their grand fleet has now been inactive for some years, they have not, in any way, ceased their corsairing nor their programme of conquest along the North African shore, so that the Knights' policy of persistent aggression is probably the best one at the present time. It is certainly an exciting, if bloody, policy, and I count myself extremely lucky to have received no serious wounds in the many little encounters in which I've been involved with them, no quarter asked or given."

He blessed himself before taking another sip from his glass, in to which he gazed reflectively for a time.

"And that's really all I can tell you about it," he finished and, draining his glass, he stood, excused himself, and retired to his small cabin.

The little gathering broke up, Grace remarking to the

forgiven Rory: "what wouldn't I have given to have been there. It goes to show that you should never judge a man by outward appearances."

"Indeed not, indeed not," replied Rory fervently.

CHAPTER 7

The following day at dawn, the slumbering watch, who had had such merriment ashore the day before, were roused by having buckets of water thrown on them by their mates. They, having recovered from their own excesses of the previous day, were not in the least bit sympathetic to the hangovers of their fellows.

The galley made ready for sea but, before hoisting the anchor, Tibbott was brought forward and tied to the great gun in the bows to receive his punishment, which consisted of twelve lashes administered by his uncle Donal (holding back imperceptibly, but effectively) on his bare back. Tears came to his eyes but he did not cry out, which won the approval of the crew.

Grace, with strong memories of her own punishment at the same age, watched Tibbott's punishment impassively, the maternal turmoil inside her being carefully hidden. She had decided on the public punishment for a threefold reason: Tibbott would certainly be more circumspect next time he was allowed ashore, the crew would see that her judgements were impartial and, if there were any watchers ashore, they would see that the priest's word had been kept, which might prove important if ever they had cause to visit Roscoff again.

While Tibbott was led away to have his lacerated flesh seen to, they set about winning their anchor, and were soon rowing easily around the Ile de Batz for the open sea. Grace called for a course to weather Ushant, and thence directly across the Bay of Biscay to Corunna.

She addressed the priest who was standing beside her.

"I've had enough of the land and landsmen for now. I want some deep water sailing to get the crew back to a level of competence at which I can fully trust them and at which they can respect themselves again. I detest what they do to themselves every time we let them ashore. Of course you can't really expect them to behave like monks, saving your presence, when they hit some foreign port with money in their purses. If they merely rowed, sailed and fought, they might as well be back in Clew Bay tending cattle and looking over their shoulders for the MacMahons, or other such renegades, to come raiding."

She overcame her mild despair, she was not someone who could remain down for long, and grew more cheerful.

"Once we've rounded Ushant, we'll devise some games to bring them back up to scratch. They're not that bad really."

She sent Fergus forward to oversee the cleaning of the deck which, after the two days in port, was not in its customary pristine state. She herself saw to the stowage of the new stores which, because of the manner of their departure from Roscoff, were still piled haphazardly on and between the benches, and must necessarily be restowed properly to maintain the correct trim, balancing the weight of the guns in the bows. The priest remained in the stern beside Thomas, who was steering the galley and whose manner, always friendly, was even more so now.

"The crew are very pleased to have heard that you're really a fighting priest, and though most of us had never heard of Lepanto, we're all well enough aware of the Turks and their raparee ways. But what particularly pleases the men about your military past, is that it means that you're not really just an ordinary priest. These sailors, good Christians that they are of course, are a very superstitious lot, much more so than landsmen, and one of their major superstitions is that having priest on board can only bring bad luck on a voyage. They're much happier about our prospects since hearing you last night."

"You're very kind, Thomas," replied the priest, "but you should remember that when I sailed with the Knights, we were all religious and we definitely could not have been considered unsuccessful. We certainly took far more in prizes then we lost. But then, I shouldn't speak of luck, since we are all in the hands of the Almighty, who will use us as He will." He crossed himself.

"Oh, I agree with you fully, Father," said Thomas, also crossing himself but, at the same time, surreptitiously rubbing the wooden tiller, "but it's of the others I speak, mere heathens, some of them."

"I am sure of it, Thomas" smiled the priest. He paused before asking,

"I wondered if you could tell me more of our captain?"

"Certainly. She's undoubtedly the best captain sailing out of Ireland," began Thomas enthusiastically. "She's tough, as you've seen, but fair. She can handle as hard a crew of men as you'll find, though a woman, as well as any man sailing. She can fight as well as any man too. But, more than any of that, she has an instinct for the sea. She knows the weather: when we can sail, when to stay in harbour; how best to handle the galley, how much sail she'll take in a blow, how close she'll come to the wind, all that kind of thing. Mind you," he finished doubtfully, "I can't speak for her cooking or embroidery, or any of the other things that you might normally class as woman's work. She wouldn't be classed the greatest of wives either I suppose, always away from home, but she's a good mother. She loves Tibbott and her other children, and Tibbott loves her, despite the chastisements he suffers from time to time."

"What fascinates me," said the priest, "is how she became a sailor in the first place."

"She's bred to the sea. Her family, the O'Malleys, have been sailors for ever - their motto is Terra Marique Potens, which I am told means powerful by land and sea - and they've traded with, and made war on, Scotland, France and Spain, and even England, for generations. She was bound to go to sea and, when her brother Donal showed more interest in music than seafaring, it was only a matter of time. Her parents were against it, of course, so, finally, she chopped all her hair off and stowed away as a boy. When her father found out, they were too far from land to send her back, so he gave her a sound trashing and accepted it. That was how she got her nickname, Grainne Maol, Bald Grace"

"You know her well, Thomas," commented the priest.

"I do that," he replied and, glancing forward, continued "well enough to know that she doesn't like being talked about and, since I can see that she's almost finished with the hold, we'd better start talking about something else."

Grace rejoined them aft and stood looking fondly forward along the vessel.

"Well James, may I call you James?" she enquired, carrying on immediately without reply "now that you've seen a bit more of her, what do you think?"

"Well, Grace," he began, "she's different to the galleys with which I'm familiar in the Mediterranean. Thomas explained her build to me, the broader beam, the greater draught and the deeper hold space. And there's no ram of course. But she's a fine vessel and definitely cleaner lined than the war galleys on which I have served."

"That's an equivocating answer," replied Grace, "and no more than I should reasonably have expected of a priest. But Thomas has given you the right of it. The Dana has been built for the Atlantic and, though I've never been to the Mediterranean, I'm told by those who have been that the waves there are shorter and sharper than we get in the Atlantic, so the Dana is slightly a compromise between a shallow draught Mediterranean galley that will swim in Clew Bay, and something that'll stand up to a real Atlantic blow, not that I'm expecting bad weather on this trip."

She touched the tiller, glancing at him as she did so. "You mustn't think me superstitious, but the men expect it," she said. The priest just caught the flicker of a smile cross Thomas's face as Grace carried on. "For the same reason, both of our masts are stepped on the keel, whereas I'm told that the foremast in a Mediterranean galley is stepped on the deck only, although I can't see the advantage of that at all, and it must certainly make the mast weaker. Of course, having the mast set on the keel in the centre of the boat means that the artillery must be placed slightly off centre to allow for recoil, which calls for very careful placing of the guns."

"Yet, you carry heavier artillery than I have ever seen on a galley of this size. Doesn't that make it unwieldy?"

"Not as long as we're careful to keep it properly ballasted. This means, unfortunately, keeping all but the ready ammunition in the stern, and that creates its own difficulties in the event of our undertaking a longer bombardment than we needed against the O'Driscolls. But the man you need to speak to about that is the gunner. He's an educated Italian but with only a very small amount of the Gaelic, which means that he can only converse with the latinists in the crew, and there are less of those than I know you would expect," this with a quick sidewards glance, "so he'd probably welcome someone new to converse with, even a priest."

She threw another glance but he refused to rise to the bait, merely responding with a smile,

"I must go and speak with him, then," and, having made his excuses, he made his way forward.

Once they had weathered the Ile de Batz, they laid up the oars and hoisted the sails and Thomas set a course to bring them round Ushant. The noon bell was sounded and, by the time dinner was eaten, the crew was back to a more or less reasonable state of health. Grace and Rory, between them, had worked them hard, and although there were still aching heads amongst yesterday's roisterers, even these were improving and, being for the most part young men, and the fresh sea air and occasional spray working their therapy, by the time they raised Ushant in the late afternoon, having made a steady four or five knots, all were back in a state of boisterous good humour.

Taking the soundings necessary in this treacherous coastline of fierce tides and uncharted reefs, they found a small uninhabited and seemingly safe bay where they anchored. The night passed uneventfully and dawn found them under way again. Ushant was rounded well to port with plenty of sea room under their lee, and a course was set to bring them well out into the Atlantic before turning south for Corunna.

Grace now set the hands to exercise. There were no more than 30 sailors and gunners in the crew, the rest being all fighting men who took their turn on the oars when necessary. These she now divided into two watches, setting each watch to row against the glass alternately, the great drum which gave the stroke being beaten faster and faster, and the men stretching out for the extra ration of wine to be won by the watch reckoned to have rowed the fastest. In time, despite their captain's stern countenance and their own increasing exhaustion, a certain hilarity began to creep into the proceedings, and the rowing became more and more ragged until Grace finally called a halt.

It was now the turn of the gunners, who were made to go through the motions of loading and firing the demi cannon on either side of the big gun, before finally being allowed one live round each. Meanwhile, through all these evolutions, the sailors were raising and lowering the main yard, with various complications of rigging devised by Grace.

She called a halt to all of the exercises just after noon, when dinner was served, along with an extra ration of wine for all, the oarsmen having been decreed inseperable in their efforts and the sailors and gunners equally deserving of reward for theirs.

"I wouldn't give much for our chances at this moment, were some unfriendly sail to suddenly appear on the horizon," murmured Grace to the priest, "but I think that that'll have cleared any remnants of Roscoff from their systems by now."

The rest of the afternoon passed in relative peace. Evening came, the main sail was lowered so that they progressed under foresail alone, more slowly but more safely, and Grace and the crew off watch retired. She was asleep deeply and instantly as soon as she lay in her cot while, at the same time, some hidden instinct continuously monitored the movements and noises of the vessel around her. Thus it was that in the middle of the night she awoke, aware of some change in the Dana's motion. Throwing a boat cloak over her shoulders, she went on deck.

The galley was sailing easily under the foresail alone. The watch were alert. She glanced at the compass in the light of the stern lantern and noted that the course was as it had been when she retired. However, there was a barely perceptible, but definite, change in the way the galley went through the waves. She sent one of the watch to awaken Thomas, and when he came on deck, he instantly agreed that they were feeling the definite beginnings of a swell.

"I hope that my desire to get away from the land hasn't overruled my instincts, but I think we may be coming in for a blow. It's just as well we're on this course. We have, at least, got plenty of sea room if things should turn ugly."

They remained on deck until the first light of dawn, a pallid light, appeared in the East, by which time the motion of the galley was becoming distinctly lively. The rest of the crew were now quite awake. The levity of the previous day was notably absent, and grave glances were cast from time to time at the stern, where Grace was in conference with Thomas and her senior lieutenants.

The morning advanced, but there was no great increase in the light, the sky being covered with dark clouds. The swell worsened along with the wind, and flecks of white spray were now beginning to fly off the tops of the waves. Grace made her decision:

"We've plenty of sea room so we'll change course due south. I'll have the main sail hoisted but ready to be struck down at a moment's notice. We'll also need extra stays on the rigging." She motioned to Conor, "unmount the swivels and stow them as far aft in the hold as you can. You can get most of the ready ammunition aft as well and, while you're about it, make sure the gunner has double lashings on the guns."

She glanced around, assessing the worsening weather conditions before adding, "we probably have just about enough time to serve the men something hot, so can you see to that as well before the cook douses the oven?"

The large lateen was raised and the galley instantly responded, flying through the waves which hammered in on her starboard bow, while all the time the wind increased. The rain now started as well, driving in almost horizontally so that, very quickly, everyone was soaked through, despite their wet weather gear. All those who were not immediately employed in sailing the galley were huddled as best they could in the meagre shelter of the benches, while the sailors themselves clung to the man ropes set up along the central platform as they went about their duties.

Grace, alone, seemed to be enjoying it, standing tall at the tiller with her long red hair streaming out behind her.

Noon came and, although there was no possibility of an observation, the log was cast anyway, but such was the speed of the galley by this stage, that the line ran right off the reel before the hapless sailor who had cast it could nip it. Grace admonished him for slackness, but the admonition was purely for form's sake, she being quite delighted at their careering flight.

Thrilling though it was, it could not go on. It had become only a question of time before something major was carried away. Grace turned the galley to run directly before the wind on a course that would eventually bring them on to the coast of France unless the wind abated. She privately hoped that her assertion that they had plenty of sea room would prove, in fact, to be the case, but it was becoming more and more obvious that if they persisted in their present course, a freak wave breaking over them would drive them under, if they were not capsized first. Handing Thomas the tiller and getting another sailor to assist with it, she clawed her way forward to check that the guns were as securely held as possible. She stood for a moment, feeling the wild bucketing of the galley beneath her feet, and then spoke to the sailors cowering in the bows:

"This is going to get worse before it gets better. I'm going to have the main sail down, but before I do, I want you to get the foresail down and replace it with the storm sail. We're going to be unbalanced with the main only in this wind, so you'll need to work as quickly as possible. When you've everything ready signal me, but don't begin until I signal back. I'll try to keep her as steady as possible, but she'll get quite lively, even more than she is now, so be careful. When all is secure, signal to me again."

She made her way back to the main mast to give instructions to the sailors there, letting them know what was afoot and having them be ready to lower the lateen as soon as she ordered. By the time she had got back to the stern, the whole crew were aware of the plan and were watching the bows and bracing themselves for the inevitable buffeting.

She put another man on the long tiller and waited with speaking trumpet in one hand, the other hand clutching the rail tightly.

At last the storm sail was ready and the signalling wave came from the bows. Grace had one last glance around, judged the space between the waves, and returned the signal.

The ropes were loosed and the foresail on its yard clattered down the mast to the deck. The effect on the galley was instantaneous. Without the restraining balance, the bows began to yaw and it took all the strength of the three men on the tiller to keep the galley more or less on course. Working as quickly as they could, the sailors detached the foresail and attached the much smaller stormsail in its place, fighting all the while with the effects of the wind, which threatened to blow both sails out and knock one or more of them overboard at the same time. When they had finished, Grace ordered the main sail down and the movement of the boat immediately improved. The foresail was folded with some difficulty and stowed, while the main sail was simply lashed to its yard and the whole rig laid along the centre platform.

That Grace had cut it fine was apparent to all but those of the meanest intelligence, and these latter crew men were mainly feeling too worried to give her timing much consideration anyway. But she had gained considerable, invaluable, sea room by leaving the alteration of course and the sail change as long as possible, sea room that might mean the difference between life and death, if this storm were to get as bad as Grace was now beginning to think it might.

The new smaller sail arrangement did not appear to lessen the speed of the galley, which plunged on in the growing gloom. The endless succession of waves building up behind the stern occasionally lifted it so high that the rudder bit thin air, the bows being driven downwards at the same time, so that the sea boiled over the front of the galley and around the battened hatches before rushing out of the scuppers. The length of the galley meant that this was frequently succeeded by the stern being almost submerged while the bows, in turn, rose high in the air, until the wave racing beneath her keel reversed the procedure again. Deadlights had been shipped in the stern windows to prevent their being stove in by the waves, and the resulting darkness had driven Father James, who had earlier taken refuge in his cabin but who had not previously experienced such a storm, out on deck, feeling that he would rather die in the open air then trapped inside.

"You might say a prayer if you wish," roared Grace in his ear. He blessed himself and intoned something which was lost in the noise.

"I've never seen the likes of this in the Mediterranean,"

he shouted.

"I fear you haven't seen the half of it yet," roared back Grace, in a voice whose volume had been developed over years of Atlantic storms.

"You can give out bread and wine to the men," she shouted to Conor. "I don't think that we dare prepare anything more substantial at the moment."

Some of the men were, by now, being copiously sick in the scuppers, but the rest all wolfed down their meagre rations. Grace went forward again to confirm that all was as secure as could be. Other than those in the stern, there were no cabins on a galley - they normally expected to anchor inshore overnight (indeed, for the same reason, they generally remained in port over the whole of the winter) - so conditions were generally miserable for the crew in conditions such as these. And of the overall misery, the sailors in the bows had more than their fair share, so there was a certain sympathy in Grace's inspection of their domain, and Donal's provisions for strengthening the rigging of the foremast, the vital foremast, as well as their arrangements for the spare timbers, yards and cordage they would need should it suffer any damage from the gale, which was now ferocious. She ordered the bindings on the bow oars loosened in case they should have sudden need of them, and with a word of encouragement, left them and returned to the stern, pausing only to tell the forward rowers to be ready for possible sudden action, and numbering off replacements for those who were going to be too ill to be of use.

While she had been forward, Tibbott had also come on deck from the darkened cabin and was clinging to the hand rail. With a mother's heartfelt anger, she drove him back to the cabin.

"I've been careless with the weather, but I'll not compound that by leaving him where he might be washed overboard," she shouted to the priest.

In the gloom, darkness was descending early. The stern

lantern was lit with some difficulty, and storm lamps were lit in the cabin. By now the wind was very severe indeed, and the noise of both it and the huge waves was reaching a screaming crescendo which battered them physically, just as much as did the wild progress of the galley over the sea.

Seeing that all was as it should be for the moment, Grace went into the cabin, beckoning the priest in after her. Although marginally quieter, it was still necessary to shout to be heard above the noise of the storm. There were a couple of inches of water sloshing violently from side to side with bits of food and debris from anything that could not be actually bolted to the deck.

"She's a very good sea boat, none better," shouted Grace, "but I fear for her cargo. Even though the hatches are all well battened, some of the caulking is bound to give and, of course, we can't stop the normal working of her planking which will inevitably allow more water in."

"I marvel that we are still afloat," shouted back the priest, "I would've expected her back to have broken by now, the way she appears sometimes to have both bow and stern in the air at the same time."

"That might have been the case in a Mediterranean galley but, as I said, this boat was built for the Atlantic. I normally have the good sense to be in port during blows like this but, if we are caught out, it's good to know that we have a good strong boat under our feet. Sure, length to beam ratio is not ideal for deep water sailing but, for that very reason, and in anticipation of this very kind of storm, her keel is uncommonly strong and much more reinforced than I suppose you would need in the Mediterranean. It's for the same reason that her foremast is stepped on the keel rather than on the deck. No, she's highly unlikely to break under us," she touched the bulkhead, "the greater danger is that we're dismasted, or that the foresail blows out, either of which would lose us our steerage, and then it would only be a question of time before a freak wave caught us abeam and capsized us. We've got our smallest, most sturdy storm sail up and, in a gale as severe as this, I'd have an even smaller one rigged if we possessed one. I'd even have a couple of reefs in it but, as you know well enough, a lateen can't be reefed as can a square sail."

Tibbott had listened wide-eyed to this exchange. She patted him on the head and smiled.

"Don't worry, I'm only frightening Father James. We're perfectly safe, but you must remain in here where a bad wave won't catch you unawares."

He smiled weakly back at her as she left the cabin, the noise when she opened the door seeming even worse than when they had entered.

"Perhaps we might say a prayer together," suggested the priest. At Tibbott's silent nod of acquiescence, he crossed himself, as did Tibbott, and they offered a Pater Noster, followed by some heartfelt prayers to Almighty God, whom they did not wish in any way to inconvenience, but who might nevertheless see His way to allowing this storm to pass safely over them, Amen.

The priest did not think that either of them would sleep and, much though he would have preferred to be on deck, he felt compelled to stay in the cabin to offer moral support to Tibbott. The lad, however, seemed much cheered by their prayers (and was probably even more cheered by his mother's assertion that they had nothing to fear) and, with the resilience of youth, confounded the priest by falling asleep almost immediately, wedged into a corner of his damp cot.

On deck it was definitely worse. It was now completely dark, and the lantern which had been lit in the bows could barely be seen through the driving rain and spray. The waves had grown bigger and more spaced out so that the pitching of the galley was even more pronounced. First the stern would drop so that it seemed that it must be engulfed, but would then rise as the bows went into the troughs, which were occasionally so deep that the small sail would momentarily lose the wind and, for a heart stopping moment, the stern would begin to slide across the waves before the sail once again caught the wind and pulled the galley back on course. If proof were needed that their safety depended entirely on the little storm sail, this graphically confirmed the fact.

Grace was now back on the tiller again with two different sailors, the effort of fighting the rudder to keep the galley with wind and sea directly astern being too exhausting for anyone to be capable of it for overlong. Thus, they raced through the dark across the Bay of Biscay towards the ever looming ironbound coast of France.

Dawn came, but with no respite. The priest, who had been unable to sleep, any more than the rest of the men, was exhausted from the constant effort of remaining upright against the plunging and corkscrewing of the galley's progress, and could only marvel at the strength of will that kept their captain not only doing her spell on the tiller, but making her way, with the greatest of difficulty, to the bows from time to time to encourage the men forward. A ration of wine and sodden bread was served which, unappatizing though it might have looked, was, nevertheless, eagerly consumed by those who still had the desire to eat.

Around mid-morning, Grace, who had been studying the conditions, decided that the storm had passed its height and shouted so to the men in the stern. To Father James, to whom the height of the waves and the ferocity of the wind seemed unabated, this seemed wishful thinking, but the men, who knew their captain better than he, exchanged knowing nods and one or two even managed small smiles.

After another couple of hours, it was becoming obvious, even to the landsmen, that things were improving marginally. The waves showed no sign of diminution but the rain had eased and the screeching of the wind through the rigging had dropped a note or two from demonic banshee to just plain banshee. Grace was on one of her visits forward when, with a sudden awful crack that was clearly heard by all, even above the noise of the storm, the vital foremast split.

The yard, sail and attendant shrouds came crashing down over the side of the galley, taking an unfortunate sailor with them, who was instantly lost in the towering seas.

The tangled mass of sail and rigging in the water, acting as a giant sea anchor, immediately so slowed the bows that the whole galley swung around as if on the end of a giant sling, fortunately not capsizing on the way, and leaving her now racing stern first through the water.

CHAPTER 8

There was no question of steering the galley nor, indeed, was there any necessity for doing so while the giant drag remained behind her. The danger now was that the bows were unable to rise over the waves which came crashing over the galley, pounding her timbers, as well as pounding Grace and the sailors who were desperately working to rectify the situation. Two sailors had grabbed axes and had started chopping at the restraining rigging to free them of it, but Grace immediately stopped them. Dangerous as their situation was, it would be immeasurably worse, fatal in fact, were they to lose the stabilising effect of the drag. She had them attach fresh shrouds to the stump of the mast, half of which still remained, and refashion the rigging so that the foresail could be used as a type of jib sail, as on a ship rigged vessel. Repairing the mast by lashing a spare yard to it so that a proper yard could be raised would have been infinitely preferable, but she knew that they did not have remotely enough time for that, so they carried on as quickly as possible with their alternative. As soon as they were ready, and she judged that the rerigged mast would be strong enough to take the impending strain, necessarily a matter of prayer and guesswork, she sent a messenger aft to warn the people in the stern. She then ordered the rowers, who were already in place on the bow benches, virtually submerged, to loosen their oars from the side platforms, ready for instant use. Now she finally allowed the sailors to get to work with the axes, ordering that the port shrouds be the last to be severed. As the remaining starboard rigging was chopped loose, the galley started to swing. Instantly, the rowers got to work in an attempt to stabilise her, their oars sometimes biting the water and, just as often, flailing wildly in the air. The last remaining port shroud parted with a crack and, for a moment, the galley was beam on to the waves and must certainly have gone over, but the new sail, being freed, and billowing forward, pulled the bows around beyond the danger point, the oarsmen frantically rowing to assist, until the natural order was restored and they were, once more, bows before the wind.

The oars were laid inboard again but, as before, ready for instant action with loosened ties. In addition to the sailor lost overboard, the collapse of the fractured mast had resulted in two broken arms and a shattered collar bone. These injured were taken aft to the very relative comfort of Grace's cabin, where the arms were splinted and the shoulder made slightly more bearable with the support of a sling, the pain of all three being dulled as much as possible by the liberal dispensation of neat whiskey. A meal was served of bread, cheese and dried meat, with a sufficient quantity of wine to raise the spirits but not to dull reactions. Grace stayed in the bows, watching the improvised sail and its effect on the quickly lashed up rigging, and decided that the stump of the mast, which, by virtue of its shortness, was reducing the effectiveness of the sail, would, by way of small compensation, still be sufficiently strong to hold it, despite the tendency to yaw consequent upon the sail's strange shape.

The day wore on, with the strength of the storm now more definitely decreasing and conditions becoming more tolerable, but it was still much too rough to attempt a proper repair of the foremast, which Grace decided would now have to wait until the next day. Meanwhile, there was the business of clearing up all the debris slopping about, but this was not as bad as might have been expected after so severe a storm, the securings of the artillery, in particular, having stood up to considerably more strain than designed for, when the bows were facing backwards and the huge seas were breaking over them. The mainmast also, with the great lateen securely lashed down on deck, looked perfectly in order, as did its rigging. Pumping, which had not ceased since the onset of the storm, became less frantic and, of course, there was no shortage of spare hands to deal with it.

With a request that she be called immediately if anything changed, Grace had a last look around before retiring to her cabin, where she fell immediately into a deep and dreamless sleep.

The next morning brought much improved conditions, the wind greatly reduced and the waves, although with a heavy swell, almost benign. There was even a glimpse of watery sun through the clouds, which had changed in hue from black to off-white.

Grace, fully refreshed, was in the bows again, assessing when they might rebuild the broken mast. Thomas, by her side, was of the opinion that this swell was still too great. Grace compromised by ordering the main sail set, at which Thomas cautiously demurred, but it did, in fact, considerably stabilise the galley, certainly to the point where they could, without too much risk to life and limb, begin real work.

They were still in open sea with no signs of land but Thomas, purely on dead reckoning, felt that the coast of France could not be too far over the horizon, although which part of that coast, he could not say. Indeed, they were beginning to see the odd seagull, which appeared to confirm his thoughts. They had definitely lost a lot of the sea room with which they had entered the storm. On the other hand, with the lateen set, albeit not close hauled, and the sea sufficiently diminished to be able to use oars if needs be, the overall situation was completely different from that which had obtained when they were careering forward, to all intents and purposes out of control, under their makeshift jib.

Patrick O' Halloran, the Dana's carpenter, with Donal in attendance, gathered his small crew of helpers about him and began the task of laying out the various spars, blocks, cables and cordage which would be necessary to fashion the new temporary foremast because, even though they were probably only a couple of days sailing from their destination, the events of the past few days had highlighted the necessity of never taking anything for granted at sea. Accordingly, Grace was going to have a temporary foremast fished to the stump of the old one on which to rig a proper foresail to get them to Corunna, whose dockyard facilities she intended to avail of to have a proper mast stepped as soon as they arrived.

The movement of the galley was now sufficiently stable for Tibbott (his back still tender but recovering), the smallest, lightest member of the crew, to be hauled to the masthead to act as lookout, and it was he who, after a couple of hours, piped shrilly down that he could see two ships to the west, or seaward side, of them.

CHAPTER 9

The work had progressed to the point where the foresail had been taken in, and the new mast, composed of two yards lashed together, together with its attendant rigging, attached to the remaining stump of the old mast. They were just about to test its running gear preparatory to raising the foresail again, but on Tibbott's hail, Grace ordered all work suspended.

"If we can see them, then they can see us. We must be closer to Spain than we thought."

She called her lieutenants forward and gave her orders:

"Fabrizio," to the gunner, "I want the guns cast loose and loaded, the cannon with roundshot and the demis with grape. You can then cover everything with this sail until I command otherwise. You can also get the patereros up from the hold and loaded, but not mounted. You'll need to get as much done as possible before we're hull up, and pray that they don't have particularly sharp eyed lookouts or, better still, that they've also suffered storm damage, though if they're sailing in company this soon after the storm, I'd guess that they probably rode it out in shelter somewhere.

Pat, you can work on the rigging for the moment but I want it looking a bit of a shambles if it comes to action."

To Fergus and Rory she gave instructions that the rowers were to be ready at their benches and the remaining crew members, particularly the harquebusiers, fully armed and waiting, but well hidden below the side platforms.

"They may prove to be entirely innocent, but until we know for sure, they must believe us to be a storm damaged and very lubberly trading galley."

To Thomas, "I believe that we may entertain them with a Spanish flag. If they're hostile, it may deceive them briefly."

She returned aft where she found the priest waiting and, having explained the situation, suggested that before the men were fed, they might appreciate a blessing, in Latin preferably, with which they would be more comfortable than English, since she knew that he did not have the Gaelic. On his agreement, she called the men to order. They knelt, more or less, and the priest, as he made the sign of the cross over them, intoned: Benedicat vos, Omnipotens Deus, Pater et Filius et Spiritus Sanctus," to which there was a gravely murmured "Amen" in reply.

Before they broke up for a quick meal of salt fish, bread and wine, Grace addressed them.

"You all know about the two vessels hull down over the horizon. Their intentions may be innocent, but if they're not, I hope to surprise them. Therefore, all preparations must be complete before we come close enough for them to see us clearly. They have the wind and, with our wounded foremast, they'll doubtless also have the legs of us as well, but we'll use that to our advantage by playing the lame duck that suddenly becomes an enraged sea lion."

This drew appreciative nods and smiles - the O'Malley flag had, as its emblem, a sea lion rampant.

She continued, "you know yourselves what's wanted: the platforms packed with mattresses and blankets and whatever else you can find to absorb small arms fire, but all out of sight. If they have cannon, they'll probably try to wound us rather than sink us. After all, they'll probably see us as a fat prize ripe for the plucking by boarding," further chuckles, "and they must believe that right up to the moment we turn on them. We'll keep working on the foremast as a distraction, but obviously it'll not be of any use to us. Just before we turn, we'll lower the main sail, and then it'll be down to the rowers to pull as if the banshee was after them until we come alongside. Any questions?"

There were none, so she finished:

"as I've said, they may well be about quite peaceful

business, but I've an instinct, indeed a hope, that they are not and, should that indeed be the case, I want them to see how the men of Connacht fight."

This drew a rousing cheer and then the men returned to their tasks.

All put on leather corselets and those who had them, put on metal breastplates as well. Most had helmets and all wore Spanish espadrilles to better keep their footing on the wet decks. The harquebusiers made ready their weapons, first removing the wax cloths with which they protected them from the damp, then lighting the slow match with flint and steel before attaching the match to the serpentine. They would put the gunpowder on the pans just prior to firing. It was unlikely that they would not have time for a second volley - it was reckoned to take as long as the telling of two Paters and two Aves to properly reload a harquebus - so they would also have their short swords ready to board, or repel boarders, as the case might be. Meanwhile, the pike men were greasing the sharp ends of their pikes to make it more difficult for the enemy to grab hold of them. When they were all ready, Grace had as many of them as possible crammed into the cabin out of sight, and then they waited.

By this time, the two strange sail had come up over the horizon and were making quick progress directly towards the Dana. Gazing at them intently, Grace identified them as galliots, smaller than the Dana, their big single lateens propelling them swiftly forward. Although they showed no colours, Grace, with a strong feeling of déjà vu, was certain that they were Algerines. On her very first voyage, when she was no older than Tibbott now was, her father's carrack had been attacked by Algerine pirates in these very same waters. Captain O'Malley had played the same role of helpless trading ship that Grace was now trying. The Algerines had been fooled then and left for dead in the water. She hoped for the same outcome now should these oncoming boats also prove to be Algerines, as seemed overwhelmingly likely. The

Spanish used big galleys, and it would have been unusual for any of the nations that did use galliots to have them in these waters other than as pirates. She said as much to the priest who, still in his clerical garb, excused himself to change into more appropriate clothing for what he called the prosecution of the Lord's work.

When he re-emerged from the cabin, he had removed his habit and was dressed like the rest of the men in breeches, leather corselet, breastplate and helmet. In addition, he wore a red surcoat with a white cross, the arms of which ended in fleurs de lys, and over which was buckled a belt with sword and dagger. Grace gazed at him in admiration.

"Well now, there's finery for you. You'd certainly take the prize for best dressed man on the Dana," she looked critically around before adding, "mind you, the competition wouldn't be that great."

He smiled back, ruefully, "this is as much as I thought I could reasonably get in to my sea chest. It's lucky I have even this much. I had thought that my visit home to England would be uneventful, but one must always be prepared in case one is called upon to do God's will, as seems now to be the case."

He continued: "but, aren't you worried that they'll see through your subterfuge?"

"Not really," replied Grace cheerfully, "they'll see what they want to see, which is a big damaged trading galley. Our guns are hidden, we have no ram, and we're much broader in the beam than they'd expect to see in a fighting galley."

"Is that not a disadvantage to you, the lack of a ram?"

"Not at all. In the first place it conceals our underhand intentions. Secondly, we don't want to sink ships, but to capture them, and besides," she added mischievously, "think of all the good Christians who are doubtless chained to the benches of those galliots and who would drown unshriven if we were to ram and sink them." She continued more seriously, "we'll certainly have to disable one of them at the outset if we're to make it a more even fight, and if that results in a sinking, then so be it, hard though it be on the slaves."

The Algerines, for so they were, and they had hung out giant green and white crescent emblazoned flags as though to prove it, had quickly come up towards the slow-moving Dana and were now within extreme cannon range. Grace put the tiller over as if to flee from them and, almost immediately, they split so that they would approach from either quarter, and the portside galliot fired a warning shot that was heard but not seen, the ball dropping in the swell astern. The sense of déjà vu grew stronger.

Grace now ordered her sailors to start spilling the wind surreptitiously from the main sail to further slow their progress and allow the Algerines to come up even more quickly. She dismissed the thought of putting a drag over the side to slow them even more. The sea was not rough enough and the ruse would undoubtedly be spotted by some sharp eyed, predatory Turk.

Soon the galliots were sufficiently close for them to make out the individual sailors, with their baggy tunics and breeches and multicoloured turbans, and they could hear their shouting and the clashing of the cymbals as they worked themselves up for battle. Looking forward from the cabin where he had concealed himself, the priest could see the Dana's hidden soldiers and rowers shifting about nervously, some relieving themselves into the scuppers, others blessing themselves and muttering last minute prayers.

Another ball was fired, this one passing through the mainsail, and from the portside galliot, which appeared to be the leader, came an indecipherable order, the content of which they assumed to be that they stop. Grace quietly gave her orders: the main sail was hauled down in a very unseamanlike fashion by sailors giving a good impression of being terrified.

Judging that the galliot which had fired would not have had time to reload, and being a galliot, would only have the one gun, Grace raised her speaking trumpet and roared a great "Now."

Instantly the oars came into action, the portside oars pulling and the starboards backing. The Dana still had sufficient way on her that, with assistance from Grace, who pushed the tiller right over, she fairly spun on her axis. The Spanish colours were hauled down and replaced by the O'Malley flag with its prancing sea lion. The starboard galliot now fired, but, obviously surprised by the turn of events, fired hurriedly, the ball passing harmlessly astern.

And now the Dana's guns were unmasked, the covering sail being pushed behind the foremast. Both banks of oars were now in tandem, pushing the Dana rhythmically forward, faster and faster, to the gradually increasing tempo of Fergus O'Flaherty on his drums. Steadying the tiller, so that they were now pointing directly at the starboard galliot, Grace shouted to the gunner to fire in his own time. The galliot began to turn away from them, presenting a larger target, and the gunner, judging his moment, fired, to send the huge ball crashing into the side of the Algerine at what was fast approaching point blank range. Her frail timbers shattered, sending shards of flying wood through her crew, both sailor and slave alike.

Grace now adjusted the rudder again to allow Fabrizio, who knew his captain and was awaiting this move, to fire, first one and then the other demicannon, unleashing their murderous loads of metal fragments into the stricken galliot. Her forward platform, where her gunners were working frantically to reload, was swept completely clear. Other fragments swept the stern, killing the steersmen so that, rudderless, the galliot turned helplessly into the wind and could be discounted for the moment.

Grace next turned towards the second galliot, which was now no more than a cable's length away, the gap between them diminishing very quickly as she surged forward closehauled to the wind. The Dana's gunners were working flat out to reload but, before they were ready, the galliot fired again with what would have been wonderfully deadly accuracy had the Dana not dipped in the swell at that very moment so that the ball, instead of smashing into the gun crew, hit the unlucky foremast, shattering it further and sending jagged splinters flying through the air. Two of the crew were killed instantly and three others wounded in very ugly fashion.

Conor leapt forward with an axe to cut away the collapsed rigging which was badly hampering the gunners, and the wounded were carried aft to the cabin. Even as this was happening, judging her moment to a nicety, Grace put the tiller hard over so that the Dana turned on to the same course as the galliot, briefly running alongside her.

"Fire!" She roared.

The men manning the remounted swivels, and the harquebusiers, rose from behind their shelters and unleashed a withering fire across the galliot, cutting down a score or more of the Turks in a bloody mess.

"In oars! Grapnels!"

The oars were swung in and grapnels hurled at the galliot. Its captain, realising the size of the crew and warlike nature of the vessel which they had so rashly attacked, tried to turn away, but too late.

Enough of the grapnels held for the Danas to be able to hold both vessels together and then, screaming their battle cries, they were scrambling aboard the galliot. They were met by a ragged fusillade from the surviving Turkish harquebusiers which grievously thinned their front rank, but then they were amongst the Algerines, slashing with their swords and short pikes. The Dana's crew, being volunteers to a man, could all fight, whereas the oarsmen in the Algerine were slaves, so that her defence fell to what soldiers she carried, a considerably fewer number then the Danas, who now fell upon them with a wild ferocity. The fighting was desperate, and necessarily hand to hand, in the very confined space of the centre platform, with men falling amongst the benches or been trampled underfoot in the surge of struggling combatants, most of whom had no more room than that in which a dagger or fist or knee might be used.

The priest led the boarders at the stern, where the throng of men was slightly less, and was met by a surprised Turk who swung at him with his scimitar. He parried the blow, and then thrust forward with his dagger, driving it deep into the Turk's stomach and upwards under his ribs. The Turk dropped his weapon and, clutching his wound, fell groaning on the deck. Stepping over him, the priest cut at another Turk, catching him across the cheek so that he fell back for a moment and then, with a howl, came slashing forward with such ferocity that the priest was himself driven briefly back before, dodging beneath a wild swing of the scimitar, he swung his sword into the Turk's neck. Blood spurted from the wound, his eyes bulged, and he too fell dying. He was now attacked from the side by a pike man, whose blade caught the priest a glancing blow on his armour. Turning to meet this new threat, his feet slipped on the bloody deck and he fell to his knees. The Turk, teeth bared ferociously, raised his pike for the killing blow. The priest tried to roll away but, just before the blade descended, a sword was driven through the Turk's back with such force that it came right through him. With a look of utter bemusement, he dropped the pike and fell forward on the deck, the sword still protruding from his back. The priest turned to his rescuer. It was Grace who, seeing his plight, had jumped over from the Dana just in time. He shouted his thanks, which she acknowledged with a dismissive wave and then, giving up trying to retrieve her sword, she picked up a fallen scimitar and returned to the Dana. The priest turned to the battle again, but it had already reached, and passed, its climax. The Dana's soldiers, augmented by their comrades from the oars, so outnumbered the Turks that there could ever have been only one result no matter how hard the Turks fought, and they fought hard, expecting no quarter. Having been boarded from forward, amidships and aft simultaneously, they had been reduced to small ineffective groups, and were now being cut to ribbons by the Danas. Some jumped overboard and some tried to surrender, but the bloodlust of the Danas was up and the killing continued until there was not a Turk left standing except their captain and galley master and a few remnants of the crew who, realising that the galliot was lost, had managed to retreat into the cabin, barring the door behind them.

The galliot secured, Grace now ordered the release of the slaves from their benches in response to their cries, which had not ceased from the first moment of battle. The keys to their shackles were nowhere to be found however, and were presumed to be with the galley master in the cabin. There they would have to remain for the moment because the first galliot was underway again, not noticed by anyone but Thomas, who now shouted in warning.

"Get back, get back," screamed Grace to her men on the defeated galliot, who were busily engaged in looting the dead and dying Turks. Perceiving their danger, they quickly returned to the Dana and the grapnels were cast off. They pushed away from the galliot until they had sufficient room to get the oars in the water, and then rowed away as hard as they could, the cries of the still fettered slaves following piteously behind them. They were no sooner clear than the approaching galliot, which had somehow found enough uninjured men to reload its cannon, fired at point blank range, fortunately with ball and not grape. The ball passed wickedly through the Dana's hull from one side to the other, cutting down a complete bench of oarsmen, scattering vicious splinters which caused even more destruction, and briefly destroying the rhythm of the oars. One standing man was sliced completely in half. The upper half of his body fell, scattering blood everywhere, but the legs and torso remained grotesquely standing for what appeared to be an age, before also crumpling on the deck.

"That Turk does not lack for courage," said the priest, to no one in particular.

"No," agreed Grace, "but, by God, he'll pay dearly for it before we're finished with him".

She raised her speaking trumpet to call to the gunner who had, oblivious to the fight on the enemy deck, carried on with the cumbersome business of reloading.

"Aim at her hull."

Catching the swell just so, he fired at the approaching galliot, the huge ball going through her strakes on the rise so that, as she plunged forward again, the sea gushed through the newly made hole, her forward impetus forcing even more water into her.

"The demis now," called Grace, and once again, the galliot's decks were swept by grape, leaving hardly a man standing.

During this brief action, the captain of the second galliot had re-emerged with his remaining men from the cabin in which they had taken shelter and had managed to get her underway again, her mast and sail being relatively unscathed.

"In oars. Mainsail." Commanded Grace.

The big lateen was hauled up and Grace settled down to the pursuit of the galliot. It was soon obvious that, even with her rigging only slightly damaged, the galliot could not sail as close to the wind as the Dana, even without her foresail, so that they soon began to overhaul her. Realising the hopelessness of his position, her captain ordered her sail lowered, and she lay rocking gently on the swell until the Dana came up alongside.

Grace sent a dozen men across with the Rory to disarm the crew, and then ordered the slaves freed. Her captain looked back at her, opening his arms in a show of incomprehension. She was attempting to indicate what she wanted by sign language, when the priest stepped up to the rail and addressed them in Arabic. There was an immediate storm of protest. Rory seized the captain and put a sword to his throat and the protests ceased. With a shrug of resignation, the Turkish captain spoke to his rowing master who began, sullenly, to release the slaves. Without any warning or apparent premeditation, and before Rory and his men could intervene, the slaves, upon being freed, spontaneously seized discarded weapons from the deck and savagely attacked their erstwhile captors, hacking them all to death.

There was a shocked silence on the galley, from which Grace was the first to recover.

"Put down those weapons or I'll kill the lot of you."

She indicated the reloaded swivels but, after their brief frenzy of revenge, the ex-slaves seemed suddenly bereft of energy, and most sat on the deck in disbelief at their unexpected freedom, some weeping openly.

"Release the rest of them, Rory, and give them something to eat and drink."

She addressed her crew:

"We'll go alongside the other galliot now. I don't think she'll give us much trouble, but keep the swivels ready, just in case."

In fact, there was no fight at all left in her crew. Her captain had been killed in their first cannonade, and it was her senior lieutenant who had instigated their return to the fray. He too was now dead and, with him, any possible spark of resistance had also died. The dispirited remnants of the crew, who had suffered shocking losses from the wholly unexpected devastation of the demis, laid down their arms. The slaves on this vessel were in an even greater frenzy to be released, their cries being made more frantic by the water flooding through the hole made by the Dana's shot, the flood increasing with each rise and fall of the now stationary vessel, so that it was already beginning to settle.

"We'll not have a repeat of that last slaughter," said Grace, ordering the surviving unwounded Turks on to the Dana, where they were shackled to the ring bolts which she carried beneath the forward rowing benches for just such an eventuality. The wounded were then transferred to join the Dana's own wounded in the cabin and only then, with severe warnings about their behaviour, were the slaves released. Some of these had also been wounded but their casualty rate had been much reduced because of the slight protection afforded them by the galliot's hull.

Grace herself went on board the galliot at this stage to assess the damage, and quickly decided that Fabrizio's gunnery had been too efficient by far. The galliot was already lower in the water and, although repairs and pumping would probably keep her afloat, she was not prepared to risk any of her men in the attempt. Accordingly, she sent the freed slaves over to the Dana and ordered a systematic search of the captured vessel. This proved extremely lucrative, the holds yielding up, from the swilling water, chests of coins, gold and silver, bales of fine cloth, spices and, in all, such booty that Grace could only wonder at the greed that had led them to attack another vessel, the Dana, rather than return to Africa with a haul, undoubtedly from a homeward bound New World galleon, sufficient to have set them all up in some style in Salee or Tripoli or in whatever port it was from which they had sailed. Well, now it would go to Ireland where, even after Black Tom had had his share, there would be more than enough to improve Grace's comfort.

The treasure, along with all the arms and chandlery that could be crammed into the Dana, was quickly and efficiently transferred to that vessel by her smiling crew, who were already assessing their own personal shares of the haul. They were also beginning to surmise what might be found in the other galliot, as was Grace herself who was cautiously concluding that, as the other galliot appeared to be the leader of the two, it might yield even more. However, there was no urgency with that for the moment. The first priority now was to do a head count of the Danas which, she feared, might prove their little victory to have been very expensively bought.

There were also the freed slaves to be considered, all of them clamouring for attention, but they would just have to wait until she had time for them. In the meantime, she ordered them fed with moderation from the supplies taken from the galliot. They fell hungrily on the food and drink, everything else driven from their minds, as they applied themselves to making up for the near starvation which had been their lot so very recently.

They pulled alongside the other galliot again, where Grace set Donal with some of his mates to repairing the damaged rigging. They had fixed their position by now with a noon observation of the sun, which came and went behind scudding clouds. They had been carried much further south during the storm than previously thought, but there were at least another couple of days sailing ahead of them to their destination and Grace was determined that the sailing gear of both boats should be in as good repair as possible for those remaining days. The Dana would then, of course, need to have recourse to the boatyard facilities of Corunna before they could contemplate, with any equanimity, their return voyage to Mayo.

She had managed, more or less, to keep to the back of her mind until now, contemplation of the number of Danas who had been killed or wounded in the short action, but she could no longer postpone the bad news. She moved across to the galliot's cabin, the Dana's being full, and more than full, with injured men, her own and Turks, as well as those unfortunate slaves who had been caught in the cannonade and subsequent fighting. She called on Thomas to follow her across and prepared herself to receive the list of casualties.

They were as bad, indeed worse, than she had expected. They had lost twenty seven men killed, with another score or so injured, some very seriously and some less so. Thomas was very sad to have to tell her that the dead included his nephew Fergus, killed by the harquebus fusillade as they boarded. Rory was amongst the walking wounded, having taken a deep gash from a scimitar in his right thigh, but this was being attended to at this very moment by Father James who, it appeared, was as accomplished at suturing as he was at swordsmanship.

What an invaluable man to have in a crew, thought Grace, allowing her mind to drift in contemplation of her passenger for a moment or two before returning to the grim business in hand.

She told Thomas how very sorry she was for his loss, their loss, before sending him back to the Dana, asking him to send over Rory, when he was restored, as well as Patrick O'Halloran.

CHAPTER 10

James had been busy. Having helped move some of the wounded into the cabin, he put aside his weapons and, donning his stole, administered the last rites to the dying, as well as to the dead of both faiths, all children of Abraham, and all is likely to benefit he felt, as not.

The ship's barber, Phelim O'Connor, in his secondary role of ship's surgeon, had already started in to his grisly work. Most of the wounds were gash wounds caused by slashing swords and axes, as well as flying splinters from the effects of the cannonade on the wooden hulls. But worse wounds had been caused by the balls from both the demicannon and the harquebuses, deep ugly wounds with torn, powder burned skin, compounded by the bits of filthy material from the soldiers' clothing lodged deep within them. There were also fractured limbs and one depressed cranial fracture, as well as two Turks who had been virtually disembowelled, but these he had already blessed, as being beyond treatment.

Having quickly assessed that the barber's very crude treatments did not extend much further than cleaning with seawater and bandaging, James offered his services, in sign language, the barber speaking none of the languages in which James was fluent, to assist or take over, as the barber wished. The barber grasped quickly and gratefully at the offer. He had, he tried to convey, in Gaelic and signs, no experience at all of this type of slaughter; it was far and away the worst battle most of them had seen, and the height of his competence and ambition being the splinting he had performed after the storm, he would be very happy for the Reverend Father to take over and would, of course, be equally happy to act as his assistant.

The priest saw Tibbott, crouching frightened at the back of the cabin, and invited him to help also, reasoning, on a kill or cure basis, that what he was witnessing would haunt the child for the rest of his life if he was merely an observer, whereas if he was put to some slight task, he might accept it as part of life at sea and, while he would certainly have nightmares, they might, in this way, be the more transient. Accordingly, at Tibbott's mute nod of acceptance, he set him to cutting strips of linen for bandages.

He inspected the patients, reaffirming his earlier opinions of who would survive, who might survive and who definitely would not. The disembowelled Turks were among the latter group, along with some of the more serious gunshot and splinter wounds, all of them moaning piteously.

"What do you have for pain relief?" He enquired of the barber, who looked back blankly at him. To his astonishment, Tibbott, whom he had hardly heard speak before - in the drunken escapade in Roscoff, his speech, what was comprehensible of it, had been in Gaelic - hesitantly translated James's English request into Gaelic. Whiskey, was the reply from the relieved barber. James was amused to realise that the translation of uisce beatha into whiskey was one of the very few translations that he would have found unnecessary from his time in the Dana.

He gave instructions to the barber, through an increasingly confident and willing Tibbott, for all of the less serious Danas to be given whiskey if they wished, which all of them did, no surprise there. For the others and for the Turks, he got a bottle from his chest which he tried, with limited success, to explain was tincture of laudanum, an opium derivative, much more effective than mere alcohol as an anaesthetic, and less likely to be injurious to the religious sensibilities of the Turks who, although infidels, still had rights, possibly even more so than the heretical Protestants, they, the Turks, being generally compassionate in their dealings with other faiths (the Knights aside) than the

Protestants, who tended to burn all who did not agree with them.

The barber, quite reasonably, had started treatment on the lightly wounded, these being within his sphere of competence. The others he had intended leaving for Grace to deal with, knowing that she would sew those that she could, while the remnant would, in the natural order of things, be given alcohol and comfort to ease their dying. The priest, he quickly realised, had much greater ambitions. He had the barber and his mates arrange the cases in order of severity, beginning with the gash wounds. One of the first of these was Rory. Exposing the wound, he cleaned it thoroughly with linen dipped in wine and then sutured it neatly, leaving a ligature at the bottom through which any bad humours might drain. Next he bandaged it with some of the linen being assiduously cut into strips by Tibbott at his encouragement, showing the barber exactly how he wished it done.

They carried on in this fashion, James cleaning and sewing, and the barber bandaging, until all of the more are less walking wounded had been dealt with, the Danas returning to their work, and the unfortunate Turks, who, after the perfect fairness of their medical treatment might have expected better, making the short journey forward to the rowing benches, where they were chained beside their unwounded comrades.

The little team then moved on to the gunshot wounds which were altogether more grave in prospect. The Dana's medical chest contained very little in the way of instruments: some ligatures, but not enough for their requirements, some blades and saws, and some leather bound chains with which struggling patients might be held down. James had to go to his own chest again, where he kept a small collection of specialist tools for the removal of deeply embedded small objects: bullets, bone fragments and the like.

He had the first patient lifted and strapped down on the

cabin table, with a leather strap between his teeth to stop him biting through his tongue. The man was already in a dreamlike, semi-delirious state from the small amount of laudanum that James had been able to spare from his meagre supply, and he lay relatively still while his wound was opened and delicately cleaned. But when James started to probe for the bullet, which was lodged in his side against his ribs, he jerked so convulsively that it required all the strength of the barber and his mates to keep him steady while James continued to probe remorselessly, deeper and deeper into the wound until the ball could be seen, up against the now exposed, glistening white bone . He got the ball out quite easily with a forceps but then had the more difficult task of picking out the fragments of burned cloth. However, in time this too was accomplished to his satisfaction, the wound liberally splashed with whiskey and stitched up, the barber then taking over the bandaging while his mates prepared the next patient. Thus they slowly progressed.

Meanwhile, Rory and the carpenter had joined Grace, Rory limping somewhat, his heavily bandaged thigh showing where his breeches, which he had not had time to replace, had been cut away for access to the wound. He was fulsome in his praise of the priest.

"He's becoming a more and more invaluable addition to this crew, even if only temporarily", agreed Grace.

"Now, give me an update on our state of readiness."

"Well, you know of our dead, and poor Fergus, God rest him. Of the wounded, the Father considers some of them so gravely injured that they'll not see out the day, and others need to be hospitalised as soon as possible, but the most of them are wounds like mine and will be back in action fairly quickly. The boat itself is in good order and the main armament undamaged. The ball we took was sufficiently above the waterline not to be an immediate worry. Having said which, we were lucky that they fired ball and not grape. That bloody ball itself was murderous enough. We have, of course, taken about a dozen unwounded of the Turks who will fill some of the bench spaces and there are sufficient freed men to fill the rest, on both boats, if need be." He paused a moment before continuing, "you'll have to speak to them soon, you know."

"Yes, but they're the least of my worries for the moment." responded Grace.

"Now, I believe we may have the men stand down and get on with tidying up the boats. Get Fabrizio to secure the guns and then you may have the ovens relit and something hot prepared for everyone. And tell Father James that I'll be with him as soon as I can."

Rory left and she turned to her carpenter.

"Well, Pat?"

"Well Captain, as Rory said, we were lucky they used ball. The mainmast is fine and its rigging is pretty much intact, a few small pieces to be spliced, but nothing serious. The poor foremast is a different matter entirely. We've begun to repair it again and we'll certainly be able to raise a sail on it in time, but it will remain weak and I couldn't honestly answer for it in any kind of a blow. I don't suppose we could make time to take the mast out of the galliot you're abandoning?" He asked hopefully.

"No." Replied Grace. "You'd need to rig sheers to get it out and there's still too much of a swell for that kind of work. Right fools we'd look if we managed to drop it through our own hull. Besides, I want to get our wounded to Corunna as soon as possible. No, we'll carry on as we are. What about this boat?"

"Well, you can see that we've started on her already. The sail and rigging were badly cut up by our fire, but the mast and yard are intact and it shouldn't take too much effort to get her shipshape again. I'm assuming that she'll have spare sails in the hold but we haven't looked yet, not until you yourself have given us the word."

"Well done, Pat. We may as well have a look straight

away, although since we took canvas out of the other galliot anyway, it's not a problem if this one doesn't have any."

She had the hatches raised and they inspected the hold, starting forward and working aft. There was an abundance of stores including, as well as the spare sails and cordage, great quantities of dried meats and fish, dried fruit, and also large sacks of rice kept in lead lined containers to keep out the damp; in short, provisions for a long cruise, ended prematurely when they had been unlucky enough to fall in with the Dana. Going in to the final hold compartment below the cabin, Grace found that her guess, which she had hardly dare allow turn into hope, was correct. It too was full of treasure, even more full than the abandoned galliot had been. Once again she found herself marvelling that they had not been satisfied with their haul, and returned home to enjoy it.

Instructing Patrick to feel free to take whatever he and his men needed for the repairs, and to lose not a minute: the wind and tide were taking them eastwards and further away from Corunna with every passing moment, Grace had the hatch into the after hold replaced and locked, pocketing the key herself. She then returned to the Dana, going straight to the cabin. There she found the priest, his surcoat covered in blood and, unexpectedly, Tibbott assisting him, and he also liberally daubed with blood.

"Mama," he greeted her proudly, "Father James is allowing me to help him and says that I am very useful to him, and I've hardly felt sick at all, well, only a little bit at the start."

"I hope you don't mind, Captain. He was in the cabin, obedient to your orders, when I arrived, but looked to be on the verge of being overwhelmed by the horror of it all so, rather than send him away and have him dwell on it, I thought it better to get him involved. In fact, he's showing such an aptitude for the work that you may well consider sending him away to Italy to be trained as a physical gentleman if he doesn't take to the seafaring," this last with a smile.

"It wouldn't be at the top of my plans for him, but I'll bear it in mind. But, that aside, I'm uncommonly grateful to you for your care of the wounded. You're a continual surprise."

"It's just another part of my Knight's training," he replied simply.

"Well, whatever the reason, I'm very glad of it," replied Grace. "Normally, this would be my work. The men seem to think that I should be better than them at sewing, just because I'm a woman, but they've certainly fared considerably better under your care than they would have under mine, so, can I say again how grateful I am to you."

"It's I who am most grateful to you, Grace. I regret that I haven't yet had a chance to thank you for saving me from that Turk when I was down."

"Oh, forget that. You'd have done the same for me," replied Grace. She changed the subject.

"Can you give me any idea of how you're progressing? I don't wish to hurry you, and indeed, you can have all the time you need, but it seems to me that you might find things easier if we were under way and the boat relatively steady, rather than bobbing up and down on the swell as we are now."

"I've virtually finished what I can do for the light and intermediate wounds. It's true that the gravely wounded would be better tended in more stable conditions. In fact, I do confess to being worried about any further work in this current sea."

"I'll speak to Pat and hurry him up if possible though, knowing Pat, he'll do his work thoroughly and at his own pace which, I suppose, is what I would wish of him. Still, I'll see what I can do."

The priest, who had continued to work all through the exchange, nodded his thanks and re-applied himself to his task.

Grace left the cabin and went forward to speak to Patrick O'Halloran, and having been told, rather testily, that he was working as quickly as possible but was determined that the repairs should not be slipshod, left him and his team to it and went aft again to finally address the freed slaves.

It was immediately apparent that, although some of the more recently taken were in reasonable shape, some of the others were in a very sad way indeed. However, all were as one in having nothing but gratitude for their deliverance. One old man, who had been nodding and smiling at Grace, now surprised her by speaking to her in Gaelic.

"You'll not remember me, your honour, Tadgh O'Flaherty, but I sailed with your father Dubhdara, God rest him. I should have stayed with him but I was led astray by my ambitions. Fat lot of good they did me." He indicated the benches. "I'd given up all hopes of rescue but now, with the blessing, I may yet see Clew Bay again."

"It's a pleasure, Tadgh, to have been your deliverer and, never fear, you'll see Connacht again before the summer is out," replied Grace with obvious pleasure. "Thomas, look after Tadgh here, he's one of our own."

The rest of the slaves were a very mixed bunch from all of the countries of the Mediterranean and speaking as many languages. There were even a couple of Englishmen who, even in the general squalor of their situation, tried to remain aloof from the others, from which Grace deduced that they were probably Protestant heretics, not that she would penalise them for that. She addressed them all in Spanish, trusting that the Spaniards, who appeared to be the most numerous amongst them, would translate for the others.

"Welcome to the Dana. I am Captain O'Malley. We're on our way to Corunna, where I intend to put you all ashore.

Ours is a Christian galley, with Christian notions, so you'll all be given a few pence when we reach Corunna, to set you on your way. One thing, I sympathise with, but cannot condone, what you did to the Turks on the boat alongside. If any of you attempts anything similar on our remaining prisoners, I'll have you chained to the benches beside them. Is that understood?"

There was a mute nodding and then they all broke into a ragged cheer.

"Good," said Grace, "we'll be under way quite soon, I hope. I intend to anchor offshore tonight and tomorrow we'll resume our journey to Corunna."

With that, she dismissed them. She then called Rory to divide the freed men more are less evenly between the Dana and the galliot, telling him, in an aside, to keep on board the Dana, where they might more easily be watched, those whom she had already privately labelled as possible troublemakers: it was her experience that it did not take long for the newly grateful to forget their gratitude, particularly to an unknown woman. She then sent Conor on board the galliot with a strongly armed contingent of Danas, although she did not expect any trouble from that quarter.

At length, the carpenter was satisfied with the re-rigging, the two vessels were unmoored from each other and pushed apart, the lateens were raised and, with Grace steering the Dana and Thomas the galliot, they set course for the North coast of Spain, leaving behind the abandoned galliot, which was settling lower and lower in the water, the waves already beginning to break over her decks.

Late that evening they anchored in a small cove, west of Santander. Their progress had been slow because Grace had not wished to overburden the makeshift foremast unnecessarily, and, although he now had the stability that he needed, the fading of the light persuaded James that the very serious cases that remained in his care would be better dealt with in the morning.

Grace sent the skiff, which had remained miraculously undamaged during the action, ashore to find fresh water, supplies of which had become dangerously low due to their unlooked for but protracted spell at sea. It was accompanied by the galliot's skiff which had similarly remained undamaged by virtue of its being towed astern.

This was a notoriously lawless region, the Moors had been driven out years earlier but central authority had not yet been properly imposed, so the swivels were mounted and loaded and a strong watch set. Then all, Danas and freed men alike, sat down to a hot meal. Normally, after this length of time at sea, this would have consisted of salted meat and fish but was, on this occasion, memorably enlivened by spiced dishes of rice cooked up by one of the ex-slaves who had, before his capture, been cook to a Spanish nobleman, but had not been considered worthy of ransom at the same time as his employer. Having already allowed the freed men to eat sparingly after their release, just to accustom their bellies to proper food, Grace now gave them their head and they applied themselves, silently, wolfishly, to making up for lost time. She also allowed them free rein with the wine. Obviously none had seen alcohol in captivity, and having eaten their fill, they all got roaring, not to say paralytically, drunk very quickly, and soon subsided into stupefaction from the combined effects of the food and wine, as well as sheer exhaustion, physical and emotional.

The Danas, no slouches themselves when given a free hand with the liquor, old hands at the trade indeed, but, through long practice, considerably more hardened to its effects, smiled in benign tolerance at the piles of corpselike bodies lying around the platforms and benches, as they themselves, those not on watch that is to say, drank themselves to the same insensibility, but at a more measured pace and with a studied deliberation.

Grace had had the awnings rigged on both vessels when they anchored so that there was some shelter for those of the wounded for whom there was no room in the cabins. She had also distributed the wounded between the two boats, the less seriously wounded being put aboard the galliot and the severe cases kept on the Dana where James could keep an eye on them. He had limited himself to watered-down wine, the better to have a clear head in the morning. Grace also had been relatively abstemious as had, on her orders, the Dana's officers. She now joined James in the Dana's cabin to share a small whiskey with him before retiring for the night.

"Lord, I do hate the aftermath of a battle," she said, "even one as successful as today's. Oh, the prize we've taken and the treasure are a great consolation, but our losses, our losses. Except for Thomas of course, they're all more are less young enough to be my own sons. I suppose I even have to admit to a motherly feeling for them, unlikely though it may seem. I know that they all feel the same: they're all friends, many of them related, which is why I've indulged them this evening. Unfortunately, the whiskey doesn't seem to work for me anymore." She smiled ruefully. "I doubt that I shall sleep tonight."

They sat in reflective silence for a while, quietly sipping, before Grace asked about James's medical training.

"Well now, Grace," he began. "I mentioned how I went rashly off to Spain to join the Calatravians, whose glories, I quickly discovered, were no more. I remained in Spain until after I was ordained and then asked for leave of absence to go to Malta. This they gave me readily enough. They're not over fond of the English, you know."

"Them too? You surprise me," Grace said.

He smiled and continued.

"I got on well with the Knights. They're rather a proud lot, but once they'd satisfied themselves that my breeding was sufficiently elevated not to demean the social standing of the order, they made me very welcome. They perceived an aptitude for medicine in me, I don't know how, decided that I might be more useful to them with some formal training, and so they sent me off to Padua for a while where it transpired that their perception was correct. I did have some instinct. And that's really all there is to it. As someone said, I merely bandage them and the Lord heals them. But, while we're on the subject of medicine, may I say Grace, that your medical chest is sadly undersupplied."

"Don't for a minute think I don't know it," replied Grace, "but you must remember that what it does contain represents the sum total of what Phelim O'Connor and myself are competent to deal with, and barely competent at that. I've tried once or twice to get one of the Galway leeches to ship with us, but they're all too comfortable to embark on a life at sea, so we've had to make do with what little knowledge we have."

"Well," said James, "when we get to Corunna, I'll find an apothecary and get him to make up a proper medicine chest, and I should also be able to find you a more extensive range of surgical instruments. I would not be critical, but what you have is fairly primitive."

"Oh, you can be as critical as you like. I'm not particularly proud of our limitations and would be happy to avail of anything you can suggest that might lessen them."

"Certainly," said James, "tomorrow then, when we start operating, I shall make a beginning on Master O'Connor's surgical education. We have some quite grave cases but I'll only treat the absolutely essential ones; the others we'll try to nurse to Corunna where, I presume, there is an infirmary. Anyway, that's another day's work. So if you'll excuse me now, Grace, I must read my Office, and then try to get some sleep."

"Of course, James. I'll leave you to it. Good night to you now, and very many thanks again for all you've done today."

"Don't mention it, Grace. I hope that you too get some rest tonight. I'll pray for it."

CHAPTER 11

The following morning, James made his rounds of the wounded, first checking those who had already been treated, smelling the wounds for any indication of putrefaction, and then, when he was satisfied, going on to those who were now to be operated upon.

The two Turks, and one of the Danas, had died during the night and their bodies had already been moved forward to be prepared for burial. Grace had simply wanted to put the Turks over the side, but James had firmly reminded her that he had already anointed them and that they were now to be treated, nominally at least, as Christians, and buried as such.

He selected his patients from those remaining according to the severity of their wounds and, with Phelim O'Connor and his mates to hold them down, he dosed them in turn with his remaining laudanum before getting to work.

Grace, at his request, had had the two boats lashed together again to give a more stable operating platform and the loggerheads were already in the galley's copper oven, getting to red heat in preparation for melting the pitch with which he would cover the stumps after the amputations. He explained to Phelim O'Connor, as he cut and sawed, that Dr. Pare's new method, which he would demonstrate to him in time, involved the ligaturing of the arteries and dressing of the stump with a mixture of egg yolk, rose oil and turpentine - the turpentine being a very powerful anti-infective - but in the absence of the necessary ingredients, they would have to make do with molten pitch as in the past which, although good enough in its own way, killed as many as it cured due to its terribly shocking effect on the already weakened patient. The barber had never before seen an amputation, let alone performed one - crushed and shattered limbs had invariably been treated by making the victims as comfortable as possible before their inevitable death - and he was stunned by the speed at which the monk operated, cutting back the skin to get to sound bone, sawing through the bone, and then neatly trimming and suturing the skin over the bone, before covering the stump in the pitch, all a matter of minutes for, as he further explained, even in their drug induced stupor, the patients felt every bit of the operation - witness their struggling under the leathered chains - and the longer the surgery went on, the more likely it was to kill them, so speed was of the essence. He also washed his hands in sea water between patients; Phelim O'Connor hardly washed his hands at all at any time, and again the priest explained that it seemed to improve the healing, although he had no idea why, it was one of the many things the Knights had picked up from the Turks who, infidels though they might be, nevertheless seemed to have some very sound ideas on medicine, and on navigation and all other manner of things for that matter. He worked as quickly as he could through all the cases that were capable of being treated with the limited facilities on board until he was finally faced with the depressed cranial fracture.

He had already had a couple of chests lashed together as an operating table out on deck, in the bright mid morning light. The man, one of the Dana's sailors, had been caught by the falling foremast, fortunately only a glancing blow, although James privately considered that he would have been better to have been killed outright. He was in a deep coma, his skin waxy white and his breathing so shallow as to be barely discernible. He was obviously not going to struggle. He was now laid carefully on the makeshift table and James had the barber shave his head all around the wound which he then splashed liberally with whiskey.

A small crowd of the less squeamish had gathered around the operating area, taking a ghoulish interest in what was about to happen. They were not disappointed. First, James cut back the scalp, exposing the wound and the surrounding bone. He then used a trephan to drill a hole through the centre of the depression in the unfortunate sailor's head. This, he explained to Phelim O'Connor, was to release pressure and ill humours from inside the head. It also seemed, to the more fanciful of his audience, to expose the brain itself, something which gave them grave satisfaction. The edges of the fractured bone around the hole he then gently raised, and with a small spoon-like instrument, he patiently scoured the underside of the skull to clean away any fragments that might cause complications and make his patient's survival chances, already slim enough, slimmer still. When he was satisfied that all was as it should be, he took a gold coin from his pocket, carefully wiped it in whiskey, dried it, and placed it directly over the hole, before finally stitching the scalp over and around it to create a firm cover for the hole. He then washed all again before bandaging the head with round after round of linen strips to keep the repair, and its cover, stable.

"By God, Father," exclaimed Rory, one of the fascinated bystanders, "that's more money than Finian Burke has ever had before in all his life."

"I hope he survives," replied James, seriously, "to consider himself wealthy. Although," he continued with a smile, "I shall certainly need recompense for that good Spanish doubloon."

"And you shall certainly have it," said Grace, who had joined them, "even if I have to stop it from his wages," glaring ferociously around lest anyone think her not serious, and getting from her crew, the older ones of whom knew her through and through, smiles and chuckles at this assumed ferocity, it being what was expected of her.

"Is that some new practice?" She asked. "I've never heard the likes of it being done in Galway, or even Dublin."

"Oh, people have been drilling holes in other people's heads for all the ages, mainly to treat fractures, but sometimes just to relieve the humours in those unfortunates suffering severe headaches or even mild insanity. It's something else we've got from the Arabs."

"I've always thought the Turks to be no more than piratical heathens," said Grace, "and now you shock me by telling me that they're at least as learned as us Christians, if not more so. Why do we not make peace with them and exchange ideas and trade?"

"Because they'll not make peace. Their threat doesn't yet extend to England or Ireland. Indeed, the late King Henry refused to join any alliances against them because he didn't perceive them to be a threat, and I've heard that Queen Elizabeth not only still pursues the same policy but does actual trade with them, but it's their general intention to impose their infidel faith on the whole world if they can, and by the sword if necessary. It's hundreds of years since Christianity lost the Holy Land to them, and ever since, they've been expanding all across Africa, Byzantium, into Spain itself and even up to the gates of Vienna. Certainly they received a huge setback to their ambitions at Lepanto but they have not relinquished these ambitions. They have a huge advantage in that they operate mainly as one fleet with one army, whereas we are an unreliable alliance, made up of many factions, each trying to steal an advantage on the other, with only the Knights carrying the fight to them continuously." He paused. "But I do agree that if we ever did have peace, we could learn enormously from each other. That's my opinion, of course, and not one that I would dare voice with the Knights."

"Well," said Grace, "I'll look forward to discussing this further at another time but now, if you're happy with the comfort of your patients, I'm afraid we must see to the dead and then get underway."

James had the bedridden cases lined up under the awning where they would get warmth and a pleasant breeze without being burned by direct sunlight, and setting the barber and his mates, with Tibbott in attendance, to sit with them, he told Grace that he was ready for the burials.

While he had been working, Grace had had the bodies prepared, stitching them in shrouds made from their new abundance of canvas, with round shot from the demi cannon stitched in to bring them to the bottom - Grace's husband's nickname, Iron Richard, stemmed not just from the fact that he tended to dress in antique armour, but because he also owned a foundry, meaning that there was no shortage of ball on the Dana. (Indeed, it could be argued that it was the weight of ball in the Dana's ballast that had prevented their capsizing when the foresail had blown out.)

The bodies had been arranged in line, up on the fighting platforms. James read the service from his breviary, the crew answering the Amens at his prompting, moving among the bodies and casting water, which he had just blessed, over each of them, Turks included. Finally he started a Pater Noster, the words of which they were all familiar with from attending Mass, that same familiarity being wonderfully consoling, and then, with Donal playing a lament on the pipes, the bodies were lifted, one by one, and gently dropped over the side. Fergus was the last to go over, by which time many of the crew had tears coursing silently down their faces, Grace included, it not being considered in any way unmanly by the men of Mayo to allow their grief to show for their lost friends.

The two vessels were cast apart again and, Dana leading, and under sail alone in a favourable breeze, the gentleness of which totally belied the storm of but two days previously, they resumed their journey to Corunna.

The long delayed mid day meal was served, and as they put the leagues behind them in the perfect sailing weather, the men, whose spirits had been sadly put down by the burials, began to revive again, and the innate cheerfulness which James had often marked in sailors, resurfaced in the usual boisterousness of the hands at dinner. He was taking his meal amongst his patients where he could watch them more closely and was already cautiously relieved to see a very slight lessening in the pallor on young Finian Burke's face. Grace joined him and once again thanked him, not only for his care of the wounded but for the solemnity which he had brought to the burial service, a great comfort to the men, and immensely more powerful then she could have achieved, this being one of the very few times when the men cared that she was, in fact, a woman. Although they knew that, as captain, it was her duty to read the service, it somehow did not sit quite right, they, in their unstated prejudice, feeling that only a man could perform a religious ceremony properly.

"You'd be a great addition to this crew, James," she said. "The men would love to know that they had someone to physic them properly if they were injured and, even more so, to be buried with Latin prayers if it came to it. They're a very superstitious lot, you know, and they will persist in the belief that prayers in Latin must necessarily be more powerful than prayers in Irish, the Gospels being written in Latin and God and His Holy Mother being more likely to listen to Latin than anything else."

He smiled.

"I'll be forever grateful to you, Grace, for rescuing me in Waterford, but I must make my way back to Malta. I will though, make sure that you are fully equipped with instruments and medicines before I leave you, and if I can possibly find a copy of Dr. Pare's book, I will teach Phelim O'Connor all I think he should know about surgery and anaesthesia. After all, Dr. Pare himself started life as a barber's assistant, so there's no reason why your barber can't aim as high."

"I think you might possibly be over estimating Phelim O'Connor's capabilities, but anything you can teach us is bound to be an improvement on our current practices. Even if it just meant that he could take over from me in the stitching line, sure, that'd be a great thing."

"Well, I'll do what I can. We can certainly arrange that the sick and hurt have something more efficacious than whiskey to dull the pain, not that I've anything against whiskey. Indeed, I believe that I'm developing a certain partiality for it."

"Oh, tis a great drink, all right, and I might even let the freed slaves have a drop before we set them down in Corunna, but not this soon. It's much stronger than wine, you know, even the wine they sell in Galway after they've doctored it."

"I had noticed its power," said James wryly, "and it would certainly be more then those poor men could bear at this stage of their freedom. Which reminds me, I haven't yet examined them properly after their ordeal and I suppose this is as good a time as any. What do you think?"

"Of course James. I need to speak with Pat O'Halloran myself anyway, to see how the repairs are coming along."

CHAPTER 12

After the ferocity of the storm, the weather had settled in to sunshine with light breezes and, after four days of gentle sailing, anchoring each evening, they rounded Cape Prior, and the Lighthouse of Corunna finally came into view.

Grace had large Spanish flags hoisted on both vessels to allay any fears the townspeople and garrison of Corunna might have had of an impending corsair raid, unlikely though that might have seemed against such a well defended town. The need for this precaution was confirmed by the view, when they got close enough, of soldiers moving purposefully among the guns on the town's ramparts and those of the newly completed fortress of St. Anton, as well as Forts San Diego and Santa Cruz.

They dropped anchor amongst the assorted shipping in the harbour at what Grace considered to be a prudent distance from shore, and the skiff was made ready. The freed slaves, almost to a man, were clamouring to be set ashore immediately but Grace informed them, with some asperity (I'm getting very intolerant lately, she chided herself), that they would have to wait until she had met with the port authorities at least, if not the governor himself, to appraise those people of the situation, before she could consent to their demands.

Calling on James and Rory to accompany her, she had herself rowed ashore by a well armed crew of oarsmen. She explained to James that, while this was not her first visit to Corunna, and the Dana was, she hoped, recognisable to the citizens of Corunna from previous visits, their prize was so obviously an Algerine that she was taking no chances on the possibility of a hostile reception. His own presence, apart from his excellent Spanish, was explained by his priestly dress which ought to completely satisfy the authorities of their peaceful Christian intent.

"Let's hope then," said James, "that they recognize it before they shoot us."

In the event, the welcome was friendly, becoming even more friendly when the nature and circumstances of the second vessel were explained. Grace sent Rory back to the Dana to get the ex-slaves ready to be shipped ashore, while she and James arranged suitable transport with the port authorities. They, for their part, insisted that the pair meet with the sub lieutenant of the district, Senor Munoz, the Governor himself being away. He, Senor Munoz, further insisted that they take wine and sweetmeats with him while they recounted the manner of their famous victory. Grace, who knew the Spanish even better than James, indulged the sub lieutenant just long enough not to insult the very prickly sense of honour for which that whole race were notorious, and then begged leave to return to the Dana to oversee the setting ashore of the freed men, and to organise the galley's reprovisioning.

By the time that Grace had got back to the shore after her reception, and with Senor Munoz in insistent attendance, Rory had returned, and the skiff was now drawn up amongst other small boats which the unusually energetic townspeople had provided for her use. She was rowed back to the Dana, having promised Senor Munoz that she and her officers would be his guests for dinner that evening, and that she would bring the Dana to be moored against the harbour wall to facilitate her unloading.

Meanwhile James, with a guide provided by the Sub Lieutenant, had made his way to the hospital of San Andres, which he found to be a light, fine and airy building and of a level of cleanliness almost on a par with that of the Knights' hospital on Malta and infinitely superior to anything which he would have expected to find in his native land. He was introduced to the Franciscan Prior who ran the hospital, and he instantly agreed that James's remaining patients - they had buried two more before reaching Corunna, almost certainly killed by the application of the pitch - should be moved ashore, the chances of survival been immeasurably greater in the hospital then on the sparsely equipped galley.

He returned to the harbour to find both the Dana and the Algerine moored against the jetty, surrounded by a great throng of people, townsfolk and ex-slaves, the latter looking bemused at their final and absolute deliverance, the fact of which some could hardly still believe. He reported to Grace, who brought him up to date with their progress. Senor Munoz had virtually guaranteed, subject to the Governor's approval, to buy the Algerine galliot into government service. She was obviously smaller than a Spanish galley, but would still be of great use for local coastal defence. Grace, in turn, had repatriated a certain amount of the treasure from the Algerines which, given its provenance, seemed only fair, although, as she reminded him, under the immemorial customs of the sea she had been under no obligation to so do. However, it had increased Senor Munoz's already good humour even further, so she felt it worth the sacrifice.

She had already organized a small handout of money to the ex-slaves and, looking at them now, she noticed that a score or so of them, including the two putative Englishmen, had hung back, seeking to conceal themselves amongst the Dana's crew. They, seeing that she had noticed them, had then quietly approached to enquire whether they might join that crew. She fully understood why the Englishmen would not wish to be cast ashore in Spain: not all Englishmen were wellborn priests and deserving of respect. The others, all Spaniards, she presumed to have already been slaves on Spanish galleys before their capture by the Algerines, and having chosen not to renounce their faith to escape the infidel galleys, a relatively frequent occurrence, they were now determined not to expose themselves to the risk of being returned to the benches of their native country again.

She accepted them all. Apart from wishing no man chained to a galley bench, no matter what the crime that had sent him there in the first place, she had need of men to replace those sadly lost in the recent battle. She had, however, warned them in the sternest of terms that any untoward behaviour would see them chained to the Dana's benches: they could see for themselves where their recently transferred captives (another favourable purchase by singer Munoz: the Turks were very quickly going to find themselves slaves on the very galliot they had so recently commanded) had been held for the last few days. That transfer of the Turks to Spanish captivity was another great relief to her. James would have noted - indeed he would have known from first-hand experience - that the stench from a slave galley was abominable to those unused to it and, even in the few days that the Turks had been held captive, the Dana had started to turn into a very odorous place indeed. She was too experienced a campaigner to allow them any freedom whatsoever; men cast down in the immediate aftermath of defeat quickly recovered, and just as quickly, started to plan their escape. She had, therefore, kept them chained, so that the normally clean decks of the Dana had, even this quickly, become filthy and quite stench ridden from the Turks' necessary functions.

She had next arranged for the trade goods which had prompted their original voyage to be stored in the town's warehouses pending their sale, and she had also arranged for their remaining treasure to be stored in the town's vaults. Now she had to organise the repair of the storm and battle damaged Dana. She hoped to careen the galley and that, of course, meant emptying her and finding accommodation for the crew, something else with which the Sub Lieutenant had agreed to assist.

But that was another day's work. In the meantime, they were invited to dine with the Sub Lieutenant and she very much hoped that James would accompany, his very good Spanish being a valuable adjunct to their own more workmanlike efforts.

"We have to move our patients," James reminded her. "There's an excellent hospital under the patronage of the Seafarers Guild and the Prior has agreed to take them under his care until they are well again."

"I hadn't forgotten them," said Grace, "though I fear that Senor Munoz will not countenance our Turks going anywhere other than the prison, wounded or not."

"Perhaps I'll speak to him."

"Not until tomorrow, please. Remember that the Spaniards have much greater reason to hate them than we have. Senor Munoz has been very agreeable to us thus far and his goodwill, pending the return of the Governor, is of the first importance. Besides, we can't begin moving them until tomorrow anyway, so it won't harm to leave the subject overnight."

"All right," agreed James, "until tomorrow then. Now, the Prior has extended his hospitality to include me as well as the patients, which is particularly suitable since it means I'll be on hand to care for them. The difficulty, of course, is my lack of the Gaelic with which to communicate with them and I had hoped that you might, perhaps, see your way clear to allowing Theobald, or Tibbott I should say, to accompany me. It might also be helpful for Phelim O'Connor to observe, at first hand, the workings of a modern hospital. I am, by the way, very impressed by what I've so far seen of Corunna and can foresee no difficulties with the purchase of all that you need for an up to date medicine chest."

"It is, for sure, a fine town, at least as fine as Galway, and a sight more hospitable and it's got this truly excellent harbour and the opportunities to trade. I suppose that only the Venetian galleys which come to Bruges every year can boast a greater variety of exotic goods than are readily available here, and with which I mean to load up before returning to Ireland. And yes, you can certainly have Tibbott and Phelim. It'll be good for Tibbott. Phelim might feel differently about it, of course, but I'll insist."

The barber did, in fact, feel very differently about staying in a hospital with a crowd of monks for company, who would, doubtless, be praying, and expecting him to be praying with them, at all hours of the day and night. As one of the Dana's junior officers, he had expected to be one of the first ashore with prize money jingling in his pockets, and he was not at all happy with this change to his plans. Grace, however, did insist, mollifying him slightly by pointing out that he would, obviously, be excused harbour duties and the labour of careening and repairing the galley.

James returned to the hospital and made his way to the cell that had been set aside for him. There, he prayed briefly before succumbing to the almost sinful pleasure of the bath that had been drawn for him, and to which he realised he had been looking forward, almost since fleeing England.

At seven thirty, Rory arrived at the hospital to collect him, having decided that he was unsafe to be left to his own devices, it being obvious to Rory that a man with so many talents would be unlikely to concern himself with anything so prosaic as time. In fact, James was quite ready, feeling wonderfully scrubbed and pink, and looking as smart as a monk can, given the plainness of his clothing, although his habit had been dusted and sponged for him while he bathed. Not knowing the location of Senor Munoz's house, he had been on the point of requesting the services of a guide from the Prior, Father Xavier, but Rory's arrival relieved him of that task.

Rory himself was looking quite smart in his shore going rig and, as they walked, he disclosed that Senor Munoz had been kindness itself in arranging billets for the crew in the barracks serving the garrisons of Corunna's forts. General leave would not start until the morrow, when the patients had been moved ashore and the galley shifted to where it was to be careened but, in the meantime, the crew were making up for their surfeit of hard tack of the last few days with the best provisions available to a captain with gold in her pockets. The site of their feast, Rory further informed James, had been moved to the house of the Governor, the Count of Lemos, it being larger than Senor Munoz's and the Count being rarely present, preferring to perform his administrative tasks from his palace in the town of Lemos itself. Finally, the good Father was not to worry about his patients: the barber was looking to their comfort, ably assisted by Tibbott, who seemed to be visibly growing before their eyes with the responsibilities that he had been granted, and of which he was becoming exceedingly proud. He was becoming quite assertive in the makeshift sickbay and even proclaiming, out of Phelim's hearing, that in the priest's absence, they were his patients. James smiled, being only too able to imagine the precocious Tibbott lording it over all and sundry if his mother was not around to administer the odd beating to keep him in check. The boy would go for, James decided, provided Grace kept him on a strict leash and kept him unspoilt while he was growing and learning his responsibilities as the privileged son of an important chieftain, and also, of course, provided he lived to see manhood.

They arrived, after a gentle stroll, at the Count's house, which was, undeniably, the finest house in the town, and occupied an obviously important position, adjacent to the customs building and the town hall. They were the first of the guests to arrive and were effusively greeted by Senor Munoz himself who offered them sweet wine from Jerez while they awaited the arrival of their fellows, who turned up en masse along with some of the local dignitaries and traders who, with their wives, had also been invited.

Grace was resplendent in a scarlet gown whose bodice was liberally encrusted with enough pearls to have graced the Queen herself, and a giant ruby pendant necklace which, James suspected, had probably only very recently been acquired from the Algerines. She wore long white gloves which hid her calloused seaman's hands, and her normally ruddy, weatherbeaten face had been feminised above her elaborately ruffed neck by white powder and rouge in the London fashion. With her height, her upright seamanlike posture and her bold, confident glance, she was very much the most striking woman in the gathering, her preeminence only being approached by a much younger, more plainly dressed woman who stood staring, almost illmanneredly, at her with open admiration. Grace introduced her officers, who included all of those with a smattering of the local language, other than Conor, who was in charge of the watch on board. Senior Munoz then introduced his Spanish guests. When he got, finally, to the young Spanish beauty, he laughingly introduced her as Maria Pita, explaining that, in view of her very low background, she really should not have been part of such a distinguished gathering, but he owed a small debt to her father from their time together in the militia, and she had positively demanded to be allowed meet the great Irish lady captain. He went on to say that her pride and temper might even have matched those of the Infanta and he did not dare refuse her demands. The girl blushed furiously and muttered at the Sub Lieutenant, making him laugh even more and exclaiming that, already widowed, if she were not married again soon to a man with a strong hand, she would prove ungovernable. He himself would gladly undertake the task were it not that he was already very happily married, smiling at his wife, whose response was colder than it might have been.

That is another lady who will go far, thought James to himself, nodding approvingly as Grace took the young woman's hands, smiling warmly at her as she led her to the side of the room to converse with her.

The freely flowing wine quickly dispelled any inhibitions that the Spaniards may have felt: many were already on nodding acquaintance with Grace and her crew from previous visits, and the Irishmen, like sailors of all nations, were quickly into their stride and making game, if not necessarily coherent, attempts at conversation with their fellow guests, particularly the ladies, so that a fine hubbub quickly filled the room. James found himself in conversation with the Mayor and his wife who were grateful to be able to converse in Spanish and who told him more about the young lady, Maria. She was undoubtedly a young lady of fiery temperament who, in different circumstances, might well have led troops herself like their revered former Queen, Isabella. Although, the Mayor's wife darkly hinted, it was more normal for a young woman to be at home, not sailing the seas like the good Father's captain, behaving like a man and even wearing men's clothes, if reports were to be believed. She looked hard at Grace for a moment as if assessing whether something so scandalous could really be true before continuing that, by the looks of things - Maria was laughing happily - she was certainly, at this very minute, putting unwholesome thoughts into that young woman's ear. James nodded gravely, thinking that all provincial ladies probably looked askance at any other woman who appeared to break the mould, as Grace had definitely done, and as young Maria, by the look of her, was also quite capable of doing. And, not for the first time, he thanked God for his vocation and freedom from the machinations and interest of the female sex, Grace excepted, he suddenly found himself thinking.

Before this thought could develop or, indeed, before any further conversation could take place, they were called in to dinner.

There were, by the nature of things, more males than females among the guests, and James found himself sitting on the Sub Lieutenant's left with Rory on his other side. He, in turn, was seated next to Maria, who was already laughing, to the disapproval of the older matrons, at his attempts at Spanish. Senor Munoz (please call me Pedro, he enjoined both Grace and James) had placed Grace on his other side. He now called for silence and invited James to bless the gathering and what they were about to eat. This done, the familiar Latin phrases being answered by respectful Amens, a noisy babble broke out again as the food was served.

Senior Munoz's attention being wholly centred on Grace: as a military man he wanted a blow by blow account of the battle with the Algerines, and Rory's attention been equally wholly centred on the beautiful Maria, James resigned himself to the feast, quite different to the Moorish influenced food of Calatreva and the South. It was preponderantly sea food as became Corunna's position as a fishing as well as trading port. Mussels, langoustines, lobsters, squid replaced each other in quick succession, to be followed by sole and tuna steaks, before suckling pig was served - no Moriscos here, although the Moors had actually once got as far as the walls of Corunna - the whole feast being washed down by copious quantities of the local Rebeira wine. The level of noise had risen in the dining room in proportion to the serving of the wine and was now running at a level approaching that of a small gale through a ship's rigging. Raising his voice to be heard above the noise, Senor Munoz now called for music, and desert was eaten, or not, depending on the level of inebriation of the individual guest, to the accompaniment of a pair of Galician pipers howling shrilly over all. Not to be outdone, Donal, who never travelled far without his uilleann pipes, now joined in, extemporising to the Galician tunes which were remarkably similar to his own Gaelic music.

Around midnight, surveying his fellow guests, some of whom were fast approaching incoherence, not to say, comatosity - the whiskey which Grace had brought was now being thrown back with gay abandon and the poor Spaniards, in particular, were not dealing with it at all well - James, who had been relatively abstemious in his eating and drinking, decided it was time to leave, and with a last glance at what was swiftly becoming a bacchanalia, he quietly exited the room.

He wandered slowly back to the hospital with a soldier to guide him. He was not, of course, unused to seeing his fellow man in varying stages of intoxication, but he was intrigued by the obvious good humour of the gathering. He would have expected a similar event in England, after that amount of alcohol, to have sparked at least one murderous insult and, as for the Spaniards themselves, whom he knew to be unbelievably touchy on matters of honour, he was certain that more than one dagger would have been drawn by now. He considered that the very bad Spanish spoken by the Danas and the total lack of Gaelic speakers amongst the Spaniards would be as likely to lead to misunderstanding as not and, equally likely, to continue inexorably down the road to bloodshed, and yet it had not done so. This intrigued him and he found that he had to conclude that it was the innate cheeriness of the Irishmen which had caused the evening to be one of such good fellowship, that and the appalling music which they all loved so much and, of course, the goodwill of sailors with money to spend and that of those who hoped to help them to spend it. He had also to admit that Grace, even in her ladylike persona, was such a commanding figure that her example, which was on this occasion one of unfailing good humour, was bound to carry the company with her in equally good humour. (The events in Roscoff could even be reasonably put down to the fact that she had not been in the tavern at the time of the fracas.)

She was obviously a very remarkable figure. Since the somewhat imperfect beginning to their relationship and the subsequent days off Baltimore and indeed, up to Roscoff, before that relationship had warmed, he had been able to observe her dispassionately, and despite his bias, had had to concede that she commanded men as well as any other leader he had seen. Since his acceptance by Grace after Roscoff, he had gleaned lots more small items of information about her which had only served to confirm his initial view. Her childhood had been remarkable. He had already heard from

Thomas of how she had cut her hair off and mingled amongst the compliant crew as a boy, in order to get to sea on our father's ship, totally against his wishes and orders. He had heard of her father's resigned acceptance and of her schooling in seafaring - for which she had shown a great aptitude - with the proviso that her schooling in the humanities be not in any way interfered with by her voyaging. He had further heard, of course, of the circumstances of Theobald's, Tibbott's, birth in the midst of a desperate fight with Algerine boarders, a fight that was all but lost before she appeared on deck swinging her sword with all the concentrated fury of a mother whose newborn son is in danger, and rallying her men to victory: to all intents and purposes, a latter-day Joan of Arc.

That she was loved by her men, as well as respected, was also obvious. They had total faith in her ability to lead them and make them rich, with dashing extravagance or, when necessary, with prudence. They still even believed in her infallible intuition regarding the weather, despite the way that she had led them straight across the Bay into the recent calamitous storm for, they argued, had she not done so, they would never have met their lovely prize, and even if by some huge fluke they had met them hugging the coast around the Bay, they would never have lured them into the lack of caution they had shown had the Dana not been so obviously damaged by the storm. And although a fighting commander had to expect losses in the very nature of things, she had impressed him with her attention to detail before the recent action as well as her obvious distress at the number of dead and wounded as result of that action, much though she tried to hide it. All in all, the only other woman he could think of who showed anything like Grace's mettle was the Queen herself and she, of course, had never been to sea and had certainly never fought with sword in hand. Furthermore, despite the persistent rumours to the contrary, he did not believe that the Queen had ever given birth, let alone at sea.

118

He tried to imagine what they would make of each other were they ever to meet, an idle conjecture since the idea of the Protestant Queen of England meeting a minor Catholic Irish sea captain, female to boot, was quite impossible. Nevertheless, it was a fascinating thought - the virgin Queen of England, proud, awesome, the love and fascination of her subjects, and the equally proud Irishwoman, most certainly not a virgin, but certainly as well loved by her clansmen. What would they discuss? And in what language? He was very impressed with Grace's Latin and he knew the Queen to be also extremely proficient in that language. English? Grace could definitely hold a conversation in English although she would be at a disadvantage with a native speaker. Does the Queen speak Spanish, he wondered? His train of thought was interrupted by his arrival at the hospital were, having bid his escort good night, he made his way to his cell for a few hours sleep before Matins, for the monks at the hospital observed all the monastic prayer hours.

CHAPTER 13

Father James arrived at the quayside the following morning to find the Dana a hive of activity. Most of the galley's officers, it is true, looked grey and lumpen whereas the men, particularly those who had been most drunk in Roscoff, wore satisfied, not to say smug, expressions on their faces. That they also spoke in exaggeratedly quiet tones to emphasise their moral superiority over their officers did nothing to improve those officers' humours. At least all of the revellers appeared to be present. James wondered how many of the Spaniards would be abroad this morning. Very few, he decided, particularly after the whiskey.

He greeted Grace, who responded sourly, mentioning rats and sinking ships and commenting unfavourably on the type of person who would leave their shipmates in the heat of an engagement just to get a comfortable night's sleep. He protested mildly that he had been up for both Matins and Lauds and had had, in all likelihood, no more sleep than the rest of them, but Grace stumped away, muttering about the general untrustworthiness of the clergy, bloodsucking tithe gatherers the lot of them. Thomas's welcome was more friendly, even if his smile looked rather weak and fixed, but Phelim O'Connor was positively bouncing with good health and self righteousness as he reported all of their patients comfortable after the night. James informed him that he expected a train of carts from the hospital within the hour, the Prior had promised as much, and so, after he had made his rounds to confirm Phelim's observations, they began to move the more seriously wounded off the galley and on to the quayside, willingly assisted by those of the crew who could be spared, James's stock with the men being still considerably higher then it appeared to be with Grace for the moment.

True to his word, the Prior himself arrived with a train of mule pulled carts, on to which the bedridden were gently transferred, and the small caravan set out again for the hospital, accompanied by James, Phelim, Tibbott, and the walking wounded.

When all had been comfortably installed in their rooms, James set off to discuss the Algerine patients with the Sub Lieutenant, not without some misgivings. The Prior had been no more enthusiastic than Grace about Senor Munoz.

He found Senor Munoz at the Town Hall, adjacent to the Count's house where they had feasted so well on the previous night. He was ushered in immediately to the office of the Sub Lieutenant who greeted him in a much more subdued fashion than he had on the previous day. He was as courteous as James would ever have expected of a well bred Spaniard, but his pallor was sickly and he was undoubtedly suffering from a hangover of Herculean proportions. Wishing that he had left his visit for another day, James made his request and was not unduly surprised when it was refused. He tried to sway Senor Munoz with appeals to his Christian conscience but Senor Munoz was adamant in his refusal. They were infidels who made war on Christians and would suffer the consequences, besides which, what the padre sought was not something that he, Senor Munoz, could grant: it was a matter for the Governor who was, as the padre well knew, absent from the town.

Aware that his cause was lost, James thanked the Sub Lieutenant for his kind attention and took his leave, acutely aware that Senor Munoz's opinion of him had plunged dramatically and that the Turks would die in prison or on the benches (with the latter of which he could not disagree), no matter what he did or thought.

He returned to the Dana, which was as busy as when he left, and where he found a not too subtle change in the demeanour of the crew. The officers had recovered to a point wherein, not necessarily entirely free of their hangovers, they were nevertheless sufficiently enlivened to be treating the men in a suitably robust fashion in recompense for what they perceived to have been the lack of respect shown them earlier in the day. Grace herself had all but recovered and there was a particular cheerfulness in her shouted abuse of the crew for a shower of layabouts, worse than Sassanachs. She was indeed, at that particular moment, informing them that had she had kept one of the Algerine slavemaster's whips, she would surely be using it to lay into them if they did not buck up.

She greeted James for the second time that day, and explained the nature of the activity. They were emptying the Dana of her weapons and stores in preparation for careening her on the beach opposite. This was not as onorous a task as it would have been on a ship rigged vessel since the galley's holds were so much shallower. They had already discovered more water in the hold than was acceptable and there was evidence that the overworking of the hull during the storm had opened gaps in the planking which would have to be repaired before their return journey. Quite apart from that was the battle damage, not as bad as might have been expected and fortunately nowhere near the waterline, but still in need of serious attention. The items that had been taken from the boat would be securely covered in their heaviest sail cloth and a standing guard of sailors and soldiers from the local garrison would guard it twenty four hours a day until it could be restowed.

James, in turn, reported on the wounded and his raised expectations for their recovery, given the excellence of the local hospital. Finian was conscious again and beginning to take soup, while all of his amputees were showing clean stumps. One or two of the gunshot wounds were still illsmelling and inclined to ooze pus, but he was confident that frequent changing of bandages and application of the very advanced medicines in the apothecary's shop, together with the dry atmosphere and lack of sea motion, would have them all back in action quite soon, possibly, he dared hope, by the time the Dana herself was ready.

"I'll visit them myself," said Grace, "as soon as we have some order here. The men are doing very well in fact, but I wouldn't have them know it. They had their fun at our expense this morning, you know, and now we're having ours but there's no ill feeling really. Besides, the first half of the crew will have their leave tonight – they're currently drawing lots for starboard or larboard - and they're more concerned with that than any perceived heavy handedness from the officers. I only hope that we have no repeat of what happened in Roscoff. I don't suppose that you'd consider leading a patrol to keep them in order: they probably respect you more than me at this stage," she asked with a smile. James politely declined.

"Well, I'd better get back to work", said Grace, "we don't want them slacking," she added loudly, and returned to the unloading of the galley, which was already riding high in the water.

James watched for a while before making his way back to the hospital. The Prior was at prayers, but Phelim and Tibbott were in the wards and seemed to be getting on well with the Spanish nursing staff. Tibbott was able to converse up to a point while Phelim, with the confidence of any man dealing with mere foreigners, was simply talking loudly in Irish and gesticulating with large gestures and dumb show in absolute expectation of being understood. That the Spaniards were obviously amused by his antics was not having the slightest effect on him: if anything, it was encouraging him to even greater efforts, much to Tibbott's embarrassment. However, everyone appeared happy so James merely suggested that they make their rounds.

Back at the harbour, the Dana was finally empty and, under bare masts, the lateen yards having been struck down to join the piles of gear on the quay, was having her oars shipped to be rowed to the beach opposite at the height of the making tide so that, when it ebbed, she would be left, literally, high and dry.

At the appropriate time, they set out across the harbour, building up speed as quickly as possible. At the very last moment, Grace called "oars in," and the galley shot up the beach, propelled by its own impetus. The heavy work now began. Aided by mules provided by Senor Munoz, they attached cables to the hull and, using logs as rollers, they hauled the galley up above the projected highest tide level, and there it was allowed to subside onto its starboard side. They then moved the cables to the masts and carefully hauled it further over before driving huge wooden wedges under it to stabilise it at an angle of about 45 degrees, where all of the larboard side was accessible down to the keel.

Grace and Patrick O'Halloran with his mates now went round the hull, carefully inspecting it for openings in the planking, of which there were considerably more than they felt comfortable with and which indicated that their safe arrival in Corunna had been due as much to good luck as skill.

"She must have been badly wrenched when the foremast went and she spun," said the carpenter. "I'd say that we're very lucky indeed to be standing here at this moment. Thank God her timbers stood up to the strain." He pursed his lips gravely.

"Don't look so glum Pat," said Grace cheerfully, "she might have broken in two, but she didn't and that's all that matters. A bit of tar and oakum will work wonders but we'll have to look closely at her frame when she's dried out. I wouldn't be surprised if her futtocks haven't opened as well, but we're in as good a place as any to sort everything out and make her as good as new again, so never fret."

Corunna was, in fact, exceptionally well provided for in the matter of shipwrights. Its position on the cusp of major trade routes meant that it had a constant stream of shipping from both the old and new worlds, many of them in need of greater or lesser repairs after crossing the Atlantic or, as in the case of the Dana, the notoriously stormy Bay of Biscay. Additionally, the Spanish Navy maintained a large facility at Ferrol, just crossed the estuary, and there was the fishing fleet in Corunna itself, all in need from time to time, of the services of carpenters, armourers, blacksmiths, coopers and the like. There was also a great profusion of naval stores: masts, cordage, everything that a seagoing vessel might require.

Grace could quite easily have left all of the repairs to the locals but, apart from the fact that Patrick O'Halloran would be mightily insulted at been superseded by a mere Spaniard in the matter of the Dana's repairs, she felt that her attentive presence might avert the more gross profiteering that the locals were bound to indulge in as being their perceived right: dockyard hands were the same the world over. So, with Patrick and the senior Spanish tradesmen in tow, she slowly went round the galley again, this time taking notes and measurements and making estimates - there were, indeed, gaps between the futtocks amidships, but the galley's knees had survived unscathed, a tribute to her builders - before settling down to some serious haggling with the Spaniards, whose opinions of those repairs and the time they would take to complete, differed quite remarkably from Grace's own. Both, of course, had entered the discussion with quite artificial estimates in the expectation of having to give way to a certain extent. Furthermore, the Spaniards were able to argue that, whereas they could see both the internal and external damage to the larboard side, they could only see the internal damage to the starboard side, there could be very serious damage externally which would be invisible until the galley was tilted on to her other flank. More tellingly, and although delicacy prevented its being mentioned, both parties knew that Grace had considerable funds at her disposal and, having perceived that she was not going to be robbed more than reasonably blind in the matter of materials, the tradesman were determined on a hard bargain on the labour front. At length, matters were concluded and, with an aside in Gaelic to Patrick to keep a weather eye on those thieving raparees, Grace had herself rowed back across the harbor in the skiff, before setting out on her promised visit to the hospital.

She found James sitting with young Finian Burke in the cell where he had had him placed in isolation, the better to avoid contamination of his wound. The young man struggled to rise, smiling wanly at Grace, his face decidedly lopsided from of the pull of the sutures in his scalp, and apologising as she urged him to lie back again: no ceremony expected in a hospital. His recovery was certainly more advanced than James would have expected after such a traumatic injury and the subsequent operation, a tribute to the hospital and its facilities, as well as his patient's youth, and depending how quickly the Dana was made ready for sea again, he might well be expected to sail with her. Grace congratulated him on his recovery and promised that they would wait for him, no matter how soon the Dana was readied. She was rewarded with another healthier smile: being left behind was a dread that had been playing on his mind ever since he had recovered sufficiently to give the matter consideration.

James called Tibbott from the adjoining ward to take over the company keeping and, having sent Phelim O'Connor to collect the walking wounded, they went to see the other patients.

Grace offered cheerful greetings to them in Gaelic. She knew them all personally, of course, and there was an easy familiarity in her approach which James could not help but see was already acting as a tonic for them. She went from bed to bed with encouraging remarks and jokes for the individual patients, some of the jokes, James judged from the reactions, being quite ribald. Ignorance is often a great thing, he thought, as Grace made a laughing gesture at him which brought hoots of laughter from her audience. He shrugged and smiled which, it appeared, was all that was expected of him, and was rewarded with smiles in return. At the end of her tour Grace addressed them all again, the bedridden and the walking:

"I'm very pleased to see you all coming along so well. A lot of that is thanks to the good Father here who we've been very lucky to have had on board to look after us," there were sober nods in James's direction, "but," she carried on, "it's his opinion, and one with which I totally agree, that the more severely wounded of you will not be able to sail with us on the Dana when she's ready for sea again."

There were dismayed looks and an outbreak of protestations. Grace held up her arms for silence before continuing,

"Don't think for a moment that I'll be abandoning you. You know me too well for that. No, my plan is that when we're ready to leave, Father James will assess you all individually and, based on what he tells me, I'll decide who can come and who must stay. Now, I think you'll all agree that the Prior, Father Xavier, and his staff will give the best treatment anyone could wish for to those who'll have to remain, and I absolutely promise that, when Father Xavier judges it right, you'll return to Connacht on the first available ship, even if I've got to pay for a Galway ship! I'll also leave you with some money for your comforts and you'll have your full shares of whatever our voyaging brings in when you return home."

This brought the cheerful response that Grace had hoped for and, with a last few jokes and a promise to return to see them next day, she and James left them, Grace explaining to James what she had promised.

"You have a great way with people," said James. "there's no doubt that your visit has advanced the men's recoveries immeasurably. A cheerful patient is a healing patient and you certainly left them cheerful."

"And I will look after them, you know." Grace responded. "Any who are fit to sail again will continue in the crew if they wish. The others will all be found positions in one or other of my households. But enough of that."

The downcast look that had flitted briefly across her face as they left the hospital disappeared and her customary good humour returned.

"Would you like to see the lighthouse? It's one of the great wonders of the world, built by the Romans they say. It would be something to tell your grandchildren about," she added innocently.

James did not rise to the bait, merely replying that he would be honoured to accompany her.

Grace had inspected the lighthouse on a previous visit but James was quite unprepared for the size and majesty of the tower when seen up close. He was, obviously, fully conversant with the Roman occupation of Britain but had always assumed that they had crossed the continent by land, taking to the sea only for the crossing of the Channel. He had never considered where their ships had come from assuming, if he had thought about it at all, that they had been built in France, or Gaul as it then was. He now found himself deeply impressed, not only by the lighthouse itself, but by the necessity of its existence to guide Roman galleys, even more frail, he supposed, then the Dana, around the treacherous north-west corner of Spain on their voyages up and down the Atlantic from the Mediterranean to Britain.

"I'm amazed," he confessed.

Grace nodded a cheerful greeting to the small army garrison who occupied the buildings around the base of the tower.

"It has a double function now," explained Grace, motioning to the soldiers.

"Its prime function is as a lighthouse, of course, but it's also a wonderful watchtower. They'll have spotted us, for instance, miles further away than would the forts in the town, which could give them vital extra time in preparing for us, had we been unfriendly. May we?" She indicated the top of the tower to the soldiers, who were more than pleased to allow the famous Irishwoman, victor over the very galliot even now tied up in the harbour, to enter the tower and begin the arduous climb to the top, 300 odd steps Grace thought, although she had never counted them, James following.

The view was, indeed, spectacular. Seabirds floated and wheeled below them and waves crashed against the cliffs which, from this height, looked much smaller than their actual size. Notable also was the distance of the horizon, near which boats, fishing presumably, were visible which would not have been visible from the town's ramparts.

"I've never seen a more perfect example of the Earth's rotundity," said James. "I wonder that the human race could have for so long believed that it was flat. Surely someone standing on this tower must have pondered it and, if not here, why not on the great lighthouse at Alexandria which, I presume, must have been about this height also and which, we are told, existed in the midst of great learning in the sciences and astrology, certainly more than must have been accessible on a rocky outpost such as this."

"Ah now," replied Grace, "that's getting too deep for me. I'm only a simple sailor, you know."

He turned his gaze inland. The excellence of the harbour on the other side of the spit of land was now revealed. There the sea was completely flat, whereas on this side, even on a calm day, the long rollers came up onto the beach in spectacular surf.

"You know that the Milesians came from here," said Grace.

James looked blank.

"Surely you've heard of the Milesians?"

He shook his head.

"The ignorance of the English. Well, an ancient king of

these parts built a tower before this one, and one night his son, standing on top of the tower, saw Ireland in the distance and decided to invade it. He was defeated and his body sent back here. His nephew, Milesius, a great warrior who had won victories all over the Mediterranean, remembered an old prophecy that he would one day lead his people to a better land and, there being a famine in Spain at the time, he took his uncle's vision and death as a sign that this was where he was to go. In any event, he set off with his army, met the Tuatha De Danann, who were the rulers of Ireland at the time, and defeated them. The country was to have been divided between them, but one of Milesius's followers pulled a sly trick which gave the invaders the land overground and drove the Tuatha underground, into the underworld, in fact. That's where they live to this day, coming up occasionally to cause mischief, and remind everyone that they have not gone away entirely. All modern Irish people are descended from the Milesians, and my own family, the O'Malleys, can claim direct descent through the High Kings of Ireland all the way back to Milesius himself."

James looked sceptical.

"It was all written down by the monks three or four hundred years ago. You can confirm it if ever you visit Ireland," said Grace haughtily. "I presume you'll believe the monks' records?"

"I do apologise for appearing disbelieving. I know so very little of Ireland, as I've told you previously. But what of these Tuatha people? You can't truly believe that they still live underground? "

"It would be a very unwise person that disregarded the Tuatha De Danann." Grace looked automatically for something wooden to touch.

"There's more to heaven and earth than St. Patrick ever told us. We're all Christians, of course, and the O'Malleys, and the Bourkes for that matter, have endowed monasteries for generations but, nevertheless, there are things which cannot be explained in the normal way, crop failures, cattle disease and that kind of thing. No, it's as well not to ignore the people of the underworld. Tuatha De Danann, by the way, means the followers of Dana who was the major goddess of the people before the Milesians. The galley is named after her", added Grace in case that was not self evident to James who was, it could never be forgotten, an Englishman. James nodded sagely and decided not to pursue the subject.

In time, they descended the tower again and made their way back to the town.

"I neglected to ask you," said James, "how the galley is and how you got on with the shipwrights."

"The galley will be fine and, as for the shipwrights, they're the same as shipwrights everywhere, trying to wring every last penny from poor sailors, but", she added grudgingly, "I have to admit that they're competent. We know each other now and they'll do their work properly, even if expensively. I'm going to take the opportunity to have the galley recaulked while she's beached. A fair bit of caulking was sprung in the storm and, rather than just doing patchwork repairs, I intend to have all the old stuff burned out and replaced which, along with all of the other work, will leave her as good as new. Sure, she'll be the most seaworthy galley afloat", she continued enthusiastically. "I wouldn't normally undertake major repairs of this nature except at home, but I wouldn't wish to face the Bay again without them. Besides, Senor Munoz has been wonderfully generous in the matter of billeting. He's also been kind enough to accommodate myself in his own house, not, I think, without some resistance from the wife, and the men, as you know, are billeted with the military. I just hope they behave better than they did in Roscoff."

"Will you not find employment for them to keep them from idleness, a very vicious sin? I'd be very happy to arrange lengthy prayer sessions to occupy them."

Grace glanced sharply at James, who was smiling.

"No," she smiled back. "That wouldn't do. I don't mean any offence to yourself but it would probably lead to mutiny. They'll keep their watches, larboard and starboard, for shore going, meals, and work, just to maintain an element of discipline. But I do have plans for their employment. The watch on duty will provide guards for the galley and our material on shore, as well as assisting the carpenter and sail maker, and the shipwrights if needed. I also want them all more proficient with firearms so I'll organize practice to that end. Guns are becoming more and more important in sea fights and I wouldn't wish us caught out for lack of practice. I also have an idea to get them to build a second smaller skiff to fit in the existing one. That will improve their boat building skills, never a bad thing in a sailor. And, oh, I've lots of other things in mind so, never you fear, they'll not be so prey to idleness that they'll have to pray."

She glanced sideways at him to gauge the effect of her weak pun, but it appeared to have passed him by. She sighed inwardly and resumed: "and what about yourself? The hospital won't keep you totally occupied."

"Well, as you say, I'm not particularly needed at the hospital. Father Xavier is a good saintly man and the men can be left in his care with a clear conscience. They also have Tibbott and Phelim O'Connor to keep them in touch with the Dana. So, with your leave, I plan to make a visit to Santiago de Compostela. It won't be a proper pilgrimage, of course, but I would like to go there, nevertheless. We're so close and the opportunity might never arise again.

It's where St James the Apostle is buried, after whom I'm named. It seems that, after his death, his disciples, fearful that his body might be desecrated by the pagans, put it on ship and sailed with it all the way down the Mediterranean and up the coast of Spain, eventually landing near here and making their way inland, before finally burying the body. Since the tomb was rediscovered, it's become one of the great pilgrim destinations. St Francis came all the way from Assisi. Various

Popes have made the pilgrimage, and at the end of the last century, after they'd expelled the Moors, Ferdinand and Isabella came here and built a hospital to care for the ills of the pilgrims. Since I first heard of it, I've longed to visit and pray at the grave, and that's what I now hope to do."

"How interesting. I'd love to go with you – I'm afraid that my life hasn't been so blameless that I can easily forego saintly intercession - but I must see to the refitting of the Dana. You'll pray for me, I hope?"

"Of course I will, and for all of the crew."

By now they had come to the town gates, where they parted company, James to return to the hospital and Grace to the harbour.

CHAPTER 14

A couple of weeks later, Grace was standing on the quayside, awaiting the skiff to take her across to the Dana, when a familiar looking carrack entered the harbour. As it drew closer, Grace recognised the Desmond flag flying from the main mast, which confirmed it to be the Arganya, James Fitzmaurice Fitzgerald's ship. This was the man, cousin to the hated Earl, of whom Tom Butler had warned her and of whom Tom was seeking news. She had not seen the Arganya since it had carried Fitzmaurice and his family to the continent after the failure of their rebellion. She watched it with a certain ill-defined foreboding as it took in its sails and dropped anchor.

Her skiff arrived and she made her way across the harbour by a circuitous route designed to take her well away from the carrack, upon which she kept a close eye. Her vigilance was rewarded by the sight of Fitzmaurice himself, standing waiting on the poop, while the ship's boat was lowered to carry him ashore. Her foreboding increased.

She spent the day supervising, and assisting with, the repairs to the Dana, which were proceeding at a very satisfactory pace. The larboard repairs had been completed and she had been tilted over to the other side to allow access to the starboard side of the hull. The Spanish workmen, when they had realised that they were dealing with a sea going captain who knew her business through and through, and not some haughty Hidalgo, had shed their reserve and were working with a particular enthusiasm to impress this Irish lady who, though undeniably tough, was also friendly and approachable, and who they were determined to show that, when it came to galleys, the Spanish were the experts, a notion with which Grace was quite happy to comply.

That evening, she returned to the home of Senor Munoz, where her forebodings were confirmed, for there, awaiting her return, was Fitzmaurice.

"I believe you know each other?" Said the Sub Lieutenant.

"We do indeed," said Fitzmaurice in Gaelic. "Your servant Madam," he continued, making a courtly leg.

"I trust I see you well, sir," replied Grace, with a curtsy of her own.

Senor Munoz was looking puzzled at the exchange, so Grace explained to him that it was a singularity of Fitzmaurice's that, when possible, he invariably spoke in Gaelic, no matter what the company, to assert his Irishness. But, as Senor Munoz was perfectly aware, he spoke Spanish as well as the next man when necessary. Senor Munoz nodded in understanding as Fitzmaurice continued:

"Your presence in Corunna is most fortuitous. I've been granted aid by Pope Gregory to bring troops and arms to Munster to renew the fight against the English. Your galley will be of great use to us in transporting some of the soldiers and the arms."

He looked expectantly at Grace, who answered less enthusiastically then he appeared to expect.

"I was warned by Tom Butler that you had some such scheme on the go."

"Ormond!" He exclaimed. "What dealings do you have with that renegade?"

"Sure, he's as Irish as yourself. He just doesn't wear it on his sleeve. Anyway, quite apart from the fact that my husband rents lands from him, it was he who got me out of the jail that your cousin, Desmond, put me in when he was trying to curry favour with the English. Why wouldn't I have dealings with him?"

"He's a Protestant for a start," he replied, "but forget about Ormond. This is a legitimate crusade, blessed by the Pope, to return Ireland to Catholic Irishmen. You know, don't you, that the Pope has excommunicated the Queen and all her followers, and that would include Ormond, by the way, so that, as a heretic, she no longer has any right to sovereignty over our Catholic nation."

"I know that you've been trying to usurp Desmond's position. I also know that the King of France and Philip have both refused you, and you'll not have me believe now that the Pope's holy help is going to get the people up in arms again. You'll need the real soldiers that Spanish or French assistance might have implied for that to happen."

He almost looked hurt by her candour but carried bravely on anyway,

"the Pope will provide soldiers as well as money. We've also got Captain Stukeley with his company, and the Pope is sending a nuncio, Father Sanders, to confirm the legality of our venture. More to the point, you obviously haven't heard that King Philip has changed his mind about assisting us. He doesn't wish to be seen to be acting openly, he's too busy in Flanders, but he will provide Spanish soldiers and another captain, Don Guzman de Soto, a very experienced soldier, lately home from the Americas."

Again he was disappointed by Grace's response.

"I know nothing of your Stukeley and De Soto other than that one is obviously an Englishman and unlikely to be trustworthy and as for the other, if he's going to Ireland, it must be to seek the fortune he didn't find in the Americas, which makes him a mercenary rather than a visionary, not that I've anything against mercenaries you understand, many of my good friends are mercenaries, but they tend to be more concerned with gain than patriotic motives."

He made one more appeal to her.

"Madam, you're an Irishwoman. Can't you see that this may be our last chance to reassert ourselves as a nation? We have right on our side. Will you not join us?"

"Listen now, Fitzmaurice, and I'll tell you how I see it. You're a soldier who's been dispossessed of his lands by the English and wants those lands back, and I sympathise with that. I also sympathise with your wish to be rid of Protestantism from the country, indeed from everywhere, if it comes to that. But for your invasion to succeed, you need far more than foreign troops and foreign adventurers. You need all of the clans united behind you and you're very unlikely to get of that. Apart from people like Ormond, many of the smaller clans will blow with the wind and some will openly side with the English from the start. You've surely not already forgotten how your own support drifted away last time you rebelled as soon as the English got a united force in the field and all of the individual clans looked to their own well-being rather than the common cause. Besides which, there's no point in being successful in Munster only: you've got to expel the English from the whole country or they'll just attack you from Leinster again as soon as they've built up an army, and for a national rebellion to succeed, all the clans have to put aside their differences and come together for the common good, and that won't happen in a hundred years. Why, in our own country we've had trouble with O'Donnells raiding from Ulster, and we don't even have a quarrel with them. How do you expect us to stand beside them in battle and trust them to stand their ground? And even if you do get everyone behind you, how many of them do you think will be happy with the idea of a foreign King and the possibility of a foreign standing army? Apart from the fact that the country would be officially Catholic again, we would still be a subject nation. But, even leaving all that aside, the leader of any Munster rebellion must be Desmond himself, and he's far too comfortable with the English to wish to annoy them. Sure wasn't he responsible for the lease of your own land to St Leger? And didn't he imprison me to impress them? No. Despite all the difficulties I've proposed, I would still probably have joined you, but I'll never help Desmond."

There was a finality in that statement that persuaded

Fitzmaurice that further entreaty was useless. He arose, and with formal thanks to Senor Munoz for his hospitality, and a good day to Grace, he took his leave.

During the exchange, Senor Munoz had been looking more and more puzzled and not a little anxious, so Grace now gave him the gist of what had been said. He was quite sympathetic. Whilst obviously abhorring the English in particular, and heretics in general, and being, on the whole, quite sympathetic to Fitzmaurice, he totally agreed that it would be impossible for Grace to support Desmond, an obvious brute to have treated her so dishonourably.

"Fitzmaurice isn't a bad man, you know," said Grace, "but he's a dreamer with a grievance and is so determined on this course of action that he can't see the pitfalls. From what I can see, it seems only a question of time before either France or Spain attacks England, and that's the great time for a rebellion, not now, when England is at peace and can concentrate all her resources on putting one down."

"You're right, of course, Grace. But now, if we might speak of happier pursuits, it so happens that I had arranged to go boar hunting tomorrow, and I've already invited Senor Fitzmaurice to join me. Would you like to come also? I'm sure you'd enjoy it."

"Yes, I'd love to. And don't worry that Fitzmaurice and I will quarrel. I'm sure we can enjoy a social occasion together. He's certainly sufficient of a gentleman not to pursue his plans on the hunting field."

Next morning, the party assembled at the Sub Lieutenant's house and made their way to the stables to collect their mounts. Fitzmaurice, who had been honoured with the use of the Governor's house, was civil but reserved. Senor Munoz was in bubbling high spirits and Grace, who was beginning to chafe at the necessary but uninspiring work on the Dana, was also in very good humour at the prospect of the day's amusement, and put herself particularly out to be friendly to Fitzmaurice who, after all, had no great love for the Earl of Desmond either, despite being his cousin. In time, as they jogged along on their horses, his reserve began to melt in the face of her persistent cheerfulness and they found themselves discussing hunting in Ireland, mutual acquaintances, and all of the other topics that two compatriots will discuss when they become acquainted away from home, especially when one of them has been away for a long time and is avid for news of that home. After a while, Fitzmaurice apologised for his arrogant presumption of the previous day and Grace responded by apologising for the less than friendly way in which she had responded. She could see him looking wistfully at her and knew that he would have wished to reopen the debate had not politeness prevented him from doing so, so she broached the subject herself, confirming, in as kindly at fashion as possible, that she could not get involved for all of the reasons that she had previously mentioned.

"Madam, I thank you for your candour. I gave consideration last night to all your observations and I have to admit that what you say makes sense. But we have aid now, less than I anticipated, but aid for all that, and I feel that we must strike before it is dissipated. But let's speak of it no more. We are two Irish people abroad, and it better behoves us to be friends rather than enemies. Come, let's enjoy the day."

"Yes, let's. And you must call me Grace. I'll address you as James, if I may."

"Of course you may, Grace."

They exchanged smiles and settled back to enjoy the sun drenched countryside as they climbed deeper and deeper into the forested hills behind Corunna.

Senor Munoz called a halt and Grace turned back to view the valley behind them, beyond which she could just see the sparkling sea, so blue and innocent on a day such as this and at such a distance.

The little cavalcade of wagons that had followed them were now unloaded of their tables and chairs and the food and wine on which they would picnic after the hunt. There were two Spaniards as well, local dignitaries, and Senor Munoz now led all four guests to a hollow clearing in the forest, all around which the trees rose up to surround them, a sylvan amphitheatre in fact, down the slopes of which any boars that could be pushed towards them would come charging at full pelt.

They readied their bows and stuck their spare arrows into the ground in front of them, flights upwards so that they could be used in a hurry if necessary, and they then settled down to wait. In the woods in front of them, the servants and attendants could be heard beating the trees and calling, as they sought the boars. Birds were disturbed and one deer ran into the clearing, took a startled look and ran out again, but there was no sign of their real quarry.

The waiting was becoming interminable, when suddenly they heard a hunting horn and the enraged bellowing of a boar which, moments later, came bursting from the undergrowth straight towards Senor Munoz in the centre of the group. With only seconds to prepare, he coolly loosed his arrow at the boar, striking it ineffectually in its right shoulder but causing it to turn in its charge towards one of the other Spaniards. As Senor Munoz drew his dagger, the other four all fired, three of the arrows burying themselves deep in the boar's flank and slowing him down. As it staggered in circles, not knowing which of its assailants to attack, they quickly loosed another volley of arrows into it and it slowly subsided on to the ground, where Senor Munoz, with studied expertise, slit its throat.

They were in the midst of their self congratulations when the horn sounded again, urgently, and much closer, and they had barely snatched their arrows from the ground before another, even larger boar, came charging headlong from the trees straight at Fitzmaurice. He hurriedly notched his arrow

140

and let fly, missing the boar, which then launched itself through the air straight at him. Of the others, Grace had been the quickest to react and, even as the boar cannoned into Fitzmaurice, she shot it through the neck, wounding it desperately, so that its brutal charge lost some of its impetus and, instead of killing Fitzmaurice, just knocked him over. Grace, alone among the hunters, had also stuck her sword in the ground along with her arrows, much to the merriment of Senor Munoz, who allowed that a woman might be granted this extra protection, she being weaker. Now, while Fitzmaurice struggled to draw his dagger, and before the others could get near, she grabbed her sword and drove it deep into the boar, which, with agonized bellowings, subsided dying on Fitzmaurice. They pulled the animal from him and helped him to his feet, shaken and bruised but otherwise not seriously hurt.

"Someday you'll all stop underestimating women," she said as she retrieved her sword. "Weak indeed. More intelligent, I'd say."

"I believe I owe you my life, Grace," he said.

"Faith, I don't want it," replied Grace with a grin, "you can hang on to it yourself, but be more careful with it now."

He smiled and turned briskly to Senor Munoz and asked, "Now, are we ready to carry on?"

"But James, are you sure? Should you not like to rest after your escape?"

Senor Munoz was positively old womanish in his desire to comfort his guest, much to Fitzmaurice's irritation.

"No, no. Of course not. We haven't come this far to be cheated of our sport over such a minor incident. No, we must carry on. Besides, we have Captain O'Malley here to look after us."

Senor Munoz relaxed, smiled and indicated to the beaters, who had been standing anxiously by, that they should return to their task. In the event, the rest of the day produced only one further small boar which was neatly despatched by one

141

of the Spaniards, after which they made their way back to the wagons for their picnic, an affair so jovial that the hunting party all returned to Corunna in those same wagons, their horses being led behind. The two Spaniards were dropped off, with many expressions of undying friendship, and they proceeded on to the Governor's house, which they found to be ablaze with light.

"I believe that the Governor is returned," said Senior Munoz. "Quickly, James" - to Fitzmaurice - "I don't wish to meet him tonight. Leave your gear with us. We'll sort it out in the morning."

They exchanged good nights and even before Fitzmaurice was on the doorstep, Senor Munoz was urging the wagon driver away.

"The Count is a very fine man, none better," began Senor Munoz, somewhat apologetically, "but he is a stickler for etiquette and it is very important that he doesn't perceive us – me - to be in a state of anything other than utter sobriety and perfect dress when we wait upon him."

They arrived quite quickly at his house where, to Senora Munoz's obvious displeasure, he insisted that they share a light supper and another bottle or two before retiring.

Grace awoke next morning, less than clearheaded, and went down to breakfast to find Senor Munoz already abroad and resplendently dressed, altogether the court official. He bade Grace a good morning and explained that he was off to attend upon the Governor General to bring him up to date with the affairs of the town and to confirm, among other items of business, the buying in of Grace's captured galliot together with the purchase of the captured Algerines, mere formalities he happily assured her. For her part, she informed him that, much though she had enjoyed the previous day's sport, she felt that the humdrum work of the galley's refitting was probably much more conducive to her good health and so she planned to spend the day with the workmen, not getting involved he was to understand, but quietly overseeing them. They left the house together, Grace turning down the hill to the harbour, and Senor Munoz uphill to his meeting with the Governor.

After a couple of hours, Grace was feeling herself again, and resolved to be more circumspect in her host's company on future occasions. She was happy with the progress of the Dana. She was also happy with the behaviour of the men who, apart from the occasional drunkenness, nothing out of the ordinary in a town used to sailors, were a credit to herself and the galley. She took a light lunch of freshly caught sardines, washed down by some local wine, in the company of Patrick the carpenter, and the leader of the Spanish workers. A further pleasure to her was the way in which the two groups were getting on, as typified by her two companions, neither of whom spoke much in the way of the other's language, but both of whom understood ships and shipbuilding and respected the other's views on the subject. There was a distant sound of small arms fire from where a group of the Danas were learning the art of musketry in the hills where they were a danger to none but themselves, while in the lee of the beached Dana, a number of aspiring carpenter's mates were making progress on the new skiff.

As the mellowing effect of the wine flowed through her, she was thinking that life was good and Corunna was as good a place as any, and better than most, in which to while away the days during a refit. At the present rate of work, she estimated that they would be ready to sail within about another four weeks. It was time to start making serious enquiries of the local merchants to assess what she might bring back to Ireland for greatest profit. The task was made more urgent by the need to be able to show a full hold to Fitzmaurice if he were to appeal to her patriotic feelings again, although she felt it more probable that he would not: he was too much the gentleman.

She idly watched a boat being rowed across the harbour

and, as it got closer, recognised her landlord seated in the stern, waving cheerily to her. She walked to the water's edge and caught the painter that was thrown to her by one of the oarsmen, holding it while they ran the boat up the shingle to prevent Senor Munoz getting his feet wet. He was in ebullient mood, still as elegantly dressed as when she had lost seen him, his crew's care explained by the shiny silver buckled shoes in which he now stepped carefully on to the beach.

"Senora Grace, I trust I find you well," he began.

"Very well now," replied Grace, " although it took an hour or two. And yourself?"

"Oh, very well indeed." He waved an arm expansively at the scene.

"What another beautiful day. It's hardly June and it already seems to have been summer for ever."

It seemed to Grace that he had had a more substantial lunch than her own light repast.

"You appear to be in very good humour, Pedro. Is it just the admittedly fine weather or did your interview with the Governor go particularly well?"

"Both Grace. Both. Was pleased with my report and was very gracious about your galliot whose purchase he immediately confirmed. He also purchased your Turks - he does hate the Turks so, he was wounded at Lepanto as a volunteer - and when the galliot is ready for sea again, he'll have them chained to the exact benches over which they so very recently lorded it. He's amused by the irony of the situation, finds it extremely droll. And speaking of the galliot, he is beside himself with curiosity to meet the lady who overcame the galliot that he can see in the harbour, and the second that was sunk, for I quickly informed him that there were two, and he wonders whether you would do him the honour of dining with him this evening."

"I'd be delighted. Do you think now, that it'll be as riotous an affair as your own? What I mean is, do I need to snatch an hour's sleep or two or are we likely to get to bed at a Christian hour?"

"Never fear Grace, that you won't be hale and hearty tomorrow morning. Count Lemos may be an old soldier, with an old soldier's sympathies, but he'll never let himself be seen carousing like an old soldier, or keeping a lady from her just sleep."

"A dry night then?"

"On the contrary, but it will be a measured and stately occasion, not the kind of feast that I would provide or, with respect, that I feel that you yourself, Grace, would provide."

Grace smiled as she replied,

"Your nobility sounds to be of somewhat the same outlook as that of the English nobility, who seem to me, from the little I know of them, to be completely constipated in thought and action, though this Queen of theirs seems to be getting to grips with that by promoting the lower born to high positions of state. They may yet become formidable."

"Never!" Senor Munoz positively spat of the word out. "They are a petty people, heretics who will never be accepted by civilised nations."

Senor Munoz was warming to his theme but Grace held up a hand:

"Enough Pedro. You're speaking to the converted, you know. Now, if I'm to dazzle the count, outgun him even, I should be getting back to begin my preparations."

She briefly excused herself to say goodbye for the day to the carpenter and his men, and then returned to take her place in the boat beside Senor Munoz for the gentle row back across the harbour.

At eight that evening precisely, they presented themselves at the door of the Governor. Grace, who believed that she would never get to grips with the late hours at which the Spanish chose to dine, was very glad to have had lunch, only wishing that it had not been quite so light. They were led in to the well remembered reception hall and were announced to the assembled company, who numbered fewer than on her previous visit, but who were considerably more finely dressed, the men as well as the women.

Senor Munoz introduced her to the Count, who bowed gravely to her in the elaborate Spanish fashion and Grace, who had been waiting to match her response to his, was sufficiently satisfied to return the bow with a deep curtsy of her own. He then introduced her to the other guests, beginning with his wife, the Countess, who appeared younger then Grace as, indeed, did the Count himself. She was beautiful, almost as tall as Grace herself, haughty, with high cheekbones, large dark eyes and long black hair held up by silver combs. They eyed each other as they curtsied. Grace was dressed as she had been on her first visit to the house, which was marginally more expensively and fashionably than the Countess, a fact not lost on either of them. She felt a slight regret, not at outshining the Countess, but of doing so in the Countess's own home. Quite apart from what her woman's instincts told her, she was enough of a diplomat to know that potential allies were not to be thrown over likely, and in dressing to impress a Spanish Count, she had neglected to consider his Countess, not her finest bit of forward planning. Well, it was done now, and she would turn all her charm on the Countess later to try to redress the balance. Meanwhile, the introductions were continuing. Fitzmaurice was there, of course. They nodded amiably to each other. Then it was the turn of another Spaniard, who turned out to be the Don Guzman of whom Fitzmaurice had spoken, one of the soldiers of fortune committed to the expedition. He was tall and graceful, golden haired and pale skinned, with pale blue eyes, delicate but thin lips, and hands as white and small as a woman's. Grace decided that he would merit careful consideration later. The introductions proceeded, some more Spanish gentlemen and their ladies, the Count's son, a brash leering youth to whom Grace took immediate dislike, the blame for which dislike she automatically laid at the feet of the boy's mother, then the boy's companion, an altogether more innocent and likeable looking boy, and finally, the Papal Nuncio, Father Sanders, an ascetic looking Englishmen whom she was prepared also to dislike, until he smiled in greeting, a soft gentle smile so infectious that she had to smile back.

They indulged in small talk for a while, until a discreet cough from the major domo announced that dinner was served, and then, taking Grace on his arm, the Count led them into the dining room. He took the head of the table with Grace on his right and one of the Spanish ladies on his left, and directly opposite him, at the other end of the table set the Countess, with Fitzmaurice and the Nuncio as her immediate companions. Grace had Don Guzman on her right and the rest of the guests were seated in what she assumed to be order of rank, with Senor Munoz around the middle. The two youths had not joined them.

After Father Sanders had said grace, the first remove was served, by coincidence the same fish on which she had lunched, but presented with considerably more style. She noted with approval that there appeared to be no shortage of goblets amongst the very ornate dinner service with which the table was laid, and was very pleased with the white wine which her servant, there was one for each guest, poured for her to accompany her fish. After more than half a lifetime of tasting and buying wine from France and Spain, Grace was fully aware that this one was a considerable cut above that which she had drunk on her previous visit to the house. She complimented the Count, while mentally noting that a few tuns of it might well form the first purchases for her return cargo. The Count waved it away disparagingly, promising much finer reds to go with the meats which would form the rest of the meal. They would not normally eat fish, he explained, except of course on Friday but, since they were in Corunna and fishing underpinned the local economy, and he was, after all, the Governor of the province, they almost always had a token fish course as a form of encouragement to those he governed.

"You surprise me," said Grace. "In Ireland we eat quite a lot of fish and we don't have anything like the variety that you have here in Corunna. Do you not like fish?"

"It's not really a question of liking", replied the Count, "although I have to confess to a certain partiality for shellfish, but fish is the food of the poor, and so, therefore, we eat meat, preferably meat that has come to the kitchen via the hunting field: venison, boar, wildfowl."

"Well, we eat all of those same meats in Ireland, but we also eat fish, as being plentiful and God-given. And, oddly enough, since I sell licenses to Spanish boats to fish in my waters, I suppose I had always assumed that the Spanish also ate lots of fish."

"It's because it's plentiful that it's considered the food of the poor and thus unsuitable for the aristocracy."

"I've heard that the English nobility have the same views, and even extend it to fruit and vegetables."

"Now you are jesting, Senora," replied the Count with a smile, "but I will not rise to your bait. I am not a fish," he finished triumphantly.

Grace laughed and allowed him his point.

"But let's speak of meat," he continued, "particularly of the boar which Senor Fitzmaurice assures me you dispatched so perfectly yesterday. Is it also normal in Ireland for ladies to hunt with the gentleman?"

"No. I'm somewhat singular in that respect. When my first husband was killed, circumstances conspired to send me home without my dowry. My prospects didn't seem to amount to much more than sitting around in genteel poverty, so I took over my father's ships and vowed to never again be at the mercy of tight fisted in-laws. I am since happily remarried, but quite independent this time round"

"That is singular indeed," said the Count, "but I cannot see that it would be acceptable in Spain. Forgive my saying so but perhaps your families are not as old as ours?"

"My family, the O'Malleys, can trace their lineage back over a thousand years directly to a High King of Ireland, while my husband's family came with the Normans, de Burgos they were then, Bourkes they are now. I believe I can certainly say that both our families were prominent when many Spanish families were unheard of, or if they were, were firmly under the thumb of the Moors," she replied with just the slightest hint of asperity.

"Senora." He held up his hands in mock surrender and laughed.

"Please forgive my presumption, which is born of the purest ignorance. But come, tell us about your affair with the Turks. It sounds, from Senor Munoz's description, as the most complete little victory."

"Yes, please do," added Don Guzman, addressing Grace for the first time.

Grace glanced at him before beginning her tale, which she kept brief and succinct. The Count smiled approvingly at her when she had finished.

"How much you omit, eh, Don Guzman? But we old soldiers can read between the lines. It was certainly a famous victory, particularly when one recalls how damaged was your galley after the storm. It fairly does my heart good to hear of these Turks being paid out in such fashion."

Conversation around the table, which had all but ceased while Grace had been recounting her story, was resumed again. The Count, ever mindful of his duties as a host, turned to the lady beside him and Grace found herself in conversation with Don Guzman. He was very attentive to the answers she gave to his quite penetrating questions about firstly, the Turks, and then the situation in Ireland and what he might expect to find there, because he professed an even greater ignorance of his destination than that of their host, and was not altogether satisfied with the answers he had received from Senor Fitzmaurice to similar questions to those he was now addressing to Grace.

Despite his languid manner, Grace was well aware of a steeliness in her neighbour, and she picked her way carefully through his questions, being completely factual in her answers, and offering no opinions. She could see that her care seemed to be causing him some secret amusement and abruptly changed the subject.

"But tell me something of yourself. What attracts you to Ireland? Hardly the weather?"

"No, not the weather," he confessed with a laugh. "I was born poor. There are many such as I in Spain, of lofty descent but of extremely limited means. What money our parents have tends to go on educating us in the classics, swordsmanship, and a very deep appreciation of what we can't afford. We are then cast loose to make our way in the world and, hopefully, restore our families' fortunes again. We almost all end up as soldiers of fortune with varying degrees of success. I myself had amassed quite a neat little fortune in the Americas, where I was born, but as with so many of my fellow soldiers, managed to lose it all in Naples, pursuing the high life and a particular woman who, when she had spent my gold, left me for another man. I had to kill them both of course, and, although there is sympathy with such actions on a personal level, on an official level they cannot be condoned so here I am, on the first step, I hope, to my next fortune."

"I fear you won't make your fortune in Ireland," replied Grace, keeping to herself her surprise at the man's careless callousness. "There are no fabulous cities of gold hidden in the bogs."

"No matter. If the venture is successful, there'll be land, as well as the gratitude of King Philip, and the Pope of course, whose nephew we are to set on the throne of Ireland. If it proves to be unsuccessful, then it's back to the Americas. In fact, it's probably back to the Americas anyway, where El Dorado still awaits discovery. It's simply a matter of whether it'll be back as a wealthy man, or as a poor one."

Grace wondered to herself whether Fitzmaurice was aware that, were his venture to succeed, he might be merely exchanging English rule for Spanish rule, albeit that it would be Catholic rule, or had he blinded himself to the fact. There was no doubt that Don Guzman anticipated the acquisition of estates if the English were expelled, but did not seem to have considered that these estates had been but recently stolen from the Irish themselves, who could not be expected to view their passing from English to Spanish ownership with any enthusiasm. Furthermore, England was but a small nation compared to Spain and, while it was possible to imagine the English presence in Ireland being brought to an end, the same could not be said of a Spanish presence, given Spain's huge wealth, her professional army, the best in Europe, and her huge fleet to transport that army to Ireland. That, of course, would depend upon their first managing to bring their affairs in Flanders to a successful conclusion, and establishing even a temporary treaty with the French, but it could not be discounted as a possibility.

She was suddenly aware that, while her thoughts had strayed, Don Guzman had continued to address her. He was now laughing as he repeated:

"You haven't said what your part is to be in all of this."

"I beg your pardon. I was considering that very thing. But, you won't be aware that I have no love for the Earl of Desmond, on whose fully committed support any invasion is entirely dependent, and for whom I wouldn't lift a finger. This is quite apart from the fact that I couldn't possibly get myself and my crew involved in Munster, without knowing how my family and that of my husband fare in Connacht so, in short, I don't wish or intend any part of the venture, something of which Fitzmaurice is well aware."

"How disappointing. Having heard of your exploits, we're to be denied observing you in action at first hand."

"Just so," replied Grace, aware that this Spanish grandee had drawn more from her then she would have wished. She was also again aware that beneath his smiling exterior, there lurked a most ruthless man, one whom she would avoid for the rest of her stay in Corunna, rather than confronting on his terms and territory.

The rest of the evening wore companionably on, remove succeeding remove with ever more delicious wine, the desert being accompanied by music, as during Senor Munoz's feast, but of a much more gentle nature, more of an accompaniment to the evening then a raucous striving for centre stage. In time, while all were still reasonably sober, there was no whiskey on this occasion, the Count brought proceedings to a graceful close, as Senor Munoz had predicted.

It had, all in all, been a very enjoyable occasion, although Grace was left with the feeling of unspoken undercurrents which she could not quite place, but of whose presence she felt some confirmation in the slightly triumphant manner in which the Countess bade her good evening. Senor Munoz, on the other hand, thought the evening a complete success. Grace had been a big hit with all, which could only make her present visit and all subsequent visits pass easily, the goodwill of the Count of Lemos being of inestimable value in Galicia. Grace herself was still not so sure. She could not be entirely relaxed that there was not some significance in the Countess's changed attitude towards her after dinner. Still, she could not disagree that it had been it had been a most enjoyable evening.

On the walk back to Senor Munoz's house they were accosted by a mixed group of Danas and Irish sailors from the Arganya who insisted on escorting them in riotous fashion on the short remaining part of their journey, their somewhat inebriated good humour finally dispelling the tiny remnants of Grace's uneasiness so that, when she made ready for bed, it was to find deep untroubled sleep immediately.

`CHAPTER 15

Next day, she was back at work across the harbour when Senor Munoz visited her again to ask that she come with him at the Count's request. He was stubbornly unresponsive to her enquiry as to why the Count should wish to see her, and in the silence of their journey, she was again aware of the uneasiness she had felt on the previous evening. At the house, they were ushered in to the reception room where the Count was deep in conversation with Don Guzman, Father Sanders, and Fitzmaurice. He quickly rose to greet them, offering wine which Senor Munoz accepted but Grace refused. There was a momentary silence while the Count appeared to collect his thoughts and then he addressed her:

"Senora Grace, you're aware, of course, of Senor Fitzmaurice's intended expedition to Ireland. You may not be aware of how few ships and men he commands. It is the King's wish that we do all in our power to help him, but we can't spare any more men at this moment. What we can do is to supply large quantities of arms with which Senor Fitzmaurice may equip your countrymen to begin the fight, until we can reinforce him with Spanish troops. For this we need ships. Senor Fitzmaurice tells me that he's made an approach to you which you have refused, and I would now wish you to reconsider that refusal."

Fitzmaurice spread his arms in wretched helplessness.

"I'm very sorry, Grace. I didn't wish this, but my tongue was unacceptably loosened last night by drink. Please forgive me."

Fitzmaurice had set beside the Countess and she must have drawn this information by a combination of wine and charm. Grace now understood the triumph in her demeanour as they parted company after dinner.

"My dear Count. I've already explained to Fitzmaurice and Senor Guzman why I've no wish to help."

"And they've explained the very good reason for your antipathy towards the Earl of Desmond, but surely you must recognise this as being too great an enterprise to admit of personal feelings?"

"I wouldn't recognise that, at all," replied Grace stubbornly.

The Count looked slightly aggrieved as he continued,

"then I regret, Senora Grace, that I must demand your assistance."

"And how will you impose this demand?"

"It pains me to say that, if necessary, we can impound your galley and also the items that we're holding on your behalf, some of which we're aware were taken in the first place by the Turks from Spanish ships and to which we could quite reasonably lay claim. Of course we would much prefer that you assisted voluntarily but......"

He had the good grace to look uncomfortable as he made this threat.

"I was under the impression, erroneous obviously, that the Spanish were an honourable people. I suppose there's no point appealing to that honour? This carry on would be beneath the dignity of even a Galway cattle rustler."

The Count was obviously stung by her reply and hastened to proclaim that, when the needs of the state demanded, personal honour had to be subject to those needs, something with which he hoped she would sympathise.

"I don't sympathise."

She looked at the assembled company but saw nothing encouraging. She tried another tack.

"Let me make my own way home, and I'll talk to the local clans and see what I can do to stir up enthusiasm."

But he was adamant. It would have to be as he had asked.

"Alright. I'll do as you demand. I don't seem to have much choice, do I? But it's under protest."

The priest was impassive, as though this did not concern him which, in truth, it did not. Fitzmaurice and Senor Munoz looked miserable. The Count looked defiant. Only Don Guzman appeared unaffected, his secret smile playing around the corners of his eyes.

"It pains me further to say that the items we hold will travel on Senor Fitzmaurice's ship and will only be returned when the arms are safely landed in Ireland," finished the Count.

"Dear God," exploded Grace, "you're telling me now that you don't even trust me, just as you expose yourselves as no more than a shower of bloody thieves yourselves. And you call yourself a gentleman. Damn the lot of you"

She stormed from the room, only pausing to throw a withering glance at the Countess who had appeared in the hallway, causing that lady to shrink from her fury.

She strode towards the harbour, pursued by Senor Munoz, who came running after her imploring her to speak to him. She calmed down quite quickly. Mastery of her emotions was something she had learned early in her career as being a very necessary adjunct to being a successful sea captain. Senor Munoz was all but overcome by shame at the behaviour of the Count, which he declared to be completely unacceptable in a man of his rank, demands of state or not, and which he suspected of being totally due to the machinations of the Countess, which made it even more shameful. He begged that she would not include himself, Pedro Munoz, as being in any way party to the Count's underhand behaviour to someone who had shown herself a true friend of Spain.

Grace relented. She found that she could not decide, if she had both her hard won treasure and the arms on board the Dana together, whether she might not have made off to Clew Bay with the lot and devil take the invasion, so it seemed inherently unfair to continue to visit her fury with the Count on Senor Munoz, who was, she felt, probably blameless in the whole affair. She also had to admit to herself that, in the Count's place, she would probably have behaved exactly as he had, although she did not pretend to his code of honour. Of one thing she was sure. Of the Count of Lemos's previous goodwill towards her, there was probably very little left. He must have been under extreme pressure from above to behave as he did, his wife notwithstanding, and he would find it very hard to forgive Grace for forcing him into such a demeaning position. Grace hoped that he would take his discomfort out on the Countess, the contemplation of which improved her humour considerably, although she was aware, even on their short acquaintance, that he was, at heart, much too good a man for that. She could only begin to guess at the agonies he was suffering in the service of his King. She allowed herself one final piece of malicious pleasure at Senor Munoz's expense by informing him that she would sleep by the galley with honest Irishmen for the remainder of her stay in Corunna, only relenting when the poor man had pleaded and pleaded otherwise.

She left him at his house and crossed the harbour again to the galley, gathering all of the crew who were present to appraise them of the situation now pertaining and solemnly warning them not to do anything that might allow the Spanish authorities to cause them further problems. She had a moral advantage over the Count which she had no intention of relinquishing and woe betide any of them who might cause her to lose that advantage. They nodded gravely in assent. They were not particularly interested in moral advantages but were very concerned not to do anything which might cost them their treasure.

They men were returning to their work when Fitzmaurice was seen, being rowed across to them. He came straight to Grace and began by continuing from where he had stopped at the recent confrontation.

"I can't begin to express the depth of my regret that I should have placed you in such a position, Grace. My only excuse, which is no excuse at all, is the amount of alcohol I had consumed which led to my betraying what had earlier passed between us. I hope you'll accept my apology."

Her regard for him, diminished by his lack of discretion, was restored by the fact that he had taken all the blame himself and had not implicated the Countess other than as the guiltless recipient of his confidences.

"Yes, of course I will. Sure, don't I know that you were led astray by that guileful creature" (he flinched) "but I don't blame you for that. You're just another poor man, far from home, unable to resist the charms of a pretty woman, and she is a pretty one, I'll grant you."

"Please Grace," he began, but she held up a hand to stop him.

"It's done now, so we must make the best of it."

"There is some good news. The Count is going to divert men from other work to speed up your refit and he believes it only proper that Spain, in imposing itself on you to act in its interest, should pay for the refit. He doesn't wish you any ill, quite the contrary. He sees you as the injured party but begs to be excused from waiting on you for the remainder of your stay."

"Well, in the circumstances, I suppose that's uncommon decent of him. You may tell him that I bear him no grudge, that I respect that what is sometimes necessary in the name of statesmanship doesn't necessarily coincide with what is decent, and that I thank him for his gesture regarding the Dana. You may also convey my sincere regrets that we won't meet again, if you don't think that to be going a bit too far"

"I don't understand how I ever thought I would have you do my bidding," smiled Fitzmaurice. "I'll convey all you've asked."

He bowed, and returned to his boat, followed soon afterwards by Grace to hers.

The Count was as good as his word regarding the repairs and, although he stayed away from the harbour, aloof in his house, he did send occasional presents of food and wine to Grace and the crew. Don Guzman was not so reticent, however. He started coming to view the refit on an almost daily basis. He gave as his reason his wish to know how a galley was put together, since he would soon command one. This was quite unlike the practice of most Spanish captains, as far as Grace was aware. They, as a rule, saw themselves as being somewhat above the menial matter of handling a ship, preferring to leave that to a master to whom they gave orders, while they readied themselves for commanding the vessel's soldiers as and when required, there being glory only in battle and the ship being merely a conveyance by which they might go to battle. Grace foresaw a time when they might well regret their failure to become better acquainted with the rudiments of sailing. That was not a criticism that she could level at Don Guzman, however. He seemed genuinely interested in the progress of the refit, watching the various stages of re-rigging, and asking properly intelligent questions regarding the functions of the shrouds and stays, and the merits and disadvantages of the lateen rig as opposed to the square rig. Despite her previous resolve to avoid him, Grace found that she began to enjoy his visits, although she would never trust him. She even wondered whether he might have amorous designs on her but rejected that on the grounds of her age, which she judged to be an inadmissible number of years greater than his. The Countess would be more his target as being both younger and more wealthy and, Grace had to admit, more feminine in her gowns and jewelry then herself in her seafaring gear. Whatever his reasons, he kept visiting until the day arrived when the Dana was eased back into the water to the cheers of both Spanish and Irish and rowed gently across to the quayside to receive her guns and stores. It was then time to take her out on trial to assess what final adjustments would be necessary to allow her to perform at optimum speed and stability.

She did not yet have her cargo: pikes, swords, muskets

and ammunition, but Grace had seen the arms in their containers and could make a very rough estimate of their weight, and so was able, from experience, to judge how the galley might behave when fully loaded. There had been a tentative suggestion from Fitzmaurice that she carry some soldiers as well but Grace had firmly refused, stating that her own crew was large enough already and that in the event of their falling in with enemy ships, she did not want inexperienced landsmen getting in the way.

The galley made her way to the open sea, first under oars and then, when they had cleared the headland, under sail. First impressions were promising. Grace went forward, checking the masts and rigging for any untoward slackness, and pronouncing herself more than satisfied with the beautiful, newly tarred ropes and cables with which they had been supplied. Leaving the guns to the gunner, who knew them in all the complications of their carriages and housings better than she did herself, she lastly went down into the hold which, being empty, allowed her to get right down to the timbers, all of which looked properly joined and caulked, as she knew they would be at this early stage. It would only be when they had put some hundreds of miles under her keel that they would really know how good the work was, whether the bilge water was foul, which would indicate no dire necessity for pumping, the water building up rather than leaking through the sides, or whether it smelt fresh which would signify the opposite. Initial signs were good however, which was heartening.

She returned to the stern and discussed her findings with Thomas and then they settled back as the crew put the galley through its trial evolutions, tacking, wearing, raising and lowering the yards, taking in and putting on sail, all in a perfect breeze with blue sky above and an azure sea spreading out all around them, broken only by the thrust of the galley's bows and the white wake stretching out behind them.

"I could sail like this indefinitely," said Grace.

Thomas nodded his approval of the sentiment.

It was dusk by the time they tied up once again in Corunna, all somewhat fatigued, particularly the oarsmen, but all happy with the performance of the refitted galley and all looking forward to an evening's entertainment as their visit drew to a close. Everybody in the crew had been as incensed as Grace at being practiced upon so shamefully by the Count but, with the stoicism of all sailors, they had quickly come to accept it, especially as the good feeling of the townspeople towards them appeared unaltered. Indeed, such was the good fellowship on both sides, there would be more than a few sad faces when they departed.

Next morning they completed the minor works that the trials had shown to be necessary before they could judge the boat perfect, and then took on their remaining stores and cargo. The troops who would sail with the flottila, a mixture of Spanish, Italian and Papal, had already arrived in the port and would begin embarking at first light the following morning. A conference was called by Fitzmaurice on the Arganya where the order of sailing was agreed: Fitzmaurice, with the three Spanish shallops that he had been given, would sail directly for Ireland, while the Dana and Don Guzman's galliot, now renamed the Marquesa in memory of the galley on which the great Cervantes had fought at Lepanto, would follow the coastline in the traditional manner of galleys. This was deemed necessary because the oarsmen on the galliot, all slaves, had had only a few days working up and, although there was a leavening of experienced oarsmen among them, it would take time to weld them into a cohesive group, the attentions of the slavemasters notwithstanding. Don Guzman had been given an old level headed master and a sailing crew who all knew what they were about but he was himself, as he freely admitted, unused to galleys and wished to do his learning in coastal waters rather then in the unpredictable waters of the Bay. This, it was thought, would be more safely accomplished in company with another boat to provide support in the event of battle, and to act as a deterrent to the newly enslaved oarsmen who might yet attempt to overpower their captors, a highly unlikely occurrence but not entirely unknown.

After the conference, a dry affair, Grace returned to the Dana to hear the pleas of those of the crew who felt they needed, and could afford, one more night with their friends in Corunna. She gave their final orders to her officers in advance of their departure on the morrow, and then retired to her cabin to prepare herself for her visit to take her leave of the Sub Lieutenant and Senora Munoz. It had already been arranged that Grace, although she had already moved her gear back to the galley where she would sleep that night, would dine with the Munozs on one final occasion. Senora Munoz had extended that invitation to include as many of her officers as could be spared from their duties and she had accepted that extension on Rory's and Thomas's behalf.

Over the month or so that Grace had been their guest, the Senora had gradually accepted that Grace had no intent on her husband and a friendship had grown between them, albeit somewhat guarded still on the Senora's part. Even so, it was with pleasurable anticipation that she looked forward to their final, less formal, dinner together.

CHAPTER 16

James paused in his ascent of what memory told him was the last hill before Corunna and let his mind wander back through the sights and sounds of his visit to Santiago: the pilgrims with whom he had travelled, the hospital in which he had stayed and worked and, of course, the magnificent Cathedral, the splendour of which was unsurpassed in his previous experience, so much so that one could have fancifully imagined that the entirety of Spain's plundering of the New World was all collected in this one place.

He adjusted his pack and sword for comfort and resumed walking, finally reaching the summit, from which he was able to view Corunna and its harbour again, basking in the sunshine. He paused a moment to take in the scene, the same one that Grace had enjoyed a few weeks previously on her hunting trip.

The sea was a wonderful blue stretching far away to his left, while on his right, the estuary running among the green hills was a hardly lesser blue. The harbour seemed more crowded than when he had left but, at this distance, it was hard to tell. He could not see the Dana on the beach but, again, that might have simply been due to the distance. He carried on.

Another hour's walking brought him to the new town, the Pescaderia, from where it was obvious that the harbour was, indeed, more full and that the Dana was actually against the quayside, taking on stores.

"Grace must have worked them hard," he thought to himself. "I didn't think she had expected the repairs to be finished for another couple of weeks at least."

The hospital coming before the harbour on his way into Corunna, he decided to call there first to see how the wounded were progressing, before carrying on to the galley. He found only the amputees remaining. All of the other wounded, even young Burke, had gone. Of Phelim O'Connor and Tibbott, there was no sign. He was welcomed by the amputees with an outburst of salutations, questions and explanations, which he was unable to understand. He thought to visit Father Xavier, but was told that he was at the monastery so, with dumb show and smiles, he tried to convey to the invalids that he would go to the galley to find out what was happening, and then return to them.

As he walked along the quayside, he was spotted by one of the Danas who ran on board to tell Grace of his return. Grace emerged from the cabin to welcome him back.

"What's happening?" He began, "there's hardly a soul in the hospital and your refit appears complete, much earlier than I thought you had allowed for."

"Come on board," said Grace, "and I'll explain all. By the look of you, a cup of wine wouldn't go amiss."

He followed her to the cabin where he realised that he was indeed quite tired from his journey. Grace waited while he drank off a long draught of watered-down wine to quench his thirst before starting more slowly on an undiluted cup. She then explained what had happened, telling him the whole story: Fitzmaurice and his plans, the Papal Nuncio's appearance, the Governor General's return and his knavish trickery, Senor Munoz's well-meaning but unavailing attempt to intervene with the Governor General's plans, and finally, her request that Father Xavier examine, and pass as fit those who could travel, and confirm which of them could not, which turned out to be much as he himself had forecast, all but the amputees. Some would be on light duties for a while, all had healed amazingly. Some still had dressings on their wounds but Father Xavier, truly a wonderful man, had instructed Tibbott and the barber in all aspects of their care and was quite happy that they go avoyaging again. He had also arranged to supply all of the surgical instruments and medicines that James had requested of him, so all that was lacking now was that James himself consider whether he might not, after all, rejoin the Dana and herself, on a regular basis. James, with a smile of genuine regret, thanked Grace for the offer, said that he had very much grown to enjoy the company of Grace and her crew, but he felt that his duty dictated that he return to the Knights.

"Ah, that's a pity," said Grace. "I'd even taken the liberty of having your sea chest brought back on board in case you changed your mind. Well, we'll all miss you but I suppose your duty is your duty. At least you got back in time for us to say goodbye.

We sail tomorrow, you know, but tonight we are guests of Senor Munoz again, a more quiet affair I imagine, than was our first feast, and in Senor Munoz's own house this time now that the Governor General, bad cess to him, is returned. You must join us." She said the last in a tone that brooked no argument.

"I'd be delighted to. I've supped on pilgrim's fare for the past month and, may God forgive me, I long for something rich and substantial. But I must return to the hospital first and bathe my body free of this dust. Until tonight then."

The feast was, naturally enough, a much quieter affair than the first one. Senor Munoz's house was not as big as the Governor General's and so there were fewer guests. Grace had only brought Thomas and Rory (the latter hoping to meet the lovely Maria for one last time again: they had seen a lot of each other during the refit) as previously arranged, in addition to James, and the Spaniards were considerably more wary of whiskey than on the previous occasion. It was, nevertheless, a very pleasant evening and when it came to a relatively early close, Senor Munoz and his fellow Spaniards were quite sincere in their wishes for a pleasant voyage and an early return to Corunna at some time in the future.

In the street, James parted from the others with a promise to be at the quayside in the morning to exchange farewells, and to have his sea chest unloaded, he reminded Grace with a smile. He was musing on Grace and her dilemma with Fitzmaurice as he walked slowly back to the hospital, and his inattentiveness to his surroundings in the dark led him to brush against two Spaniards walking in the opposite direction.

"Watch where you're going, monk," snarled the one against whom he had brushed.

A quick glance showed James that by their dress they were obviously young hidalgos and, equally obviously, they had been drinking. James offered a murmured apology which was met by a demand to speak up, priest, by the first man, while his companion tried to get him to come along.

James apologised again more clearly. His apology this time elicited a sudden suspicious look.

"You're not Spanish, are you?" Asked the first grandee slowly and suspiciously. "Did you hear him, Ignacio?" He asked his companion. "He's not Spanish. I'll warrant he's not even a priest."

He addressed James again:

"what are you, sir?" His suspicion deepened.

"You're English, are you not? He's English, Ignacio, a spy no doubt. Well, we know how to deal with English spies in Spain."

He drew his sword.

"Defend yourself, Englishman."

James admitted he was English but also asserted that he really was a priest, attached to the Dana, which Captain O'Malley and even Senor Munoz would confirm. The Spaniard would have none of it and, despite his companion's attempts to draw him away, again demanded that James defend himself, emphasising his demand with a sudden flick of his blade that drew a tiny trickle of blood from James's cheek.

"Give him your sword, Ignacio," he ordered his friend.

"I am sworn not to fight Christians," said James.

"Are you a coward, Englishmen, hiding behind a monk's habit? You'll fight or you'll die."

With a shrug, James turned to the second Spaniard who drew his sword and gave it to him. The weapon was barely in his hand before his assailant was on him with a fierce lunge that James barely parried. While he was off balance, the Spaniard swung at him again with the dagger which he had also drawn, again just barely missing. With an inward curse at the habit which was impeding his movements, James moved back and took stock of his opponent. The Spaniard was undoubtedly skilled, he had probably been taught swordplay from infancy, but he was overconfident and arrogant and his movements might just be impaired by alcohol. James suddenly lunged himself with a speed that surprised his opponent, who had to raise his dagger to deflect James's sword from piercing his shoulder. He suddenly looked quite sober.

"See Ignacio, this is no priest. Priests don't learn swordplay. They learn to pray on their knees, which is where I'll soon have this lying Englishman."

He thrust again, feinting with his sword while attempting to bring the dagger up viciously under James's guard, but James was fully conversant with the Spanish way of fighting and was ready for the dagger, which he easily avoided, before thrusting himself with a straight arm at the Spaniard who, being momentarily unbalanced, barely escaped James's point. They now circled each other warily, thrusting and parrying with neither getting the upper hand until James saw that his opponent was beginning to tire. Judging his moment, he made a sudden ferocious lunge at the Spaniard's face and, as the man, almost involuntarily, lifted his weapons to protect himself, James dropped the blade and plunged it through his belly.

The man dropped his weapons and, clutching his wound, from which the blood was already beginning to flow, sank slowly to the ground. James turned to the second Spaniard but he seemed in shock. He lowered his sword and knelt beside the wounded man to assess the damage he had caused. He addressed the second Spaniard.

"If you get him to hospital quickly, he'll live."

But the other man, recovering his composure, told James that he would now have to fight him.

"He'll die if he doesn't have immediate treatment," said James.

"All the more necessary that I avenge him," said the man, picking up his fallen companion's weapons, and attacking James headlong.

He was very determined and courageous, but not as skilled as his friend, and James, neatly sidestepping his first lunge, parried and parried until an opening presented itself and then, coldly and clinically, drove his weapon through the man's sword arm. He dropped his weapons and looked long at James before saying:

"you'd better kill me now for, if you don't, I'll surely pursue you until I kill you."

"Bah, you Spaniards and your overinflated sense of honour. You're quite ridiculous. Do you not see that I could quite easily have killed both of you?" Replied James, who was as annoyed with himself as with the Spaniards. "I didn't kill your friend, and I didn't kill you so that you could help your friend. If you value him, get him to the hospital now, or his death will be on your conscience, not mine."

He flung the sword from himself in disgust and strode angrily away into the dark, leaving the young Spaniard holding his wounded arm and gaping after him. He wandered a while through the streets, considering his future. His plan to remain in Corunna with the amputees before taking ship for the Mediterranean was now out of the question. So was any possibility of leaving Corunna overland. The men he had fought could be expected to be sufficiently influential to make sure that any pursuit was prosecuted with the utmost vigour. He thought of surrendering himself to Senor Munoz but concluded that, priest or not, he would be charged and condemned as an Englishman. He could realistically expect support from nobody except, possibly, Father Xavier, and he knew instinctively that that would not be sufficient to prevent a long imprisonment, or even death, which he thought, without any vanity, would simply be a waste of life. With a somewhat wry smile to himself, he accepted what appeared to be the only course open to him, and made his way circuitously to the harbour.

Keeping to the shadows, he cautiously made his way to the Dana. The watch brought him on board and back to the cabin, where Grace was still up, attending to her paperwork. He gave a brief account of what had happened while Grace watched him with a fond smile.

"Aren't you the right hero now?" She asked when he had finished. "There was I, worried about how the crew might behave, and all the time the one I should've been watching was yourself." She was enjoying the moment. "And, I suppose, you'll be wanting me to rescue you again now. What'll you get up to in Ireland, I wonder?" She paused, enjoying his discomfort. "Of course you'll have to come with us. Isn't it what I've been asking of you all along? I'd almost say that it's God's will, if it weren't blasphemous. But, tell me, what did these Spaniards look like?"

James described the men with whom he had fought. Grace looked serious.

"It sounds as though you may have actually crossed swords with the Governor General's son himself. Certainly his friend is called Ignacio, and he himself is a big arrogant fool of a boy. If it was him, and if you did kill him and, I suppose, even if you didn't, there'll be a great hue and cry very soon. They'll easily recognise your description at the hospital, if that's where they end up, and won't take much longer to discover your identity even if they return to their home. We'd better get you out of sight straight away. You'll not mind if I have to lie a little on your behalf?" She finished, with an innocent smile.

She called the watch to tell them that, despite what they might have thought they had seen, Father James had definitely not come on board tonight. As far as they knew, he had returned to the hospital. This confirmed what they had surmised, that, priest or not, he was in hiding from some furious husband and, with knowing looks and, indeed with a certain admiration, for they were all sailors after all, they readily agreed that no, he had not been seen all evening.

She called for her officers. Virtually all of the crew were aboard. All stores had been stowed and watering completed during the day in preparation for the little flotilla's departure next day. She gave her orders: they were to be ready to slip from the quayside at dawn and lie at a single anchor midstream to catch the ebb. She brought James back into the cabin and led him down the ladder to the small aft storeroom, her own. There she tapped a panel and a small space opened of which he had previously been totally unaware.

"I had never mentioned this to you," said Grace, half apologetically. "The fewer people who know of it, the fewer can reveal its existence."

The space was about the size of a cupboard and curved with the side of the galley, of which it appeared to be the outer skin. It was full of items of treasure from their battle with the Algerines.

"If things should go wrong with Fitzmaurice, we'll not have lost everything. Help me re-stow this in these chests." She indicated some battered boxes lying haphazardly in the hold space. "I hope that we'll not have to use it, but it's a consolation to know it's there if necessary. You should just about fit in. You'd better remain in the hold in case we have any visitors while we're moored to the quayside."

She showed him how to open and close the entrance to the space and then left him alone. He sat in the dark on one of the boxes and decided it was an appropriate time to examine his conscience and pray for forgiveness for his actions. He wondered uneasily for a while whether he should not have given himself up, but consoled himself that prayer would disclose if he should leave the temporary safety of the galley. He was lulled by the repetitiveness of his rosary and, overcome by sudden extreme fatigue, for it had been a long day, he fell fast asleep.

Meanwhile, on deck, Grace was telling the crew as much as she felt they needed to know about the events of the night. It was a godsend that so few of them spoke Spanish so that, in the event of their being visited by the authorities, there was little likelihood of their being let down by a slip of the tongue, no matter that nothing she said would prevent them over acting their ignorance of the situation.

The remaining few hours of darkness passed slowly but it was time, eventually, to rouse the crew and unmoor. She looked briefly into the hold, where James was still fast asleep. She thought that he was unlikely to sleep long through the moving of the galley on to her anchor but she let him be for the moment. They slipped their moorings and, with bow oars only, rowed out to the middle of the harbour, where they anchored. They had left one of their skiffs, they now had two, by the quayside for any stragglers still ashore. Grace sent the hands to breakfast. All around them, the other ships and boats in the harbour were awakening. The early fishing boats were already on their way to their grounds, oblivious and uncaring of the momentous events getting into train around them. People were stirring on the Arganya and Grace saw Fitzmaurice himself appear on deck.

"You'll never be a successful rebel if you get up this late", she thought contemptuously to herself.

Now there was activity on the harbour wall and Grace saw a pilot boat setting off directly towards the Dana with Senor Munoz on board. Soon, he was climbing over the low freeboard of the galley, but not before Grace had discreetly sent Thomas below to warn James of the forthcoming visit.

"I apologise greatly for disturbing you, Señora Grace", he

began, "but there was a fight in the town last night and the Governor General's son has been seriously wounded, as was his companion, though he less so. They're both in the hospital at the moment, and the description they've given of their assailant matches that of your Father James. Father Xavier confirms that he returned from Santiago yesterday but that his cell has not been slept in. Do you happen to know where he might be?"

"I wish I did," replied Grace cheerfully. "He was to have collected his sea chest before we sailed. In fact, he was going to leave us here and return to Malta where he sails with the Knights of St John but, as you see, here's his sea chest, and yet no sign of himself."

"I hope you'll not be affronted, Señora Grace, but I am ordered by the Governor General himself to search the galley. It's purely a matter of formality, of course" he ended apologetically."

"Of course," agreed Grace. "Where would you like to begin?"

Senor Munoz pointed forward, and Grace instructed her men to open the hatches so that the Sub Lieutenant's men could begin their search. She was gently humming a Gaelic air as the Spaniards moved slowly back along the galley, watched, with a decent semblance of idle curiosity, by the Irishmen. Finally, they got to the cabin. Senor Munoz looked wretched.

"Come on," said Grace, "you may as well do the job properly."

The visitors gave a cursory glance at the cabin, and she now raised the hatch to the hold and insisted, despite Senor Munoz's protestations, that they search there as well. She stood back while one of the Spaniards glanced briefly through the entrance before confirming that it was, indeed, unoccupied.

"I'm so sorry for this inconvenience. Had the decision been mine alone…" His voice trailed away.

"I understand. Of course I understand," said Grace. "Now Pedro, will you join me for breakfast?"

"No, no. I wish I could but the Count will be expecting a report." Senor Munoz was positively miserable by now. "We can't be certain, of course, that Father James was involved, but that boy was deserving of a lesson anyway, whoever gave it to him," Senor Munoz confided before taking his leave, repeating his wish of the night before, that Grace and her crew have a prosperous voyage.

When she had seen the Spaniards over the side, and almost all the way to the quayside, Grace went below to release James from his confinement.

"I'm very grateful to you," said James. "Tell me, was it difficult to convince them that I was elsewhere?"

"No." She waved dismissively. "Señor Munoz was here under protest anyway and was happy to believe, even without my telling him, that you weren't on board. What I had to say, which was only a half lie really, convinced him, for what gentlemen, particularly a Spaniard, ever doubted the word of a lady? And Pedro Munoz is very happy that Grace O'Malley is a lady, despite my being the leader of this bunch of pirates.

Anyway, enough of that. I'm afraid you'll have to remain out of sight until we're well out to sea and, even then, I think that you'll have to dress and behave as a common seaman while we're in company with the other ships. You wouldn't be too proud for that now, would you James?" Grace smiled.

"No Grace. I'll swallow all my English pride and be as common as you wish. I may even try my hand at the Gaelic, and I can't conceive of anything more common than that."

"Behave yourself, or I'll lock you in that cupboard again."

They parted on that note, Grace returning on deck to watch the embarkation of the Spanish soldiers, thankful that she had carried her point that the Dana was already crewed to capacity. It was becoming obvious that they were going to miss their tide and possibly the next tide as well, and she began to wonder whether she might not be forced to move back to the quayside while they waited. As if divining her thoughts, Fitzmaurice hailed from the Arganya to assure her that they would certainly get away that day, to please be patient. Grace acknowledged with a shrug of resignation and turned her attention back to the business of preparing a war galley for sea.

CHAPTER 17

All was finally ready on the other ships of the flotilla and, Arganya leading, they won their anchors and set sail for Ireland on their momentous mission.

As agreed, once they reached the open sea, Fitzmaurice's carrack headed north directly across the Bay, followed by the three shallops, while Grace and Don Diego turned east to follow the coastline. Grace watched the other four ships until they disappeared beyond the horizon. It was another perfect sailing day but Grace knew that were the weather to change and a storm blow up, not something to be dismissed in these particular waters, the shallops would do very well to survive. She had said as much to Fitzmaurice, but he was in such a tearing hurry to get to Ireland that he had ignored what she had to say, too cautious by far, and carried on anyway. To Grace, it was just another example of how ill conceived and misjudged the whole plan was, not that she was too worried about Fitzmaurice and his followers, who had seen enough of the world to make their own decisions without her. In a sudden fit of pique she decided that, provided he kept to his side of the bargain, as far as she was concerned he could go hang himself afterwards.

She turned her attention back to the Dana and her consort. She had suggested to the Spaniard that they row as much as was reasonable in the first few days. The galliot's new crew would need as much practice as possible to get them to the state of mechanical unison and instant response that made galleys such dangerous weapons in the right hands. She had made known that this not out of any altruistic motive, but so that the Dana would not be hampered in action by having to protect not only itself, but a badly handled companion. Don Diego was a sufficiently hardened campaigner to see the value of this so, for the rest of the day, when they might well have cruised easily under sail, they worked hard at the oars, not without some grumblings from the Danas which Grace cheerfully rebuffed, they needed the soft living of the past month knocked out of them. More importantly, she also wanted her own new crew members to become used to the rhythm of the Dana and particularly to the orders which were, of course, issued in Gaelic, a completely alien language to the Spaniards and to the two withdrawn men who had quite quickly admitted to being English once they had realised that the Irish had no grudge against individual Englishmen, only against their rulers, and their rulers' deputies. Grace suspected that they were Protestants: they had always contrived to miss Mass in Corunna by being invariably on hand for extra watch keeping duties to selflessly allow others to attend. Grace did not really care provided that they fitted in and did their fair share which, to date, they had certainly endeavoured to do. Besides, Black Tom was a Protestant and it would have been quite hypocritical of her to overlook that in him and not in others. She wondered what James might make of them if he knew.

She looked for him now and found him forward, conversing with Rory, one of the few members of the crew who had a fair bit of English.

"I've been meaning to tell you James, that we rescued a couple of your fellow countrymen from the Algerine and, since you're back with us again, I thought you might wish to take them under your wing.

You might all wish to take Gaelic lessons together," she added facetiously.

Out of the corner of her eye she saw the two men almost miss a stroke, their fellow oarsmen calling angrily to them to keep their rhythm. They kept their heads down and re-applied themselves to their rowing.

"Certainly Grace. Which two are they?"

"They're currently rowing. I'll have them brought to you

175

when they've finished. It'll probably be a pleasure for the three of you to converse together in your own heathen tongue. One thing, if they should prove to be heretical Englishmen, I'll not have them subjected to any unwanted conversion attempts. I don't want any discontent in my crew"

There was an almost audible sigh from the bench below. James frowned.

"I'm sorry that you should think so low of me. I thought we knew each other better. I'm not a Dominican."

He begged to be excused and made his way to the stern.

"Bloody men." She spat the words out and, bending down, cuffed the ear of the nearest Englishman. "Now, see the trouble you've caused. I should've left you in Corunna to have your fingernails pulled out".

She strode away after James, pursued by the thank yous of her mightily relieved new crew men who were, this time, careful not to miss their stroke despite their overwhelming sense of relief.

She found James in the cabin, studiously reading his breviary.

"I'll not apologise," she began. "I reckon myself as good a Catholic as the next but I'm not a priest, nor yet a man, and I'm not privy to what might go through a priest's mind when confronted by heretics, for they're certainly Protestants, you know. My only concern is the good of this ship and the well-being of its crew and I can't have men on the benches who, through fear of the unknown, might let us down at a crucial moment. Now, you can accept that as a sensible precaution on my part as ship's captain rather than as plain Grace O'Malley, or you can sulk for the rest of the voyage. Well?"

He paused for a while before replying.

"It was an intemperate reaction which I can't excuse. Please forgive me, Grace"

"Sure, you needn't worry about it now. I'm sorry myself. I could've put the thing better or, at least, told you privately."

Grace was, in fact, quite sorry at the thoughtless way in which she had acted. She was beginning to realise that she valued James's friendship as much as it appeared he valued hers, but the damage was done now and she had repaired the situation as best she could without actually grovelling, something which she would do for no man. She returned on deck, leaving James to his prayers.

By this time, the Dana had pulled well ahead of the galliot with its smaller, raw crew. She ordered the oars to rest easy to allow the galliot to catch up with them and then hailed Don Diego to suggest that they find a suitable anchorage for the night. He acknowledged with a low bow and a sweep of his broad brimmed hat.

Thomas's charts were fairly sparse on the nature of the nearby coastline, so they chose a likely looking cove at random and rowed in, keeping a sharp look out. The Dana was unflagged but Don Diego had a large Spanish flag flying on the galliot which Grace hoped would allay the fears of any watchers onshore and decrease the likelihood of attack, either from locals who might perceive them as Algerines, or from pirates who would not dare attack a national ship. Their choice proved to be a good one. Within the cove, the sea was quite calm and the lead showed a good depth of water under their keels. Anchors were dropped fore and aft to keep both vessels facing the open sea in case of a sudden need to exit the cove. Small parties went ashore to check the surrounding countryside, and a stream was found from which they could replenish their casks. Satisfied that it was safe to do so, Grace ordered guards placed around the cove and, leaving a strong watch on board, brought the rest of the crew ashore for the night.

To her surprise, James appeared in his monk's habit again. She remonstrated, pointing out that Don Diego and his fellow officers might wish to arrest him for the affair in Corunna, but he replied that he had been giving the matter serious consideration and had concluded that the sense of uncleanliness he felt at his cowardly behaviour outweighed the purely pragmatic considerations of his situation. He would make the voyage as planned, but would then find some way of returning to Corunna to face the authorities. She would understand that it was just another instance of foolish male vanity, he concluded with a smile, which, deadly sin though it might be, he had yet to suppress.

The crew of the galliot followed them ashore, a much smaller number, given that most of the crew were chained to their benches, so that Don Diego had had to leave an even stronger harbour watch than Grace. He now looked hard at James before addressing Grace:

"There was talk in Corunna before we left of the Count's son and his friend being attacked by an Englishman dressed as a priest. Can this be the man?"

"Indeed it is. He is English and he actually is a priest, and I believe that it was he who was attacked, rather than the other way round."

"And yet you shelter him. There would be those who would think that as a Captain of Spain I should arrest him and put him in chains until we return to Spain."

Before Grace could reply, James intervened.

"It's my intent to return to Corunna in my own time and of my own free will. I believe, in retrospect, that my departure was too precipitate, but I equally believe that father Xavier and the Abbot of the Hotel dos Reis Catolicas in Santiago will vouch for my character and that I needn't unduly fear Spanish justice, even as an Englishman. You are, of course, welcome to try to arrest me".

Don Diego looked pointedly around at the assembled crew of the Dana, who, even if they did not understand Spanish, were aware of the tension, and were moving in to surround the Spaniards. He then looked at his own heavily outnumbered men and shrugged.

"Perhaps when this is all over......"

He left the unfinished sentence hanging in the air and

smiled his half smile to Grace, but the warmth of that smile did not extend to his eyes. Grace took him aside.

"A word, Senor. You've heard of the Cistercian monks of Calatreva?"

"Yes, a soft, pampered lot more concerned with serving themselves then God or Spain."

Understanding dawned on his face.

"He's one of them?" He asked in surprise.

The smile on Don Diego's face was now a proper one.

"A worthy opponent then. You may rest assured, Señora Grace, that your Englishman will be completely safe until after our business with Fitzmaurice, even if I have to protect him myself."

He bowed deeply and, still smiling, addressed his men, ordering them to start on the watering and making cooking fires and, with another bow to Grace, doing what ever the Señora requested.

"I believe, Señora Grace, that with your greater experience of galleys, and indeed of seafaring generally, you should command our little force until we arrive in Ireland. You may consider both myself and my men completely at your disposal."

"What strange days we live in, a Don making himself subservient to a female. Whatever next?"

"Not a female, Señora Grace, if you will excuse my addressing such a handsome woman as yourself in such a fashion, but a sea captain of proven quality and achievement."

Grace looked at him hard but did not reply. She resolved though, that Don Diego would pay for his impudence, one day.

He, meanwhile, had turned on his men, who had watched the exchange in somewhat dumbstruck fashion and curtly ordered them to get on with their tasks, something they did with alacrity, the wrath of a Spanish captain not being worth incurring. His smile had quite disappeared.

The Danas were well used to the requirements of spending a night onshore mid voyage, as were the galliot's master and her soldiers, all hardened campaigners, and quite soon a hot meal was made ready. Both groups sat down separately from each other around their own fires: the obvious belligerence between the Dana's priest and the Marquesa's captain had created a feeling of mistrust between the two crews, a situation for which Grace inwardly cursed the Spaniard's calculated hotheadedness. Normally, she would have expected music and friendly rivalry between the two groups, sailors were sailors and a lack of understanding of each other's tongues would never be any hindrance, but this was a quiet evening and the sailors and soldiers unrolled their blankets for sleep without any prompting from her. This suited Grace, since she planned an early start but, for once, she would have preferred to be hunting them to bed like the big children she considered them to be.

The following day set the precedent for the rest of the voyage. The overnight camps were cleared at dawn and they sailed or rowed, according to conditions, until they found another suitable anchorage. It was Grace's wish to complete the voyage as quickly as possible, as it was Don Diego's, but she told him early on that she was prepared to be delayed by as much as he needed, in the interest of getting his crew to peak pitch by having them row as much as possible, even in conditions more suited to hoisting the lateens. At his surprised reaction to this, she was quick to inform him that this was not for his benefit, but for hers: as she had pointed out at the start of the voyage, she was stuck with him and was not going to have her own crew endangered by any incompetence on the part of his. He took this better than she had expected. He was quite professional about it and reiterated, sincerely she believed, that she had the experience and that he intended to benefit from it.

On the evening of the third day, as they sat down to dinner, he felt able to inform her that his slave masters were relatively happy with the progress of his oarsmen and that he would be comfortable with running under sail henceforth, whenever she desired.

"You must have very persuasive slave masters," she thought to herself.

Aloud, she congratulated him and raised her glass to drink to a speedy final landfall. On this occasion, and on the succeeding evenings, his manners were impeccable and the tension between the two nationalities gradually disappeared so that, in time, both captains had to intervene to prevent the development of drunken carousels that would otherwise have had both crews seriously incapacitated and the efficiency of the two boats gravely hampered. Despite his good behaviour, or possibly even because of it, Grace kept her guard up and even went so far as to warn James that for all his manners and his breeding, as he had described it to her, the Spaniard was not to be trusted. It was her instinct that some day, for something, or even someone, that he particularly prized, he would put his honour aside and do whatever was necessary to achieve that prize. On a practical basis, her two English crewmen were always left on board as part of the anchor watch and never mixed with the Spanish crewman, a situation with which they were quite happy, given their awareness of the very well deserved hatred of the Spanish for the English. They also kept quiet during Don Diego's frequent visits to the Dana, to extend his learning as he put it.

The voyage progressed quite quickly along the coast of Spain, north up the coast of France, and then west by the southern shores of Brittany. This was quite a nervous time for the Spanish and there were some nights when they anchored offshore and had to eat ship's fare rather than risk unwelcome attention from the French authorities. They met no shipping other than fishing boats, from whom they frequently bought their dinner. It was Don Diego's casual assertion that they should simply take the fish, be the

181

fishermen Spanish or French, but Grace was scrupulous that everything be paid for. Fishermen formed a brotherhood and it would be madness to risk having the word spread, possibly as far as official ears, that there were vessels of malevolent intent in the vicinity. She also insisted that they sail under the O'Malley colours only. In this instance, Don Diego was again sufficiently professional not to risk the venture by insisting on a display of Spanish colours, much though his pride would have wished it.

A day's sail short of Brest, they anchored as usual, taking even greater care than normal in selecting their anchorage, for they would not only have to fear hostile Frenchman ashore, but also the possibility of a horseman being sent to Brest to alert the French navy of their presence. This was of little consequence to Grace but would have been very dangerous to the Spanish. Consequently, they discreetly inspected two coves before settling on a third one as being the safest looking. They observed their usual precautions, sending a party of Danas ashore to confirm that it would be safe (Spaniards blundering around the French mainland did not bear thinking about) and when they had confirmed that it was, they landed and, again as usual, saw to their watering first before making their fires and preparing their dinner.

Don Diego professed himself to be quite enjoying galley life.

"You know, of course," he said, "that fresh food and water quickly become a memory on long voyages. This idea of making camp each evening, dining well, and sleeping ashore is almost civilised. And one even has one's own cabin as ship's captain. Yes, it's quite a comfortable life, not to be compared with real sailing obviously," he could not resist the slight barb, "but I can definitely see the attractions it might hold for someone of a provincial outlook."

Grace gazed at him a moment before replying levelly, "sure, I've misjudged you. There was I thinking you the provincial one. After all, you don't speak English or French, let alone the Gaelic and, by your own admission, you've ever been only in Spain and its colonies. The New World is all very well, and, indeed, I hope to visit it myself one day, but it is as yet a barbarous, heathenous place, not to be compared with Europe and its great cities, its culture and music." He hung his head in mock abashment. Grace carried on. "And as for the comforts of galley sailing, sure it's comfortable if you stay immersed in your cabin and ignore the fact that your men are making do on hard benches, for we can't always keep to the coast, as you'll soon find out. But then, it may well be a provincial thing to think that you'll have a happier more efficient boat if you mix with your men and share their discomforts. And I'll tell you something else. It won't be long before the stench from your slaves makes you wish you were far from your galley. Then you'll be wishing that you were somewhere less comfortable, but where you could breathe clean air. That's a bit of a problem on your so-called "civilised" Imperial galleys, not one you'll find on a "provincial" galley, crewed entirely by free men."

He looked at her admiringly.

"I am, as ever, impressed by the way you put forth your views, Senora Grace. You don't hold back. It's a feature of your character and one that I greatly enjoy. Of course, the same forthright manner might be indiscreet in a man, but in a woman it's refreshing."

"My sex is neither here nor there. I'm a ship's captain and to be treated as such, and if you find yourself unhappy with anything I say or do beyond what pertains strictly to this voyage, you'll find me more than ready to satisfy that unhappiness."

James and those Danas who understood Spanish heard this with some anxiety, as did the other Spaniards, they having grown attached to their fellow voyagers after the initial distrust, and not wanting any unpleasantness, particularly to the Irish captain, for whom they had

183

considerably more esteem than for their own. Don Diego merely shrugged however, and Grace continued,

"As I seem to have all your attention, this is probably as good a time as any to tell you what I plan. We'll shortly leave the French coast and head for Ireland. I hope to make landfall around Kinsale, whence we'll make our way to Dingle which is, hopefully, were we'll find Captain Fitzmaurice. That'll entail a few days away from the land," she glanced at Don Diego who remained impassive, "and we will, therefore, have to cram in as much water and stores as we can carry. I would've preferred to have done this in Roscoff, it's smaller, more discreet for various reasons but, as my own men know well enough, that port is probably closed to us for the moment, so we'll have to make do with Brest. Therefore, it's my intention to sail beyond Brest tomorrow, and find another quiet spot where the Marquesa can lay low while we return to Brest to replenish stores for the crossing. We'll be trying to fit into the Dana enough for both boats, something for which you'll understand she's not designed, so I can tell you now that we'll definitely be on short rations from tomorrow until we get to Ireland."

She addressed Don Diego directly: "do you have any comments or suggestions?" He shook his head. "It's such a pity that you don't speak French, in which case we could've brought you with us, but as you don't, well," she shrugged. She was rewarded by the half smile. Two can play at baiting, she thought.

"What about the Englishman?" the Spaniard asked, jerking a thumb towards James. "Are you going to trust him not to run when he gets on French soil?"

"James?" she queried, looking at the priest.

"I'm not sure that I need to answer that, but I will point out, Sir, that I don't believe that I've anything from which to run. I acted in self defence against the braggarts who forced me to fight, as you yourself seem intent on doing. I don't know you well enough yet to assert that you too are a braggart, time will tell." The Spaniard's right hand flew to the hilt of his sword as James continued: "but I'll certainly pray for you, a common decency and no more than I would for anyone else of such an intemperate disposition."

Don Diego jumped to his feet, sword in hand.

"You'll fight me now, English dog," he hissed.

"Enough," said Grace. "You'll not fight, either of you. I'm in command here and you'll both obey me. I have far too much at stake in this venture to have it jeopardised by foolish male pride. There'll be no fighting amongst you until we're finished with Fitzmaurice. Then you can do what you want to each other," she finished in exasperation.

"You may hide behind a woman's skirts for now," said Don Diego, "but you'll answer to me eventually, I promise."

"I've killed more Moors in God's name than I care to remember but I've never yet killed a Christian. However, that can change. I'll fight you at your convenience," replied James.

Supper was eaten in silence after that, and everyone took to their blankets earlier than they might otherwise have done.

Grace lay awake, uncertain how she could avert what seemed certain to transpire between the two men. She knew James's prowess but she could also see in Don Diego a formidable opponent. She realised, with some surprise, that if James were to fall, she would kill Don Diego herself, such was the warmth of feeling she had developed towards the monk.

Next morning, there was an oppressive silence amongst both crews as they loaded their gear from the beach and made ready to sail. The anchors were won and the two boats slowly exited the cove. As soon as they reached the open sea however, the galliot's rate of rowing picked up dramatically and the Dana was quickly left behind. Before it was out of earshot however, they could hear Don Diego exhorting his slavemasters. They were responding with indiscriminate whipping as the rhythm of the drum grew quicker and quicker, driving the slaves to greater and greater exertion at the oars.

"He's working off his temper," said Grace to Thomas, "the slaves mean nothing to him. He cannot, or will not, learn that if he drives them like that, they'll be too exhausted to row hard when it matters."

She ordered the lateens hoisted, the oars were laid inboard, and they set off in pursuit of the Marquesa, which was already dwindling in the distance. The galliot could not keep up the pace, of course, and the Dana caught up with them quite quickly.

Don Diego's humour was obviously quite restored and he waved cheerily to Grace.

"That was exhilarating. I had never appreciated how quickly a galley could move when the infidels are properly driven."

"If you drive them like that," Grace called back, "you'll kill them."

"Who cares?" he replied casually. "They're only Moors. Anyway, they can quite easily be replaced by more Moors."

"Not in the Irish Sea, they can't. That kind of driving needs to be carefully husbanded for desperate situations. I suppose you'll learn in time. I just hope you don't expect to do it at my expense. You'll be in for a surprise if you do. Now, if you've finished amusing yourself, you may raise your sail and follow me."

Grace ordered the Dana's sails let free to allow the Marquesa time to get her single lateen raised, and then the two vessels proceeded northwards until they were beyond Brest and looking for a likely cove in which to lie in concealment.

Having seen the galliot safely anchored, and trusting that Don Diego would do nothing foolish, Grace retraced her steps back to the port.

Brest was a much larger town than Roscoff and already had much bigger docking facilities. However, it was also much busier and it took some time and maneuvering before the Dana was safely tied up at the quayside.

Grace did not intend to be more than a couple of hours in port so, other than being allowed to stretch their legs along the quays, there was no leave for the crew. A port official came on board to check their cargo but, after receiving the customary presents, he took no more than a cursory glance into one of the holds, where the boxes of munitions were carefully covered with some bales of cloth to validify the trading nature of their voyage. This done, she set off to purchase the supplies that they would need for the ocean going part of their journey, accompanied by the cook, Rory, and a handful of men for the carrying.

James was allowed ashore also to see the sights of Brest with the strict enjoinder that he be back in no more than two hours. He wandered the dockside, taking in the many sounds and, particularly, the smells of the port, quite like, but not exactly so, those of the ports of the Mediterranean. Foreign sailors in outlandish garb, fishwives with their baskets of herrings on their heads, tradesmen, peasants and soberly dressed merchants all mingled, together with fishermen and peddlers of various sorts, all talking and calling out in various languages of which, of course, French was the most dominant. The shipping tied up at the docks was as varied as the sailors, but the Dana was the only galley amongst them, all the others being ship-rigged oceangoing vessels. There was even a Galway ship to whom Grace, as she passed, had called a cheerful greeting but, the O'Malley flag being instantly recognisable to the long suffering men of that city, there had been no response other than a stony faced silence. James had wondered whether there might not be trouble ashore between the two crews, but she had assured him that the thirty odd men of the Galway ship would not dare to try anything with the Dana's much larger crew, would go out of their way to avoid them, in fact.

His wandering brought him back to the quayside as the Dana completed its loading. Brest, like any other oceangoing port, had an abundance of warehouses stacked with dried fish, salted beef and pork, fresh fruit and vegetables and all the other foodstuffs necessary for long voyaging, and it had taken Grace no time at all, even with the haggling involved, to get what she wanted. It had been transported by handcart from the warehouses in such bulk that it now overflowed from the holds on to the decks, fore and aft, and even on to the gangways. There had been much amused comment from the satisfied merchants at the amount of her purchases, relatively little in ship terms, but very excessive for a galley: did she intend to row to the New World perhaps, or was the Dana so slow that they would need this amount of supplies, were the Irish gluttons? All this she accepted with an outward show of good cheer, but inwardly, she would have wished to bang their heads together.

They cast off and pushed away from the quay. They were sufficiently overburdened that shipping and using the oars was a considerably more complicated procedure than usual and it was with some relief that they were finally able to hoist their sails. They met more ships coming in and out of Brest than they had since leaving Corunna and there was some anxiety that they would be unable to keep their rendezvous undetected but, after a certain amount of unseamanlike backing and filling to amuse any watchers into believing that they were having difficulties with the galley's handling, they put in to what they hoped would be perceived as a random cove, where they found the Marquesa hidden behind the small headland for which the anchorage had been chosen.

Most of the crew of the Marquesa were ashore but, on the arrival of the Dana, they quickly floated their skiff and rowed out to the galliot, alongside which Grace was now tying up the Irish galley. Don Diego expressed surprise at the amount of supplies that she carried, but was quickly reassured by Grace that, if the winds should prove unfavourable, they might well end up on very short rations, even with this amount: the galliot was already overmanned because of the extra troops she was carrying to Ireland. They transferred the Marquesa's share of the supplies, not without some difficulty, the shallow draughted boats tending to rock alarmingly as the heavy weights were moved from one to the other but, in time, the job was done. Don Diego had already seen to the watering of the Marquesa and Grace now organised that of the Dana, after which they set about preparing the evening meal.

When they had finished, Grace invited the Spaniard and his master to join with herself and Thomas to discuss the next few day's sailing. Thomas had brought some spare charts for the Spaniards and now outlined the details. The major imperative was to avoid English ships and, to this end, Grace intended to go further out into the Atlantic then she would otherwise have done, before turning north towards Ireland. They certainly had enough supplies if they were not profligate in their use. However, a storm, or even a calm, might force them to reconsider how quickly they used their supplies, particularly the water. They could, obviously, row in a calm, but if the men had prolonged periods at the oars, they would need correspondingly more to eat and drink to sustain their strength. This thought seemed to amuse Don Diego, who commented that a galley rowed by slaves seemed a much more economical proposition, to which Grace pointed out that her crew of free Irishmen gave her an eager fighting force about three times the size of that of the Don, a fact which he appeared, amazingly, not to have actually previously considered, as evidenced by the sudden wiping of the half smile from his face.

"You needn't worry, Don Diego," said Grace, "until I get back what is rightfully mine, I've every intention of looking after you like a son."

"Your concern does you credit, Señora," he replied.

His sailing master had watched this exchange impassively, as indeed he had viewed all transactions between the two crews since they had first sailed from Corunna. His taciturnity was reassuring to Grace. He did not look like a man who would be easily panicked, which she supposed was why the Spanish authorities had appointed him to the Marquesa. He had no worries about deep sea sailing. He had crossed the Mediterranean to North Africa many times, and had frequently been out of sight of land for several days at a time in pursuit of Moorish galleys, times when everyone had been on short rations. He merely commented that he had heard that the Atlantic waves were greater than those of the Mediterranean but, if they ran into bad weather, they would just have to make the best of it. Grace warmed to him, almost a Spanish, if more silent, version of Thomas.

They would obviously try to stay together for the crossing but, if they were separated, Kinsale was where they would rendezvous. However, they were now into July and she had every hope of settled weather so that, she looked for something wooden to touch, the rendezvous should be unnecessary: they would arrive together.

Thomas and the Spanish sailing master settled down to a detailed discussion of winds and tides, particularly those at the mouth of the English Channel which, although intended to be left well to starboard, would nevertheless exert an influence, especially if it came on to blow. They were not worried about private signals, any other vessel they met could be presumed to be English, and they would run or fight depending upon circumstances but, the primary aim being the delivery of the arms to Fitzmaurice, they would accept battle only as a very last resort.

CHAPTER 18

Shortly after dawn the next day, the Dana and the Marquesa set out for the open sea. Don Diego kept to his cabin so Grace had to address her final orders to his sailing master, which were merely a reiteration of what had already been decided: Dana would lead and he would follow, keeping to within about a cable's length of the Dana; they would continue sailing through the night rather than lie to; again the Marquesa would follow, the Dana's stern lantern being its guide. In the event of an emergency of any sort, each would fire a blue light to alert the other; if they were separated for any reason, he had the rendezvous clearly marked on the chart with which Thomas had supplied him. Finally, and absolutely, they were to avoid all contact with any other shipping. The sailing master acknowledged all of this. Grace could only wonder how much the sulking Don Diego would be prepared to be dictated to, but that was out of her hands so she would not waste time worrying about it.

The first two days passed uneventfully. Once out of sight of land, the few small coastal traders and fishing boats, with which they had shared the horizon, disappeared. The weather was good, with a breeze that propelled the galliot along at what was probably her best speed, the slightly faster Dana allowing it to keep on station by keeping her lateens slightly less tightly hauled to the wind. They had two gratifyingly corresponding noon sightings, which placed them exactly as Thomas had calculated. Grace exercised the men with sword and pike to keep them alert and fit and on the second day, when they were quite alone on the ocean, having had the arquebuses and patereros loaded and fired in dumb show, she allowed them to actually fire a few real volleys. She had long decided that the gun rather than the ram was the way forward for galleys, and it was her intent that her crew fire and load as quickly as possible: she would dearly love to reduce the two Paters and two Aves down to just two Paters, or even a Pater and an Ave. Finally, having hailed the Marquesa to alert them to her intentions, they lowered the lateens and shipped oars. She then had an empty barrel thrown over the side and had the great guns fire at it, starting at five cables and gradually working closer under oars until they finally shattered it. This drew some ironic applause from the Spaniards, who had watched all these activities on the Dana without making any effort to emulate them. Grace ignored them, merely ordering the oars to be laid in again and the sails rehoisted, before resuming her station. James had watched all of this from the stern, and now congratulated Grace on the performance of the Dana, which he allowed, with a smile, was almost up to the Knights' standards, not that this was in any way surprising to him, having already seen her in real action. "Practice makes perfect," was her simple reply before lamenting that the Spaniards would not follow her example. Their avowed tactic of ramming and boarding, before carrying all before them because of the excellence of their infantry, was all very well against other galleys bent on similar tactics, but against the new type of warship that the English, in particular, were building, given any wind, they would be blown out of the water before they could get close enough to board.

The next day passed as had the previous ones, with plenty of arms drill aboard the Dana, and what Grace assumed was pleasant sailing aboard the Marquesa, although the guns were not fired again. On the day after that, just after the noon observation, Tibbott, who was sitting in his usual position on the yard where it crossed the main mast, called down shrilly that he could see a sail on the horizon to starboard, quickly correcting this to two sails. Low as Tibbott's position was, they could not yet be seen from the deck, but Grace assumed that if they could see the two strange sail, then the two strange sail could almost certainly see them. She glanced back at the Marquesa but she seemed, as yet, unaware that they were no longer alone. She decided to keep to her present course. She was fairly sure that in this wind she could quickly out sail any ship rigged vessel and she was certain, given that the two sail were coming out of the Channel, that these were English ships, and the English having given up their dalliance with galleys as far as she was aware, they would prove to be ship rigged, in which case they would have to tack at least once to have any chance of intercepting her. Thus her reasoning, and her decision, for the moment, to continue on her present course.

An hour passed, by which time the two strange sail were visible from the deck. There was a sudden clamour aboard the Marquesa where they had obviously finally become aware of the other vessels. Don Diego was now in the bows of the galliot, gesticulating to catch her attention. She ordered Thomas to spill some wind from the sails to allow the galliot to catch up.

"You've seen the sails, Captain Grace?" called Don Diego, the form of address being a new one for him, and one which gave Grace some amusement.

"Not for much above an hour", she replied dryly.

"What do you intend?" he called back.

"I assume them to be English, in which case I intend to avoid them."

"But, you can't. If they're English, it's our duty to attack them."

"Our duty is to rendezvous with Fitzmaurice and to bring him the arms and men that have been promised him by your superiors, under whose orders you are sailing."

"But we're strong and they're probably only merchant ships. We can take them and bring them with us, and whatever cargo they contain, to Ireland."

"Now we see your true intent," thought Grace to herself,

"the perceived first step in the restoration of your fortunes."
Aloud she said, "I would remind you again that you're under
orders to Fitzmaurice. I can't allow you to risk your boat and
your men in what may turn out to be a very dangerous
endeavour."

"Bah. I forget that you're a woman. You cannot conceive
of the sense of honour by which a man must live. I am a
Captain of Spain and it's my duty to hunt and kill Englishmen
whenever and wherever I find them. That includes your pet
priest by the way," he added as an afterthought, "who'll yet
give me satisfaction."

He ordered the galliot to change course to intercept the
strange sails. With a shrug to Grace, her master gave the
necessary orders and the Marquesa turned on to her new
heading. With a string of blasphemies which made no
allowance for James's presence beside her, the import of
which he understood if not the actual words (they were in
Gaelic), she told Thomas to follow the Spaniard.

Another hour's sailing on converging courses brought the
four vessels sufficiently close to each other for Grace to be
able to make a detailed study of the two oncoming ships. She
did not like what she saw. She had Thomas bring the Dana
alongside the Marquesa and called across to Don Diego:

"Have you looked properly at these sail, at all?"

"No," he replied. "That they're English is all I need to
know."

"Well, I can confirm for you that they are English and
that one of them is definitely a ship of war. If you take the
trouble to look, you'll see that the leading ship is of a much
lower build then a cargo ship would be. That's the way that
the English have started to build warships: they carry heavier
guns closer to the waterline so that they're not top heavy; it
also makes them lighter and faster. We still have the wind
advantage and, by altering course now, we can soon put them
behind us."

"That may be the Irish way," he replied, "it is not the

Spanish way. Any Spaniard is worth at least two Englishmen and, when we board them, they will not resist us." And so saying, he turned pointedly away, making an end to the discussion.

"The bloody, bloody fool," thought Grace to herself. Her instinct was to turn and leave him to his own devices but she knew that she could not. Despite herself, she was being dragged into an action from which she could see no gain. Even if they should capture one or both of the oncoming ships, she had no use for such a vessel in and around Clew Bay. She supposed, morosely, that she could sell it to the Spanish. Either way, she did not wish to bring the English Navy down on her. She was not, after all, sailing as a national galley, only as plain Grace O'Malley, for Grace O'Malley's own profit and that of her followers.

The Marquesa was heading directly for the English ships, for that was what their colours, now visible, confirmed them to be. Don Diego had already hoisted Spanish colours, thus giving away any element of surprise they might have had. With a sigh of resignation, Grace ordered Spanish colours to be hoisted on the Dana as well. Let the Spanish take the blame for what was about to ensue. Then, rather than follow the Marquesa directly, she had Thomas ease back on to their earlier course so that they would still have the wind advantage. The weather, which had been excellent since they left Corunna, continued so. It was almost as though the sea gods, having treated them so ill on their outward voyage, were now making up for that ill usage.

She decided, and Thomas agreed, that it was unlikely to change for some while yet. A storm blowing up at this time would have been disastrous, conferring all the advantages on the English ships. As things stood however, the galleys had a definite edge, if Don Diego did not choose to squander it.

There were now a couple of cables between the Dana and the Marquesa as their courses diverged, but the English ships still remained together, heading directly for the galliot.

Judging that she still had plenty of time to do so, Grace ordered hot food served before the ovens were shut down. She then called the crew aft and addressed them:

"It wasn't my intent to seek battle today. Our priority is to bring our cargo to Captain Fitzmaurice and get our treasure back from him. However, our Spanish friend," she jerked a thumb towards the galliot, "has seen fit to go treasure hunting himself and left us with little choice but to follow, since we don't know how Captain Fitzmaurice will respond if we turn up without him. There's no point in subterfuge today. We'll let the English know from the outset how strong we are: it may make them cautious. We'll have to see whether they stay together or separate, and plan accordingly, but what ever they decide I intend to stay to windward of them. The state of the sea is to our advantage so, as we get closer, we'll probably drop sail and proceed under oars to increase our maneuverability, but I'll decide that as we see how things develop. I'd guess that they'll be armed with six or nine pounder cannon, and I intend that we engage them with our big guns until they are close enough to open fire themselves. I want round shot to begin with, and then, when they're within range, grape and chain for their rigging. You can judge that for yourself, Fabrizio," she said to the gunner. "I want all the patereros loaded with grape in case we board, but, as I said, we'll have to tailor our plans to theirs to a certain extent. May God be with you all, now."

All this time the two pairs of ships had been getting closer and now, suddenly, the English ships had grown in size sufficiently for it to be discernible that they were both warships. They had evidently spied the Spanish flags and were now themselves preparing for battle. It was also obvious that the larger one had begun to turn towards the Dana, leaving her consort to do battle with the Marquesa. Grace asked James to bless them all and they knelt down while he did so, not without some feelings of ambivalence: they were about to do battle with his own countrymen. When

196

he had finished, the crew went to their stations, a murmuring of anticipation running through the galley.

The great guns were loaded from the ready ammunition pile and fresh ammunition and powder were brought up from the magazine in the aft hold. The oars were made ready for shipping at instant notice and, after some soul-searching, Grace ordered the skiffs lowered to be towed aft. This, she knew, would slow the galley slightly, but that was preferable to the hail of splinters which would result if either was hit by round shot.

It was soon quite obvious that, even with the skiffs acting as a drag astern, they had the legs of the ship and Grace now maneuvered the Dana so that they were well up wind of it, forcing it, in turn, to lie as close as it could to the wind to try to get nearer. This meant that while their opponents presented only a small head on target to them, they presented the same to their opponents, the difference being that while all of the Dana's heavy guns pointed directly forward, those of Englishmen did not, other than for a few small bow mounted guns which had a much lesser range than those of the Dana. To fire his main armament, the Englishman would have to either luff or tack completely, either evolution making him a much larger target.

Grace's course had taken them about half a mile from the Marquesa which, on its direct course, had now come within range of its opponent and had commenced firing, its rate of fire, however, being sadly less than Grace would have judged acceptable. Nevertheless, there was as yet no response from the Englishman, the range still being too great for its smaller guns. Grace could see that he was taking damage, but the distance was too great for her to tell how serious. "Well," she thought, "the Spaniard has chosen this battle, and though I wouldn't wish ill on him, he's going to have to fend for himself until I've dealt with my own man."

With a last glance around the horizon to make sure that there were no other sails in sight, she turned her attention back to deal with this opponent, who was fast coming into range. She ordered the sails taken in and the oars shipped. The transition from sail to oar was accomplished smoothly, the momentum of the galley driving it forward while the oars began to bite. Long before this, Tibbott had been brought down from his lookout position and she now sent him into the cabin where James and the barber were preparing their grisly instruments. She sent word forward to Fabrizio to fire in his own time while she kept the galley exactly in line with the ship. When he judged that they were well within extreme range, and he was satisfied with his aim, he pulled the lanyard to fire the 24 pounder, the shock of the recoil appearing to almost stop the boat in its progress. With no sails to impede the view, Grace could see the ball fall just to port of the ship. The gunners set about reloading; the 18 pounders were still outside what Fabrizio would have considered effective range so he was concentrating on the 24 pounder. Grace forced herself to appear calm although she was inwardly seething at the time being taken to reload. She might have shouted to hurry up, but she had complete faith, born of experience, in her Italian gunner. She curbed her impatience until the gun was ready again. Once again the gunner bent over his gunsight, signalling minute changes of direction to Grace until he was satisfied with his aim. The gun exploded again, and this time they saw the 24 pounder ball hit the Englishman directly on the bows, ploughing through it's timbers and causing what Grace hoped was great damage as it travelled the length of the ship. There was a cheer on the Dana, instantly suppressed by Grace, who wanted silence so that she could communicate with the guns. Fabrizio now fired his 18 pounders and was rewarded with another hit. Grace had deliberately kept their speed quite low. She wanted to maintain the advantage of her big guns for as long as possible by keeping the Englishman at arm's length. She also wanted to conserve the strength of her oarsmen for the flat out effort that she knew would soon be necessary.

Furthermore, she was quite happy to have the Dana shrouded in her own gunsmoke: it would mask their intentions, she hoped. She warned Rory now that, on her command, she would want the rate increased to maximum effort. They got off one more salvo, the lumps of wood being visibly knocked from the Englishman's hull. She imagined the carnage being wreaked along her decks, both by the balls and the flying splinters. She almost admired the way that the English captain stuck doggedly to his task. Soon, she could feel him thinking, it will be my turn. Not if I can help it, was her thought.

She called to the gunner for grape and chain and warned Rory to be ready. The Englishmen fired his bow guns, miniscule items compared to the Dana's, but lethal for all that, one ball taking the hand off one of the Dana's sailors, and another shattering some oars, causing momentary confusion before they were replaced. Grace watched her opponent attentively. Soon, she knew, he would turn to bring his broadside to bear and, at the rate at which they were closing, this would be at a range that would be deadly to the Dana's frail timbers.

She saw the sailors man the sheets and, from the slightest shiver in the Englishman's sails, she decided he was going to tack rather than wear.

"Now!" She roared at Rory. He passed the command on to the oarmaster who began to up the rate so that the galley surged forward, picking up speed by the moment.

The English ship began its ponderous turn. Grace waited and waited until she was sure that it was fully committed. Then she put the tiller hard over so that the Dana began to turn in the opposite direction. Perceiving what she was about, the English captain fired, but he was too late, the whole port broadside, except for the ball from his aftermost gun, passing harmlessly astern of the Dana to splash in the sea. The one shot on target passed through the wall of the cabin under Grace's feet. She shouted down to make sure they were all right. Tibbott called back that Father James had been grazed in the head by some flying wood but that Phelim could attend to it.

"Let's hope you've taught him well, James," she thought anxiously to herself.

Meanwhile, the English captain was trying to correct his mistake by bringing his ship back onto its original course, but the turn had gone too far and his efforts only succeeded in having him taken aback so that, for the moment, he wallowed helplessly. Having gone past the ship, Grace now put her helm to the opposite side, and the Dana swept around again in a long beautiful curve which left her facing the Englishman's aft starboard quarter, just beyond the arc of fire of its starboard broadside. From high on its poop deck, Grace could see a man staring down at the Dana, her captain she presumed, and then he was obliterated by the explosion of grape and chain from the Dana's guns at point blank range. Fabrizio immediately got on with the methodical reloading of his guns, and, as the smoke cleared, she could see that the English ship was badly wounded, her rigging in tatters and her sails flapping uselessly, although her masts appeared undamaged. She even imagined that she could see blood running from the scuppers. Slowly, she saw men picking themselves up and looking dazedly around. Judging that they were safe to leave for the moment, she turned the galley towards where the Marquesa and its opponent were locked in mortal battle.

As they got closer, they could see that Don Diego had rammed the other ship and that the Spaniards were trying to board, using the ram as a bridge. For the moment, the English were holding their own. The sea between the two vessels was awash with bodies. Over all of the noise of clashing swords and pikes and the discharge of musket and arquebus could be heard the wailing, the shrieking, of the slaves. The reason for this shrieking was that the galliot had obviously been hard hit by the English gunnery and now appeared to be settling in the water. Taking all of this in at a glance, Grace steered for the unengaged side of the ship and, with the oars backing water, hailed it, demanding its immediate surrender. A single musket was discharged, harmlessly, and then the English flag was lowered.

Grace sent Donal with a party of boarders in the two skiffs to take possession. As they clambered up over the side, they were met by a bloodied Spaniard who greeted them formally before subsiding on to the deck in exhaustion. The remaining English crewmen were bundled, as prisoners, down in to the hold which was then securely battened over them, after which Donal hailed Grace to inform her that their prize was secure. She brought the Dana slowly round to the other side of the ship where, close-up, the scale of the carnage was horrifyingly clear. The bodies in the water were mostly Spanish. Although she could not see on to the English deck, she assumed that there must be as many bodies there, both from the cannonade and the small arms fire.

"Grace?" She turned to find James at her side. His head was bandaged but still copiously covered in the blood which was oozing from under the bandage.

"My God, James, are you all right?"

"Yes. Absolutely. It's merely a scalp wound. They always bleed profusely, and when I have time I'll get Phelim to suture it for me. But, firstly, I believe I'm needed on the Marquesa. May I have a skiff?"

"Of course, of course."

She called to Donal to return one of the skiffs and then had it tied alongside while James quickly gathered a bag of instruments together. He went down the stern ladder and was quickly transported to the galliot.

What met him was a shambles that might have daunted another man, but to a veteran of Lepanto and numerous lesser battles, it was not as harrowing as it would have been to someone coming upon such a scene for the first time. He quickly confirmed that the galliot was sinking, slowly but irrevocably: it was beyond repair, and he quickly called out as much to Grace, giving an estimate of two hours at the most before it went under.

"You'll have to do what you can in that time," Grace called back. "Donal will assist in whatever way he can." Donal acknowledged this with a wave from the deck of the ship.

"I have to return to the other Englishman before he effects sufficient repairs to get under way again and make a nuisance of himself."

She ordered the oarsmen to start pulling again and put the Dana about to return to their first opponent. She could see that the crew of that ship were working frantically, knotting and splicing to get the rigging sufficiently serviceable to be able to get moving again. They had not lost their teeth either, as was evidenced by the firing of two cannon from the stern, which, although causing no damage, forced Grace to alter course to avoid them, delaying the Dana and causing her to curse with the freedom that she had been subconsciously keeping in check while James was around. She smiled briefly at the revelation while she reassessed the situation. The effects of wind and tide on the Englishman's hull were causing it to slowly rotate in a manner that she found annoying because it meant that she could not lie to off one of its unprotected quarters, since one or other of its guns was always swinging into an arc of fire which would contain the Dana.

She concluded that she would not be able to force the surrender of this ship as quickly as she wished so, accepting the inevitable, she had the Dana lie to, just beyond the range of the English guns, got Fabrizio to unload his cannon of the grape and chain with which they had been loaded, and reload with ball. She then commenced a slow but deadly cannonade on her helpless adversary. All work ceased on the Englishman as her remaining crew took shelter from the relentless battering and, sooner than Grace had hoped (she was well aware of the resoluteness of English sailors against impossible odds) the English colours were struck down.

She sent another, larger prize crew onto this vessel and, when they had quickly secured it, (more than half the crew had been killed or wounded by the Dana's guns, including the captain and his first officer, and the remainder were too exhausted to resist) she sent the carpenter after them, with his mates, to make whatever temporary repairs would be necessary to get the ship under way again. Her sails and rigging would have to wait until she could spare Donal from the other ship. She then returned to the Marquesa.

When the Dana had left, James, as a first priority, had made a quick tour of both vessels to assess who, of the two crews, were most in need of medical attention. Accompanied by the cries of the slaves, for whom he could do nothing for the moment, he now moved up and down the platforms of the galliot, getting the few remaining able-bodied members of its crew to move the wounded on to the prize. These included Don Diego, who was found bleeding heavily from a leg wound, pale and unconscious, lying across one of the rowing benches on the bodies of the three dead slaves who had previously been the oarsmen on that bench. The master had not been so lucky. He lay dead beside his helm, the same taciturn expression that he had always shown in life still expressed on his face in death. The lieutenant and corporal of the infantry were also dead, and the senior surviving unwounded soldier or sailor left on the galliot seemed to be the sergeant. It was he who now commanded the other able-bodied survivors, under James's supervision, in the moving of the wounded. If he had any qualms about taking orders from an English priest, he did not show them. On the contrary, with that special inate discipline that most long serving NCOs seem to acquire, he appeared to accept James as being their natural commander and, having been given his instructions, carried them out efficiently and with a minimum of fuss.

When the wounded had all been transferred, James said a brief prayer over the bodies of the dead, English and Spanish alike, and had them dropped overboard. Whatever anxiety that this may have caused (all sailors hope that if they die at sea, they will be properly shrouded and buried with a weight of some sort to bring them to the bottom), it was accepted by all as regretfully necessary, given the overcrowded state of the prize, with prisoners below and survivors littering the decks. Even as he tended the wounded, he was considering the position of the slaves, whose increasing, and increasingly piteous, cries for mercy had not ceased. He had Donal remove all of the light weaponry from the galliot and the patereros loaded and mounted on the prize and then aimed at the galliot. This caused even more howling from the slaves, who pulled and tugged frantically at their chains. He addressed them, shouting to make himself heard. They were going to be freed, and they would have the use of the two skiffs, Donal's and the galliot's own which, being towed astern, had hardly been damaged. But, if they made any attempt to board the ship, he would kill them all. This was all in Arabic, and those of the slaves who had been present at the capture of the galliot and who had seen James, first fighting implacably, and then tending the wounded, Christian and Arab alike without discrimination, understood him to mean what he said, as he had intended. The sergeant had listened to this exchange with a frown of incomprehension on his face. James now translated the gist of his message and the incomprehension changed quickly to defiant refusal. He would not be party to saving the lives of infidels but, if they were going to save them, it should be as prisoners for the head money. James patiently pointed out that, apart from there being no room for prisoners, many of the slaves were Spanish, all criminals of one sort or another no doubt, but still Spanish and besides, they could not possibly cause trouble, adrift in the Atlantic in a couple of skiffs. He doubted, in fact, that they would survive in the skiffs, but he could not condemn them to be drowned like rats, chained to their benches when the galliot sank. The sergeant appeared to accept the logic of this and did not interfere when James asked Donal to take the keys of the locks from the wounded slave master and give them to the nearest slave. Donal did this, stepping out along the ram and back again. James then had all the able-bodied men, Irish and Spanish, use the prize's sweeps to push the galliot away from them, no easy task, taking into account the considerable extra weight of seawater that had already seeped in to it. The effect on the prize, when freed of the dead weight of the Marquesa, was immediate and, unburdened, it began to drift away so that, quite quickly, there was clear water between the two vessels. As an afterthought, James called out that if any of the slaves were not freed by their brothers, he would open fire on them all and sink the skiffs as well.

Feeling that he could do no more for the slaves, he reapplied his whole attention to treating the wounded. As he worked, he got the sergeant to relate what had happened and the sergeant, who had accepted the situation and bore no ill will, proceeded to do so, succinctly and unemotionally as if making a report to a senior officer, in which position he now appeared to view James.

They had attacked the Englishman directly without preliminary maneuvering. They had fired their cannon but, even though they hit the Englishman, they had only managed to get away two shots before they were themselves within range of the Englishman. He now opened fire, and although he had smaller cannon, he had more of them and they were served more quickly. The galliot began to take damage, but still they kept on. They were under oars by now and moving as quickly as the sergeant could ever remember moving under oars. They took the last broadside at point-blank range but it was hurriedly fired. Had the Englishman fully depressed his guns, he must have blown the hull wide open. As it was, the galliot was hulled by at least two balls and the rest of the broadside severely mauled them, breaking oars and killing and injuring more than they could afford. The Englishman however, in the mistaken belief that he would sink them before they got close, had held his course until it was too late to get out of the way of the stricken galliot which, with a last desperate spurt of rowing, had rammed him as the Father had seen. Don Diego, who had been standing in the bows, oblivious to danger, now called for them to charge, but the Englishman discharged a final volley from his swivels which took down not only Don Diego, but about half of the attackers as well. He, the sergeant, had succeeded in getting on to the Englishman's deck, from which he was briefly in danger of being driven back, but he had been followed by others and they had managed to gain a foothold. The fighting was hard and he thought they might well have been defeated had the Senora not arrived when she did. As it was, he shrugged eloquently to indicate what the cost of the victory had been to both sides.

James could easily imagine the horror that lay behind that laconically told tale: the slashing and thrusting of a close quarters sea fight, the screams of violence and of pain, the evisceration of bellies by twisting pikes, the breaking of limbs and skulls and the utter frenzy to kill before one was oneself killed, the bloodlust raging and no quarter asked or given. He gave an involuntary shudder, thankful that he had not been involved, other than as an observer. It was well known that the Spanish infantryman was the best in Europe, despite being so ill served by his officers. That this was so, was amply demonstrated by this brief battle. He could not readily bring to mind any other soldiers who, leaderless, would have carried on fighting as these had, although, of course, their ship was sinking under them at the time and there was no great choice open to them. That they might have surrendered did not seem to have been a consideration. How different the outcome in terms of casualties might have been if the Marquesa had been fought as the Dana had been fought, wresting every last advantage from wind and sea to achieve the same result but with minimal damage. As it was, the galliot was lost with gross wastage of life.

He looked up at this thought and glanced over to where the galliot was now awash. All of the slaves appeared to have been freed, but there were as many wounded among them as there had been among the Spaniards: English guns did not distinguish between soldiers and slaves. Their only hope was that Grace might be able to pick them up, but he was certain that even that would be too late for most. Even as he glanced, the galliot slowly and finally subsided beneath the waves, the cries of the wounded who were dragged down with her being cut off on the instant. A couple of score of slaves had managed to get into the skiffs or were hanging on to the sides, surrounded by the bodies of the dead as they bobbed up and down on the swell. He blessed himself and got on with his task.

The ship's rigging had not been remotely as badly cut up as had her consort's but, without the carpenter or his own mates, there was not a lot that Donal could do to repair the damage that had been done. In the meantime, he busied himself with the gaping hole in the ship's side caused by the galliot's ram, which was, fortunately, above the waterline and was of little consequence so long as a swell did not get up. The only immediate threat it posed was that the prisoners might just conceivably climb out through it and rush the deck. To prevent this, and for the tidiness that his seaman's mind required, he had a spare sail dragged up from below and set the men to fothering it, not an easy task. To begin with, one of the men had to climb out onto the bowsprit and loop a corner of the sail under it so that the sail could then be dragged under the ship by ropes brought up on each side. As soon as the sail went below the bows of the ship and under the water, it became immensely heavy and it took all of them to drag it back, laboureously passing the ropes outboard of the various stays until it was positioned level with the hole. It then had to be adjusted so that the hole was covered before being made fast, the final attachments being to the main mast. When the Dana returned, they could use its skiff to cover the sail in pitch to make it more watertight, and they would also be able to bulk it up on the inside. This latter task would certainly have to wait until he had more men because the English prisoners would by now have got over the first morale sapping inertia of their defeat and would be looking to turn the tables on their captors at the first opportunity.

Eventually the Dana returned and Grace came up the side. She approved Donal's activities and brought some more men across to oversee the prisoners, allowing him and his men to get on with finishing the repair of the hole. She then went to see how James was getting on with the wounded.

He had taken over the captain's cabin, which was the most light and airy accommodation on the ship, and was methodically working his way through his list of wounded, assisted by a young Spanish soldier who the sergeant, who was proving invaluably competent, had selected as being the only survivor with the delicacy of touch to be of any use. This did seem to be the case and, although his pallor was as grave as that of any of their patients, he was not flinching from the task. This work was itself no more shocking than seeing the bodies pile up in battle but, whereas the heat of battle shut the mind to all else, the same could not be said of this cold-blooded sawing, sewing and bandaging. Grace pursed her lips at the paucity of survivors from either side.

"God bless the work, James," she said. "I don't believe I've ever seen worse than this for a bloody little battle."

"No," agreed James. "There are, of course, prisoners in the hold, but I'd guess that both sides have suffered well over sixty per cent of casualties. I don't speak of the slaves on the Marquesa, whose casualty rate must have been even greater. You'll have seen their survivors in the skiffs. The wounded had no chance at all and, even though I ordered all to be freed, only the able-bodied got away before the galliot went down."

"Yes. I've sent our remaining skiff to look for survivors in the water. I'll have to think about what to do with them when we've finished the repairs. The Dana will be quite shorthanded when we've crewed the two prizes and I suppose we could put some of the slaves on the benches, the Moors only of course: any Christians can join with us, or they can stay with the Spaniards on this ship."

She turned to the sergeant to congratulate him on his success in boarding unscathed, and for being of such assistance to James. He bowed formally in acknowledgement and, in turn, thanked the Senora for her assistance and for providing the Father for his men. She then did a quick headcount which confirmed that, of his men, only seven sailors and six soldiers remained capable of bearing arms. "As bloody a little battle as I've seen," she repeated to herself. James interrupted her thoughts.

"Don Diego was the only surviving officer." He indicated the still unconscious Captain lying amongst the already treated wounded. Don Diego's right thigh was heavily bandaged, his breeches cut away. "He's been very lucky. He was right at the front when the swivels were fired and the one ball he took could have broken a bone or severed the femoral artery but did neither. He's lost a great amount of blood from the wound but I'm certain that he'll survive and that he'll probably even keep his leg, with God's blessing."

Donal came up from the hold to report that the hole had been plugged to the best of their capabilities with the available materials, and that the prisoners, who had been gathered in the bows under guard while the repairs proceeded, had been returned to the hold, which was now battened down again.

Grace turned her attention to the two skiffs with the slaves again. She called across to them, ordering them to row over to the ship and reminding them, if they needed reminding, that she could sink them at a moment's notice if they provoked her in any way. Under the watchful eye of the Dana, which had all of its patereros loaded and manned, as were those of the prize, she allowed the slaves on board, one skiff at a time. To her query as to whether any of them were Christian, she was surprised to find virtually all of them clamouring to claim that distinction. She looked at the sergeant who was exhibiting frank scepticism. She sighed and told him to examine them and then turned her back has he ordered them, in Spanish, to undo their breeches to discover who of them had been circumcised, and who not. He quickly confirmed that all had been and, to the protests of those who claimed that they had been forced, he merely shrugged, "Renegadoes. Lucky not to be hanged."

They were all ordered back into the skiff and the process was repeated with the slaves from the second skiff and this time two Christians were discovered, or at least, two who could show that they were not renegades, forced or not. She gave these two over to the sergeant who took them somewhat contemptuously, commenting that they were obviously criminals, jailbirds. Grace's very sharp reply to this was that they were Christians, were no longer on Spanish soil and were now subject to her orders, not Spain's as, she reminded the sergeant, he himself was. "Of course, Senora," was his reply, keeping well hidden whatever his true feelings might have been on this turn of events.

She called down to Thomas that he was to take the remaining slaves on board, one skiff at a time and chain them to the benches. When this was done, she had a cable passed from the prize to the Dana and the slaves had their first experience of rowing in their new quarters, a hard one, albeit it was shared by the crew of the Dana, as they took the prize in tow and slowly pulled it to bring it alongside the second prize.

For a small few of the slaves, this was their second sojourn on the Dana, and when Grace ordered the ovens relit, and hot food prepared, they were able to inform their fellows that they would share the same food as the crew, a most unusual occurrence, although it would, of course, be infidel food. But, hopefully, Allah would understand. The food situation on the Dana had, in fact, been greatly improved by the capture of the two ships. These appeared to have been outward bound and were fully laden, not only with barrels of salted rations, but with fresh food as well, so that the threat of short commons could be put aside for another few days at least.

The repairs on the first prize were completed just before nightfall. The three vessels then lay to overnight and, at dawn the following day, repairs commenced on the lesser damage to the second prize. James had worked unceasingly throughout all the comings and goings of the previous day and, after a brief exhausted sleep, had now relieved Phelim and Tibbott, whom Grace had left on the first prize. He was happily surprised at what he found. Two amputations had been left for him, but all of the other casualties, including the unfortunate Dana who had lost his hand, had been properly treated, and even if some of the bandaging looked somewhat clumsy, it was effective. Certainly, their patients were appreciative of their efforts. The two amputations having been completed and, at this very early stage, showing every sign of being successful, James finally had Phelim see to his own gashed scalp. Phelim was quite reluctant, not wishing to be the man who made a botch of the Father's head, but was finally persuaded to it for, as James pointed out, even if by any chance it was not the neatest bit of work, his hair would grow over it again, and nobody would ever know the difference. Accordingly, the now grimy bandage was removed, the head shaved, the wound cleaned and the sutures placed to bring both sides of the gash together. It was then re-bandaged. James sat quite stoically throughout the procedure. It was not particularly painful, as he had finally persuaded Phelim, the scalp being less endowed with feeling than most other parts of the body's covering.

He had an attentive audience. It was obviously not like having Finian Burke's brains exposed, but it was a satisfactorily bloody procedure, it was being performed on their own priest/surgeon and, besides, it was a comfort to all to see James entrusting his own head to Phelim O'Connor. Who among them could say that he too might not need similar attention in future, and to have that treatment provided by a competent, optimistic Phelim O'Connor rather than a reluctant one would be a blessing.

When James returned to the other ship, he found Don Diego awake and being fed thin gruel by the sergeant, a somewhat incongruous sight. He suppressed the smile that he could feel trying to creep onto his face and, with a properly grave demeanour, first congratulated Don Diego on commanding such fine men as the sergeant, and then enquired how he felt. The sergeant was as impassive as ever. Don Diego, however, looked sharply at James, suspecting insincerity, but was reassured by James's solicitous expression.

"I owe you thanks, it seems. Sergeant Quevedo tells me that I looked as though I might have bled to death without your attention. He also tells me that you treated our men as well as your own English compatriots, without distinguishing between us."

"It's the teaching of the Knights that all sick and wounded are treated equally. Even the Moors, whom the Knights kill with abandon, once they are wounded, are cared for as God's children, even if misguided children. Had we been in a position to do so, I would've treated those poor devils on the Marquesa as well, but it sank before we could do anything for them."

"So, I'm not to flatter myself that you made any special effort on my part," said Don Diego, with just the tiniest hint of his cynical smile on his pallid face. "Nevertheless, I can't consider that things remain unchanged between us. Sergeant

Quevedo also tells me how you took command of the situation regarding the slaves. I can't truthfully say that the fate of Moorish slaves concerns me greatly, but I respect your view and wouldn't condemn it. It does confirm what I'd begun to suspect after I recovered consciousness and heard of your activities, that you're too honourable a man to have been guilty of the cowardly attack which was how your affair in Corunna was being presented." James bowed without showing the slightest hint of the irony he was feeling as Don Diego continued, "so what I wish to say is that I totally withdraw any aspersions I cast on your character and apologise unreservedly for them and, if you're agreeable, I'd be honoured to share your friendship."

He held out his hand and James took it briefly, declaring himself the more honoured. This touching reconciliation was rudely interrupted by Grace. She kept her voice low out of consideration for the other patients but this in no way lessened the cold, barely contained fury which underlay what she had to say to Don Diego.

"I suppose I should say how glad I am to see that you've survived your gross stupidity but, in truth, I wouldn't care had you been killed. It would've been no more than you deserved. You're a liability Sir, a vain, arrogant, foolish liability. Your actions, which I conceive to have been motivated by no more than base greed, have led to the unnecessary deaths of many good men and the loss of your ship. You've also jeopardised a mission to which you declared yourself fully committed." He tried to interrupt her but she waved him down and continued: "Fitzmaurice is awaiting your arrival in Ireland with reinforcements and arms to start on a venture which I've always thought ill judged, but whose possible success is now even less likely because of your selfishness. We've been lucky enough to have taken two prizes, but they won't replace the men you've so wantonly lost. Indeed, they've possibly made things even more difficult, because we now have prisoners, and more

213

manpower will be lost guarding those prisoners. Oh, what's the use? You sicken me, sir, with your airs and graces and grand Spanish notions of honour, but you're just as venal as those you profess to despise."

She turned and stalked from the cabin, leaving a deathly silence behind her. Even with her voice kept low, what she had had to say to Don Diego had shocked everyone else in the crowded cabin, even the English patients who, though they did not understand the Spanish in which it was spoken, could not mistake the import of the words.

Don Diego had, if possible, become even more white of face. "If she were a man, by God," he started, and then slumped back. "She's right, of course," he all but whispered, "I have been headstrong, and though I judged my actions pure, as being to the greater glory of Spanish arms, I find that there's now a thread of doubt in my mind that I acted for myself as much as for Spain."

"You're very low at the moment," James told him. "You've lost a lot of blood, you're in pain and you're feeling the inevitable anticlimactic depression that most soldiers feel after battle. But try to feel positive: you'll heal much more quickly if you do and you'll doubtless find your natural arrogance returning before you know it." He smiled to indicate that this was to be taken as a witticism, but the Spaniard looked only more downcast.

"And what about you, sergeant, what do you think?"

If the sergeant was surprised at being asked by his captain for a character reference, he did not show it. "We saw the enemy and we attacked them directly, as is our duty, Sir," was as much as he would comment.

"You see, Father, why sergeants are the backbone of the army? They take their orders and act upon them, as good discipline demands. They don't distract themselves with the scruples with which you and I might be burdened. I believe that I'll follow that example in future, certainly until I become a General," he smiled weakly, "though taking orders from a woman, no matter how battle hardened, is a trial. Still, that situation won't last much longer."

"You'll soon be your old self," thought James privately, "I only hope that you don't resent us all, particularly your good sergeant, for this display of weakness in front of us."

He excused himself to attend to his other patients.

On deck, now that they had the men with the necessary skills at hand, repairs were proceeding quickly and, by mid afternoon, they were ready to resume their interrupted voyage. Donal remained in charge of one of the prizes and Grace put Thomas in charge of the other. Both prize crews were galley men with limited experience of ship sailing but, short of letting some of their captives free to assist, that was a problem that they would have to overcome themselves. It did mean that their progress would be significantly slower with the limited sail plans of which they would be capable until they, literally, got to know their ropes, but they were sailors and they would make the best of their situation.

Before they set off, Grace called all of her officers on to the Dana to outline her order of sailing. Thomas would lead the way and, as ever, be responsible for navigation. She would have preferred him on the Dana, but he had the most experience of any of her officers of ship management so, perforce, must stay on one of the prizes. Donal would follow and Grace would bring up the rear, to windward of the other two. It was hoped to complete the journey without being brought to further action, but if they did meet other English ships of equal or greater force, and there was a likelihood of battle, she would take off the prize crews and any able-bodied Spaniards and, possibly, only possibly, Don Diego and the other Spanish wounded as well before, as a last resort, abandoning the prizes. She did not have to say, they knew her well enough, that this would be a very last resort.

They returned to their posts and made ready to set sail, the officers of the prizes being powerfully motivated to get to grips with their vessels without delay. The prospect of losing the prizes was anathema to them, all of them, officers and men, having worked out to the last coin what their share of the prizes would be when sold. James remained with Donal, and Tibbott and Phelim with Thomas. The masthead of Thomas's vessel being higher than that of the Dana, Tibbott was, as soon as his medical duties allowed, sent up to it to be the lookout for the little flotilla.

Night fell, but instead of lying to, they continued northwest with lanterns lit. In the light winds prevailing, the somewhat clumsily handled prizes were only making two to three knots and Grace thought that speed safe enough for them to risk continuing in the dark. With morning came a cold drizzling rain that persisted all day long. The prize crews, with the accommodation available to them, were hardly inconvenienced and were the subject of some envy from the crew of the galley, who huddled in what shelter they could find under their quickly sodden blankets and cloaks, their only comfort being that their new slaves had it even worse, there being no cover at all for them. This was small consolation however, and, as the day wore on, the sea began to rise and there was then no consolation at all, as the slow moving galley, its speed dictated by that of the ships, began to plunge and wallow more than it would normally have done, so that they then had to contend with spray as well as rain, and with even the occasional wave breaking over them. Visibility was much reduced, which was a double-edged sword: enemy ships would not be able to see them, but neither would they be able to see enemy ships until they were virtually on top of each other. Grace offered a silent prayer that this would not be so, and found herself wishing that James were nearby so that he could offer a more official prayer, as it were.

The day dragged miserably on until Grace had to consider whether to carry on in the murk or lie to. Fortunately, the weather at that point began to clear. The rain stopped and they began to see the odd star through the thinning clouds.

She decided to keep going. The sea was still rough but not showing signs of increasing. She felt it to be the remnant of a great storm out in the Atlantic rather than a fresh storm brewing. Before the light went entirely, she brought the galley up beside Thomas to check that his reckoning of their position agreed with her own and he confirmed that, all things being equal, they would raise Ireland on the next day. This proved to be the case and, having made their landfall, Grace ordered their course reset to keep them just barely in sight of land from the masthead as they made their way west along the coast of Munster towards their rendezvous with Fitzmaurice in Dingle Bay.

Grace was very mindful of what Tom Butler had told her about the rumours of rebellion. These rumours had been more than confirmed in Corunna and Grace, being on the one hand well aware of the reach of Walsingham's intelligence network, and on the other of the inability of any her own countrymen to keep a secret, was more than a little worried that she might encounter English warships patrolling the Irish coast, or reinforcing the garrisons along that coast. Youghal and Cork were well behind them but Baltimore had still to be passed, and although there was little to fear from the O'Driscolls themselves after their recent distress at her own hands, they had, in the past, been friends to the English, and might well be again. But the miles passed slowly by until eventually they were beyond O'Driscoll territory also and then, with some relief, were heading north past the territory of the O'Sullivan Beare, past the Skelligs and finally in to Dingle Bay. Night was now approaching so, with the caution that had kept her alive through a lifetime of seafaring, Grace decided that they should anchor in the Bay rather than be unpleasantly surprised in Dingle itself, although, from what she had gleaned from the solitary fishermen that they had thus far encountered, the land was still at peace

CHAPTER 19

Dawn of the following day found the Dana moving slowly under oars into Dingle. The two prizes had been left at anchor until signalled that it was safe to follow, but with a warning that, in the event of trouble, they were to cut their cables and run for the open sea, making their own way to Clew Bay. As they got closer, it became apparent that the harbour was empty, save only for some small coastal craft and some fishing boats. Grace had the patereros loaded as a precaution, and then went ashore in the skiff, wondering whether Fitzmaurice was somehow still at sea or had already been captured. The news, however, was reassuring. Fitzmaurice was just across the peninsula in Smerwick, whither he had gone after touching briefly in Dingle. The other news from Dingle was that the English fleet, under Winter, was known to be at large. There was not a moment to lose in getting to sea again.

Gathering the two prizes on her way, she set off around the end of the peninsula and, after threading her way through the Blaskets, arrived that evening in Smerwick where she was warmly welcomed by the waiting Fitzmaurice. He had watched them from afar, and was impatience itself to hear what had happened to them. He had noted the absence of the Marquesa but could see the two ships in her place, and initially had been unable to decide whether or not the Dana was being pursued or if the two ships were friendly, deciding finally that they must, indeed, have been friendly, given the leisurely nature of the Dana's progress.

Grace quickly brought him up to date with her news, not neglecting to criticise roundly the actions of Don Diego who, although responsible in part for the prizes, by being the cause of the fight in which they were taken, had nevertheless

218

endangered them all and had lost, by death or wounding, the greater part of his small force. While sympathising with her, Fitzmaurice proclaimed that they would shortly have so great a force that the Spaniards' loss, though sad, would not be of great consequence. Besides, he pointed out, Grace had won for herself two fine prizes. Grace did, indeed, have two fat prizes and she was very pleased with the way their crews had mastered the sailing of them in the few short days since their capture. They would never out sail a well drilled crew, but that was not necessary. They simply had to get them to Clew Bay intact where she could make plans to dispose of them, and she did not doubt her men's competence to do that. Accordingly, she arranged with Fitzmaurice that she would land the soldiers and the wounded to be cared for by his Spaniards, and then send the two prizes on their way without waiting for her. To her great relief, he also accepted the English wounded and their unwounded imprisoned compatriots, reasoning that, although no senior officers from either ship had survived, the men who did would have some small value as hostages, if at any time he needed to bargain with an English fleet or army. He was also a sufficiently fair man to still regret Grace's treatment in Corunna by the Governor General and said as much, giving that as an equally strong reason for unburdening her of the prisoners. This task and the unloading of the munitions from the Dana were scheduled for first light on the following day and so the two ships were brought up to the small jetty in readiness for that purpose, the Dana lying at anchor in the harbour with the Arganya and the shallops, until the jetty was clear.

Fitzmaurice had placed his men in the old iron age fort at Smerwick, Dun an Oir, which they were using as a base, and from which he was sending out messengers all over Munster to call the Irish to arms. It was to this fort that he now invited Grace and her officers to dine and spend the evening, and in which she could fill in the details of their voyage. Grace set a strong watch on the Dana, as was their habit when they were

219

anchored anywhere outside Clew Bay, even in Ireland, she being fully aware, and secretly rather proud of the fact, that she had as many enemies as friends in her native country. They then joined Fitzmaurice in the fort.

The assembled company included Fitzmaurice's wife and children and various of his officers, as well as the captains of the Spanish troops from the shallops, and an Italian engineer, Captain Julian, skilled in defensive works, to whom Grace resolved to introduce Fabrizio on the morrow: he would enjoy conversing with another Italian, even if he would probably become very nostalgic afterwards, even tearful, her otherwise phlegmatic gunner. The company also included Don Diego, who had not been seen by Grace since her verbal lashing of him, but who was recovering remarkably well from his wound, even if restricted by having to use crutches. He was also well recovered in his humours, bowing as deeply to Grace as his crutches would allow and honouring her as his rescuer. Behind him, James, who had accompanied him, raised an eyebrow. Although Don Diego was the designated senior Spanish officer, it was apparent that he would lead no troops for quite some time, but he did not seem deflated by the fact, reacquainting himself with his fellow officers with just the right hint of superiority to demand their deference. Grace watched with some amusement, catching James's eye, but was happy to keep her amusement hidden, now that her journey was all but complete and it appeared that she would finally be rid of him.

James Fitzmaurice was a different man on his own territory. It was as if the nebulous dream for which he had travelled Europe for the past four years having finally become real, he had found himself again. Certainly, the bumbling lack of competence of which he had appeared to be guilty back in Corunna had quite disappeared. He was now strong and confident, moving and speaking with the quiet assurance of one totally in command of his destiny and the destiny of those he commanded. His disposition of his small invasion force met completely with Grace's approval. The earthworks of the old fort were being repaired and he had placed his lookouts very well indeed, even providing for intelligence from the Dingle side of the peninsula to be brought quickly by horse. More important were the messengers he had sent out to all those who he judged likely to join them, particularly John Fitzedmund Fitzgerald, John of Desmond, his old ally from the previous rebellion. He had also sent urgent exhortations to the earls of Desmond and Kildare, but it was Grace's opinion that Desmond would probably send his to Dublin, to warn them and to curry favour with the Castle.

Grace introduced James to the Papal Nuncio (they had not previously met because of James's absence in Santiago), and she went to converse with Fitzmaurice's wife Catherine.

The evening was a pleasant one, but there was a certain distractedness about the proceedings on the part of all the major participants, and Grace was not sorry when it came to an end. She wished her host a good night and then walked with James back to their quarters.

"What did you make of it?" was her opening question to James.

"A successful evening, I thought. Captain Fitzmaurice is a new man and the rest of his company seem eager and competent. This isn't the place for his wife however."

"I agree, she's much too gentle a person for this kind of undertaking, but she's here at her own insistence so she can't lack for backbone." She paused as if in contemplation of the virtues of Mistress Fitzmaurice before continuing, "and how did you get on with Father Sanders?"

"Another person who seems to be in the wrong place. He is altogether too unworldly. You know that he was given a banner by the Pope himself? He unfurled it in Dingle when they landed, and he then blessed the whole enterprise, committing all to what he thinks of as a Holy Crusade to oust Protestantism from Ireland. I worry that he considers that

that alone will suffice for success. He doesn't seem to understand the fighting that'll be required and the deaths and misery that will result, not to mention the upheaval that'll be suffered by the poor peasantry."

"You seem well enough informed, James."

"I am tolerably well informed, Grace, having spent the past few days having the Irish situation expounded to me at length by Donal, who's nothing if not enthusiastic on the subject. For instance, I know much more now about the rivalry between Ormond and Desmond and about the previous rebellion and the devastation that ensued. Hence my comment on the poor peasantry. He also explained how this inter-family rivalry is endemic throughout the country and that the invasion may be supported by some and opposed by others simply on clan alignments existing at this time."

"He's not wrong there," said Grace, "I'm afraid we're an unreliable race of people, changing allegiances at the drop of a hat, even at the turn of the tide. I've tried to tell Fitzmaurice but, sure, he knows it himself already, he just doesn't want to acknowledge it. He's convinced that if he can get up some momentum, the rebellion will gather in all and sundry as it speeds up. And he'll not accept that Desmond has no stomach for another rebellion. That cur has had too many setbacks in the past few years, and is perfectly happy at this stage to hang on to what your countrymen have seen fit to leave him. I can tell you that for fact, as you well know, having been handed over by him to Drury like a common criminal, just to boost his standing with Dublin Castle. Still, it's not our problem. Once we get our cargoes exchanged, we're away and they can sort it out for themselves."

"Have they any chance?"

"Of course they have. The people have very bitter memories of the way in which the last rebellion was put down, and lots will flock to Fitzmaurice, though not necessarily to Father Sanders, just for a chance of revenge and to settle old scores. It all depends upon how many. It also depends on who joins in on the other side and what way Tom Butler, for instance, will lean, though I imagine it will be on the side of the Crown. He's not a bad Irishman, you know, but he can't stomach Desmond any more than I can.

But, as I've said, it's not our fight. I'll watch what happens with some interest, and depending upon who looks like winning, I may well join in, particularly if there might be some profit in it for me."

"Are you that mercenary?" asked James, somewhat coldly.

"Not really. I just like to watch you react when you think I'm behaving badly. Happily, you're still just pompous enough an Englishman to take everything seriously."

She laughed, and clapping him on the back, wished him a good night, leaving him somewhat discomfited by his naivity with her.

Next morning, Grace was about early. The prizes were being unloaded of anything that might be of benefit to the invaders, and then she wanted them away before news of the landing spread sufficiently far to prompt investigation by Crown forces. The prizes had been hard won, she did not have the men to both sail and fight them, particularly so since they had lost the few Spaniards they had rescued, so she wanted them out of harm's way as quickly as possible. James was, at the same time, overseeing the transfer of the wounded ashore. He had slightly mixed feelings about this since both he, and his by now very competent assistants, Tibbott and Phelim, would be leaving with the Dana, meaning that the wounded would be reliant on whatever care Fitzmaurice could provide. Happily, Mrs. Fitzmaurice had volunteered to tend to the dressings. He had met her early in the day and, after speaking with her briefly, felt that Grace's assessment was correct: she would not break easily, which eased his conscience somewhat. They had buried seven more at sea in the very short time since the battle and now, from a coldly professional viewpoint, he thought that the wounded who had survived to Smerwick would all heal in time, given reasonable attention, good diet and dry surroundings. He said as much to Catherine Fitzmaurice as he committed them to her care, the first time that he had ever delegated nursing responsibilities to a woman, surprising himself as he did so, and reflecting again that Ireland seemed to produce a hardier version of the female sex than his own country.

The prizes set sail at about noon, and had hardly cleared the harbour before they were replaced by two galleys being rowed in which Grace, after a long hard look, declared to be the those of her kinsman by her first marriage to Donal na Cogaigh, the O'Flaherty's of Bunowen.

They rowed in to cheers from the assembled crowd. They were the first to respond of those to whom Fitzmaurice had written, and their arrival seemed the harbinger of great days to come. They recognised the Dana as surely as Grace had recognised them, and they responded with cheers of their own, and a certain amount of ribaldry directed towards Grace and their cousins who sailed with her.

"They're a little bit free and easy," said Grace to James in mock disapproval, "but you can be sure that tonight's feast will be noisier affair than last night's."

She went down to meet the O'Flaherty officers as they came ashore in their skiffs, being met by them with hugs and handshakes all round, before all went to meet Fitzmaurice. As they walked, their leader, Richard O'Flaherty, took Grace aside to express his surprise at finding her in the company, being aware of her feelings towards Desmond. She quickly outlined the situation for him with a particular dispassionateness, remarkable given her distaste for Desmond, and explained how she had been forced into assisting the invasion, but she was careful to say nothing that might adversely colour O'Flaherty's outlook: she had no desire to see Fitzmaurice fail. She recognised that, in truth, now that the great adventure had properly begun, she would actually like to see it succeed. However, O'Flaherty found her account disturbing, especially the loss of the Marquesa and her troops. She was able to allay his doubts marginally on this subject by telling him that the English Captain Stukeley was due at any time with the bulk of the invasion force, which was coming via Lisbon, where they were hoping to pick up extra troops from the King of Portugal. But it was a thoughtful O'Flaherty who finally shook hands with Fitzmaurice.

"I hope that Grace hasn't been trying to dampen your enthusiasm for our venture," was Fitzmaurice's opening remark after they had exchanged greetings.

"Not at all, not at all, quite the contrary," was O'Flaherty's reply, "but I confess to having expected a much bigger force than I see here. You'll not achieve much with this lot. In fact, if you don't get your reinforcements soon, you stand in great risk of being driven out again by the English before you even get started."

Fitzmaurice repeated what Grace had already told O'Flaherty about Stukeley, emphasising his imminent arrival, and the fact that his troops were all hardened men who would provide a very solid core for the whole army, but O'Flaherty did not appear overly convinced, merely responding, "we'll see, we'll see."

His somewhat dampened enthusiasm spread to his men, and the night's feasting was a more subdued affair than Grace had expected, O'Flaherty himself, even though perfectly civil and even getting slightly drunk, looking thoughtful throughout the proceedings. On the plus side, they were all in their beds relatively early and in good shape to carry on with the transfer of the cargoes when they awoke on the following morning.

The unloading of the Dana had begun as soon as the prizes had left and the galley was able to be brought alongside the jetty. It had continued all through the afternoon until the jetty was loaded with enough equipment and munitions to equip at least 500 Irishman when, and if, they should finally arrive. The Arganya had also been brought in and tied up alongside, ready to begin the transfer of Grace's own cargo back into the Dana, but night had fallen by this time, and that task had to be deferred until the following day.

Morning found Grace impatiently awaiting the arrival of Fitzmaurice to permit the transfer to begin. After an hour, during which all kinds of thoughts had assailed her regarding his trustworthiness, she set out for the fort to accost him regarding his tardiness. She met him along the pathway in angry argument with O'Flaherty, who had, after a further night's consideration, decided to withdraw from the venture pending the arrival of other reinforcements, Irish or Continental. Fitzmaurice was inclined to blame Grace for O'Flaherty's actions, but O'Flaherty was adamant that he had not been in any way influenced by her, that Fitzmaurice's own message had led him to understand that he would be joining a small army, not the puny force that he had actually found upon arrival. He was at pains to point out that he was not abandoning the enterprise, that he was merely protecting his men and his galleys, but that he would leave a man with Fitzmaurice to alert him when the reinforcements arrived, at which time he would return. Fitzmaurice persisted with his arguments for a while, but finally accepting that they were fruitless, accepted the fact and, having shaken hands with O'Flaherty and wishing him safe voyaging until they should meet again, turned his attention to Grace.

"I don't suppose you've had a last minute change of heart, Grace? No? I hadn't really expected that you would but, no harm trying. Let's get back to the boats."

He led the way back down the path and was soon unlocking the specially chained hold covers to allow access to Grace's goods on the Arganya. They began the transfer at once, pausing only to watch as the two O'Flaherty galleys hauled anchors and rowed slowly out of the harbour, considerably more subdued than when they had arrived.

O'Flaherty himself gave Grace a brief wave as he passed.

Fitzmaurice was standing nearby and confessed that, for the first time, he was having doubts about the venture, not because he doubted that the Irish would rise, but because of the behaviour and attitude of his allies. Don Diego, it transpired, had been in a fury about O'Flaherty's departure. He had wanted, bad leg and all, to fight O'Flaherty, and when O'Flaherty had given him what he, Don Diego, had considered a pitying look, had demanded that Fitzmaurice turn the guns of the fort on the O'Flaherty galleys. This he had, of course, refused to do. The upshot of all of this was that Don Diego was now refusing to speak to him, and the other Spaniards were barely cooperating with him. Stukeley's arrival could not come a moment too soon as far as he was concerned.

Grace was quite sympathetic and voiced her sympathy before turning her attention back to the work in hand. This was completed in the early afternoon. She then sent the Dana back out into the harbour, preferring to have the galley at anchor rather than tied up at the jetty, where her new cargo might prove very tempting to some of the people on shore. She told Fitzmaurice that she would leave next day but offered, in the meantime, to speak to Don Diego in an attempt to effect a reconciliation. They were walking back to the fort with this intent when one of Fitzmaurice's lookouts came galloping into view shouting "the English are coming, the English are coming."

Fitzmaurice grabbed at the man as he pulled his horse to a stop and ordered him to report properly. It appeared that four ships had come into view rounding Inistooskert. The lookout, thinking that they might be Stukeley's force, had waited until he could positively identify them. When he had decided that they were English, he had then come as fast as he could ride with his warning.

"That'll be Winter's fleet," said Fitzmaurice. "How long before they get here?" he enquired, but the lookout, a landsman, could only offer the most vague opinion.

"Not long, on this south-westerly breeze," said Grace. "I must leave immediately. God be with you, James."

"And with you, Grace," he replied as she rushed away back to the jetty.

It was the greatest good fortune that she had moved the Dana to anchor so recently. Most of the crew were still on board, and those that were ashore had heard the alarm and were now themselves rushing back to the harbour. Using her own and the Arganya's skiffs, she quickly got her remaining crew members back on board and, even as they prepared to sail, had Fabrizio ready his guns.

The O'Flaherty galleys were long out of sight by now, so there could be no question of help. If they were to escape the English, they would have to do it alone. Any plan, however, would have to wait until they cleared the harbour and she could make some assessment of her opponents. She did not think for a moment that news of her Channel battle would have yet become common knowledge, but it would be enough for them to see her leaving the rebel stronghold to have reason to attack her. James, who had come on board on the last skiff, stood behind her, watching as the galley cleared the harbour and she calmly viewed the oncoming ships, deciding on her course of action.

The four Englishmen were strung out in line astern, with the leading ship a good three cables ahead of the next ship. She guessed that they had made some northing since being first seen, before wearing to keep to windward of anyone attempting to escape from Smerwick. Grace concluded that they knew their business. She went to the front of the stern platform to address the crew:

"Men, this voyage of ours seems to be getting busier and busier." There were smiles. No anxiety, noted James. They can see what is in front of them, but they have utter trust in her. "There are only four of them." Cheers this time. James hoped the sound would not carry to alert the Englishmen.

"We'll concentrate on the leading ship," Grace continued. "My plan is this. We're going to edge as close as possible to Dunacapple island there. We're going to row slowly and in an unseamanlike fashion, just like the trading ship that we are," more smiles, "but, when I say, you'll row as hard as if your lives depended on it, which they surely do. And this is equally important, the moment I order, both sails are to be instantly hoisted."

She addressed the gunner who had come aft along the central platform, "Fabrizio, at my command, you may fire directly at her hull. I don't believe we'll have time for a second shot, but prepare for one anyway."

The Dana was not showing any colours and she now ordered a Spanish flag prepared for hoisting.

"I'd prefer that they didn't perceive us to be Irish," she said in an aside to James and Thomas, adding to James that his monk's habit would greatly aid in the deception, the poop decks of Spanish ships being well known for the abundance of priests that they tended to contain. "They'll certainly not treat us any the less vigourously under Spanish colours, but they may be fooled into thinking that we'll turn south. If we get past them," she added, touching the rail.

The Dana progressed towards the island in laggardly fashion as the first ship in the line bore down on them, doing an easy five knots or so towards the apparently simple merchant galley. Noting that the guns were covered with old canvas again, the patereros dismounted, and the men concealing themselves as much as possible below the rowing platforms, all without direct orders, James was made aware again of how well the Dana's crew were used to subterfuge. He hoped that Winter's ships would be as easily fooled as had been the Algerines.

The leading ship, which at this point was not much more than a couple of cable's lengths away, now turned to port to expose her full broadside, and an officer, presumably her captain by the highly burnished glitter of his breastplate and helmet, called at them to cease rowing and prepare to be boarded. A cannon was fired across the Dana's bows to emphasise the order.

Grace called to cease rowing, and as they glided forward with ever decreasing speed, she pulled and pushed at the tiller in a haphazard fashion, as if struggling with the direction of the galley, until the bows were innocently pointed directly at the Englishman. She picked up her speaking trumpet and roared:

"Fire!"

The sail cloth was whipped from the guns and, in rapid succession, all three cannon blazed out, hitting the Englishman amidships. James, who was watching carefully, saw the splinters fly and thought he saw at least one gun dismounted. A twenty four pound ball could do enormous damage at two hundred yards range, the eighteen pounders scarcely less. He imagined the havoc on deck and found his feelings to be very mixed. Their opponent was crewed by heretics acting directly under the distant orders of an heretical Queen, heretics who would be merciless to him as a papist traitor if they caught him, but who were still, like himself, English. They would be equally merciless to Grace, of course.

Grace was now shouting at the men to row for their very lives and the galley, which had been moving ever more slowly, leapt forward under the impetus of 160 oarsmen exerting every ounce of strength of which there were capable, free men and slaves alike. She put the helm hard over, turning the galley to larboard just as the Englishman fired his broadside, a broadside that was ragged and ill aimed as result of the shocking surprise that he had been given by the Dana's totally unexpected salvo, and which passed harmlessly astern.

The Englishman now began to turn again to bring himself onto a course that would bring his broadside to bear on the Dana's stern but Grace, anticipating the move, immediately turned the galley back on to their original bearing to cross his stern. The next moments were vital. The galley surged forward in excess of ten knots as the rowers, responding to the strokes being called by Rory, pulled ever harder at a pace which would soon exhaust them. All would depend on how quickly the Englishman, who had been almost hove to before the Dana's volley, could get up enough speed to complete his turn and, even more importantly, how quickly his gunners could reload.

All watched anxiously as the English guns were run out again and the Englishman began to pick up speed, but the critical moment arrived before his guns could be brought to bear on the Dana, and he was forced to turn again or risk being taken aback. The galley was not yet safe, however, and even as they passed close enough to the Englishman's stern for the remounted patereros to loose a volley, he fired his two stern mounted cannon, the two balls smashing into the Dana just abaft the foremast, killing the slaves chained at the foremost benches and causing many more, and some of the Danas, to be wounded by flying splinters.

"Avast rowing," roared Grace. "Up sails."

The sailors had been awaiting this order, and as the oars were laid inboard, both the lateens were hoisted and made fast so quickly that hardly any of their speed was lost in the transition, and what was lost was quickly made up as the sails caught the wind and the galley heeled over to speed through the sea, its bow-wave sending spray flying over the decks.

They were not yet clear of danger. The Englishman was now trying to bring his unused larboard guns to bear, so Grace had to fix a course directly away from him to present the smallest possible target, a course that was taking her directly towards the other ships of Winter's squadron, which were now alarmingly close. The Englishman fired again, but the Dana was now making such speed that he fired at the extremity of his range and all of the balls fell short, except for one which, bouncing on a wave, neatly cut off the Dana's flagstaff so that the Spanish colours dropped into the sea astern. By this time, the damaged oars had been discarded, so there was nothing to impede the galley's speed when Grace turned her for the final time to head north for home.

The other English ships gave chase briefly in the hope that the damage that the galley had received might cause something to carry away but, perceiving that this was not to be the case, soon abandoned their chase and turned back towards Smerwick.

James, who had gone forward to see to the wounded, returned to find Grace in tearing good humour. The melancholy which she knew would inevitably succeed the action had not yet befallen her and so it was with barely suppressed high spirits that she enquired about his charges, though she did make a proper attempt at gravity as he made his report. But she was not to be deprived of her happiness at their escape from the jaws of disaster just yet, nor the joy of their imminent homecoming.

"Well James, I don't suppose you've had many more adventurous voyages than this, even with the Knights. But it's almost over. Soon we'll be tied up on Clare and I'll show you some real Irish hospitality."

"I don't wish to spoil your happiness, Grace, but I believe the captain of that ship, at whom I got a good look as we passed, to have been a man with whom I fought at Lepanto called Richard Bingham. A hard fearless man, but vengeful, Grace, very vengeful."

"Don't be worrying yourself about him now, James. He'll have no idea who we are, particularly since we left our Spanish colours behind for him. Cheer up and enjoy our escape."

And slapping him on the back, she moved away to the rail to survey her boat, looking extraordinarily handsome, and laughing to herself in the joy of the moment in a manner that, in a less formidable woman, might almost have been seen as girlish.

HISTORICAL NOTE

Grace O'Malley was a very real character in Tudor Ireland. We now know of her through what has been handed down through folklore, and also through her many appearances in the English state papers of the time. Contemporary Irish history was written by monks and was notable for its almost complete lack of reference to women, Grace included. From the writer's point of view, this is fortuitous since it leaves many gaps to be exploited.

From the point of view of this book, what is true is that she was married twice, had three children by her first marriage and one by her second. Her first husband, Donal O'Flaherty, was killed in battle. Her second, Richard Bourke, was still alive at the time of the actions described. I have brought forward their acceptance of his Knighthood by a year or so to help with the story. She did rescue Hugh de Lacy from a shipwreck on Achill and may, or may not, have been his lover. When he was murdered, she wreaked her revenge as described. The Waterford raid on Baltimore happened as described, but 30 years earlier, and Grace was not involved. (The feud would end disastrously for Baltimore in 1631 when Algerine galleys, led there by a captured Waterford man, sacked the town and took more than a hundred prisoners for the North African slave markets). Likewise, Fitzmaurice's years o n the continent, trying to drum up support for a second rebellion, and his presence in Corunna and, subsequently, in County Kerry are all genuine but, again, Grace's participation is purely speculative on my part. Equally speculative is the description of Grace's galley, which is normally thought to have been smaller than described, large galleys being supposed to have been unusual in Ireland at that time. However, the raid on Baltimore was led by what was described as the Waterford Great Galley, and the O'Driscoll galley taken in the raid was one of 30 oars, indicating that there were large galleys in Ireland, so that it seems reasonable to give Grace a galley of 40 oars.

Another speculative bit of fiction is her meeting with Tom Butler. Here, again, it is known that, as well as the lands that he ruled as a chieftain, Richard rented lands from the Earl, so that it seems reasonable to suppose that they may have met, and even been friends. She certainly met the Sidneys, father and son, who were impressed by her, the father describing her in a report to Walsingham as "a most famous femynyne sea capten", from which I have taken the book's title.

All of the Spaniards named, other than Don Diego, were real people: Maria Pita would, in time, lead Corunna's successful defence against Drake's raid.

The captain Richard Bingham mentioned on the last page of the book was another real historical character who did fight at Lepanto and was one of Winter's commanders. He would go on to cause serious problems for Grace in the future.

Given what we know, it would be hard to over exaggerate Grace's life, truth being stranger than fiction, upon which rests this tale.

Readers interested in Grace's real life will find the best account in Anne Chambers *Granuaille, Grace O'Malley-Ireland's Pirate Queen.*

Printed in Great Britain
by Amazon